The Poppy Drop

The Poppy Drop

A LILY LIST MYSTERY

C.L. BAUER

For information contact:

www.clbauer.com

ISBN: 978-1-7363460-0-6

First Edition: October 2018

Second Edition: May 2019

Third Edition: January 2021

10 9 8 7 6 5 4

The Lily List Mystery Series

The Poppy Drop
The Hibiscus Heist
The Tulip Terror
The Sweet Pea Secret

Dedication

For my family and friends...here we go!

Prologue

The "boulevard" was the most popular street in the new suburbs of Kansas City, Missouri. Popular was in the eyes of the beholder. Small trees just planted by the developer edged the new streets. Small shops with cloth awnings in different colors lined the sidewalks. The architecture featured clay tiled roofs and brick storefronts of mom-and-pop shop keepers making their American dreams realities. This new shopping area still had a lot to prove; it wasn't downtown and it definitely wasn't the Country Club Plaza but more and more citizens were taking a chance moving to the outer areas of the streetcar routes. More and more families needed groceries, housing supplies and those non-necessities like candy and flowers.

Lily's opened its doors for business on the boulevard on a bright cool March morning in 1939. Its green and white striped awnings marked the little flower shop tucked in between a five and dime store and the local watch maker.

That twelfth day of March, Ida Faust placed her plants for sale out front on the sidewalk and turned the "closed" sign over at precisely nine o'clock. Maybe it was a little cool for the plants but the sun would warm the day soon enough. Besides, Ida wanted people to know that Lily's was open for business. She hoped the business would come. Her husband, Edgar, was working at his already established jewelry shop downtown, just one block off Main Street.

She shook her head in amazement at his work ethic. Always working, always pushing ahead was what her Edgar did. He had made a fine home for their little family; just the three of them. As she went through her open shop's front door she smiled. She had wanted more children but Lily was enough of a handful. God had blessed them with a real firecracker. She could still remember the day at the orphanage as the nurse placed the bundle in her arms. Immediately she was their daughter, her screams soothed by just a little lullaby.

It was ten o'clock on the dot when the bell rang at the top of the door and the first customer strolled in. Ida popped her head up from behind the counter. The man wore a smart fedora, light camel-haired jacket and brown crisply pleated pants. His shoes were shined and he carried a cane.

"Good morning. May I help you?"

"You have any yellow roses? My wife loves yellow roses and that's all I ever buy her." His heavily accented voice gave him away as a fellow European immigrant.

Ida smiled. "You sir are in luck. They are my favorite too. I brought them in for my first day open."

She turned to the refrigerator box and slid the glass door. "How many?"

"You from Germany?"

She stopped. "Yes. My husband and I came over ten years ago. It was a hard time. And you?"

"Berlin. My beautiful Berlin just wasn't where my future could be. I still have family there but now this is my home. I'm Leo Stein and I'll take all the yellow roses you have."

And that was Ida's first sale and her first customer.

The sky was darkening by the time Edgar and Lily entered the shop that day. Her small daughter ran to greet her, hugging her around the legs.

Edgar was more interested in business. "So how were the sales today?"

"Slow but pretty good. I had six sales."

He shook his head. "You need more to stay in business, mine Liebe."

She held Lily's hand as she began to turn off the shop's lights. "I will do better but it was a good first day. I met a fellow, very nice, very good customer. He bought out all my yellow roses."

"Ah, Lily's favorites. Good. I had a good day too. So, you come back tomorrow?" She grabbed her pocket book and turned the last switch.

"Of course. I need a business to leave Lily when we are gone. It will be this shop."

Almost twenty years later, Lily Faust was sweeping in the shop when she saw Mr. Stein coming toward the door with her morning coffee. Today he had a tall man with broad shoulders walking next to him. He looked like trouble with black wavy hair.

Mr. Stein introduced Victor Schmidt and handed Lily her drink.

"Lily, Victor knows a lot about plants and I thought he could help you out now and then."

The young man stuck his hand out to her and smiled. "Pleasure to meet you, Lily. Call me Vic."

He was trouble and she married him a year later. In the bargain she also received a couple of his brothers and sisters who were great workers. Her business, now their business was really taking off and she was the talk of the town. The boulevard was the place to shop and to see Lily. What was she wearing? Did you see her hat, her shoes? Did she buy them on the Plaza? Is she doing your wedding? She did mine and she was amazing.

Vic and she had everything, everything but a baby. Her deceased mother and father had adopted her and they had been a happy little family. She and Vic had tried so many times and adoption was an option but it didn't seem like a good idea on so many levels. The two of them fought all of the time and it seemed like the only place she smiled was when she was working at someone else's wedding. Thank God for Vic's brothers. The Schmidt boys helped out so much around the shop she never had to look for real employees. Vic now had his own greenhouse which kept him out of her hair.

It was a Friday afternoon when two policemen came into the shop, their hats in their hands.

"What can I do for you today, officers?" Ed, Vic's brother came out from the back of the store when he heard the question.

"Mrs. Schmidt?"

Lily nodded. Something didn't feel right. She clutched the edge of the counter. Instinctively she reached out for Ed who was now on her left side.

"We have some bad news, ma'am. Your husband was in an accident..."

She stood motionless as they continued to describe her husband's death. She melted onto the floor and into the gentle bandaid of darkness as Ed tried to grab her. Vic was gone. Her mother and father had been dead for a few years now. Nothing was certain anymore.

She found that certainty and confidence in a bottle. With Ed's help the business continued to thrive. It became an elite wedding florist shop. Lily became a supreme actress remaining flamboyant never showing her real side of desperation. She enjoyed jazz clubs and meeting friends for dinner but she was always the odd woman out. She was alone until she arrived to an empty house and her friend, the full bottle of bourbon.

Ed was making his own life eventually marrying a lovely woman, Helen French. Life was good, for him.

On a crisp December morning, Ed Schmidt unlocked the shop's door. He held a thermos of coffee in his left hand, his job since Mr. Stein had passed away a few months back. He'd catch the bus down on the corner to go to his full time job at the steel company but first Lily needed her coffee. With Helen pregnant the full time job was necessary and the extra money on the weekend from Lily just set them closer to their goal of buying a house.

As he entered he saw the brown liquid on the floor behind the counter. What the heck was going on? He threw the thermos down when he saw her head. Lily Schmidt had successfully entered that oblivion of darkness she so badly wanted to dwell in.

The shop closed during the week but Ed kept it going. Helen miscarried and didn't want to go back to her job with all the friends who had been anticipating the baby along with her. They'd try again and if they were blessed with a girl they'd call her Lily. Eventually, Helen became the shop owner and tried to fill the very high heels of the woman who preceded her.

They named their first child John. Helen had her mind set on the name Elizabeth for their second. Ed just couldn't say no to the woman he loved, to a woman who had such difficult pregnancies.

Their final and surprise child after many years was named Lily.

1. Change display in the front window
2. Clean out buckets in back cooler
3. Begin calls for this week
4. Finish all bows props etc
5. Complete schedule
6. Make sure help knows when they are working and where
7. Finish my schedule and confirm all consultations
8. Sunday go to a movie and stop thinking for two hours
9. Make sure wholesaler has RED English Garden roses

Chapter One

Another week was beginning and so was THE SEASON. Lily Schmidt unlocked the front door, turned off the security system and lifted the blinds on the display window of her shop. The early morning sun came straight in like a laser, creating a halo to form over a mirror on the wall. Lily shielded her eyes with her hand as she stumbled through the store and headed to the back.

"When will Monday morning stop? I feel like a vampire," she said aloud. "Please Lord, don't make me wait until I'm seventy years old to retire."

God and Lily talked quite a bit, especially on Monday mornings. Frankly who else was there to complain to when you were self employed? Her assistant would be in after her one o'clock class at the university and by that time Lily's mood would change. She would be fine, or a facsimile of fine, when dear Abby would pass through the door with love in her eyes. The twenty year old Abby was in love with Jeremy Klein and if Lily heard about how wonderful he was one more time…Well it wouldn't be pretty. She would go out into the street yelling like a banshee until one of the bartenders from the bar and grill on the corner came out to pull her into the building. He would probably think she was just practicing for karaoke night. Her screaming and yelling held some similar components.

Lily took a deep breath and looked at the calendar for the week. She'd already made her list and had it on the white board beside her desk. She forgot to add in bookkeeping and that was something that was mandatory. With the stack of "to do's" getting higher and higher she had to get to it. She had to. This was just the middle of May and the wedding season was really going to hit. She'd be here on Sunday cleaning up, attempting to hit the Mt. Everest of paperwork.

She began to sing. "Climb every mountain, ford every stream…" Lily was not going to continue to the "follow every rainbow" part. When you were the owner, the boss and the sole proprietor of your existence, rainbow connections didn't really exist. Oh, and you were in charge of the family business. Of course, the family was pretty much gone but you were the last woman standing after over seventy some years.

It was only Monday. How would she live through the week? She always did but sometimes it just seemed too much. Lily just kept going. She couldn't be the one to sabotage the shop now. Besides it seemed to have a life of its own.

It was still in the mid-town of Kansas City. It still had loyal customers with history, for some, from the very beginning. Just last year she had provided the wedding flowers for Mr. Stein's great granddaughter. He had been that first customer of Ida's with a twenty-cent purchase of yellow roses. Wow, yellow roses for less than a quarter. He had been a friend of the shop with his visits of coffee and conversation for Ida and for the original Lily, this Lily's long deceased aunt. He received great, inexpensive flowers and the occasional apple strudel. Lily still had the recipe in one of her Dad's metal filing cabinets. 'Best apple strudel' was scrawled at the top.

Lily looked up from her desk to see the copy of the bill of sale on a piece of faded carbon paper. Next to it was a photograph from the Kansas City Times, page five. The headline read "Lily's Opens For Business". Not very creative but it served its purpose. The story went on to say that the shop was edged between the five and dime and the watchmaker shops. But it was one block from 'Greenie's', a plant and flower shop, and five doors down from another flower shop, 'The Painted Wagon'. What had the Fausts been thinking? But all three thrived. If you needed funeral flowers or something delivered to a house you came to mid-town. If you had a daughter marrying, you came to mid-town. If you didn't like the Painted Wagon, you went to Lily's. If you didn't like either of them, you stopped at Greenie's. It became the boulevard of blooms. Wow, had times changed.

By now Lily was just dreaming at her desk. It wasn't going to change anything. Living in the past usually didn't change the future. And it was still Monday. It was time to put on her big girl panties and go to work.

She called it the responsibility gene; what made you tick and do the right thing. It made you do your homework when you really wanted to go out and play…*Lily, be a good girl and get that homework finished.* It made you pay your taxes on time…*Lily, you don't need a penalty or a bad credit rating.* It made you send out thank you notes…*Lily, make sure you are always gracious and thankful for every little thing you receive.* It made you go to church on Sunday no matter how exhausted you were…*Lily, God will know if you aren't there.* Supposedly the responsibility gene made you a better person, but not without coffee. She needed coffee. Desperately.

She was trying to cut back on caffeine, on coffee but Monday was not the day to attempt acts of insanity. Besides she could work as she drank. Lily began with a call to the hotel venue they were decorating on Saturday. Of course the coordinator wasn't in town but a short message in her mailbox would do it. Next, she called the cake lady.

"So this bride has gone back and forth over the color of the cake," Darlene of Good Cakes complained. "First, she wanted white icing, then she wanted a cream color. I told her if she has butter cream frosting its not going to be stark white, hence the 'butter' part of the cream. She still doesn't get it."

Lily understood her complaints. The girl just never seemed to settle on anything and it was the same with her flower order. She had notes all over the final document and the post-it notes were like yellow pieces of wallpaper in the file folder. A month ago, Lily very forcefully told her she couldn't change anything once the order went into the wholesaler and the growers. The bride was still attempting to make not-so-subtle changes. Lily only hoped that after countless emails and many phone calls, some balancing on the rude scale, that the bride still liked her a little when she saw her.

Darlene and she decided they'd hope for the best. Thirty minutes later their call ended and Lily saw the email from the hotel coordinator. The schedule for Saturday and the delivery times for another wedding were now confirmed. She'd only need her assistant Abby staying at the shop to accept any walk-in work, and for the other smaller wedding to pick up their flowers.

Done and done. Abby could clean out all the buckets and the cooler when she arrived this afternoon.

Lily was suddenly feeling accomplished; the coffee was really kicking in. The phone rang and halted her happiness.

"Lily, it's Neal," her wholesale representative said calmly. Usually Monday calls from Neal were bad news. Big gulp, small prayer, and Lily waited for the shoe to drop.

"Well, it looks like those garden roses are going to have to come in from Ecuador and not Holland or California. We were having a hard time getting the red and we had to go to the South American market."

"Neal, what does that mean for me exactly?" Her heart was pounding. She didn't need any problems with this order when the bride was already difficult. If the girl couldn't figure out that butter cream was a little creamy looking then she sure wouldn't appreciate that a red garden rose wasn't red or wasn't there at all.

"It just means that you won't get those roses until late Thursday afternoon and we can run them out on the last city route."

Ohhhhh. That was it? No sweat.

"Great Neal, but I'll see you on Wednesday for my usual pickup."

"See you then, and just let me know if you need anything in the meantime."

The crisis of the red garden roses was averted and all was right in the wedding kingdom once more. She needed to check in with the difficult bride but she'd wait until tomorrow. There was no reason to make Monday worse. That girl was so nice but she just couldn't make a decision to save her soul. How did she keep her job? Did she ever make a decision during her workday? Lily looked at her notes to see what she did do for a living...a *nurse*? She didn't know whether to laugh or cry.

Lily headed to the front to begin changing the large window display. Mother's Day was over.

"Thank you, Lord, for getting me through another one of those," she said out loud. She had a look in mind for the window featuring pink hydrangea and a bone china set. The finer things in life were coming back. She was hanging midway into the window when she saw her favorite retired policeman.

John Temple, 'Big John', was smiling at her with his head crooked to the side. "What are you doing in there, girl?"

"I'm working. Get in here and give me a big hug." He threw his head back and laughed out loud.

"We both won't fit in there." He was pointing at the window. Lily shook her finger at him as he came into the store.

"John, you knew what I meant."

"Yah, but it is fun to tease, especially after Mother's Day. How's my girl? Are we going to survive this weekend?"

Lily molded into his arms as she said yes. John was one constant in her life. He was the real reason she actually came into work on Mondays. Her store hours, especially in the winter, were actually Tuesday through Friday but John knew she was catching up on things on Mondays. If he didn't see her in the store, he'd head to the back door. He was her very own large guardian angel with a gun.

"How about tomorrow I bring you a burger and we sit

outside on the bench. It's supposed to be a beautiful day."

"That sounds good. Around one would be great. I have an appointment but I should be done by then."

He finally released her. "That's perfect, little girl. I'll see you then. You want diet or real?"

"Real Coke please. It's May and I need all the caffeine I can get."

He saluted her as he turned. "Real it is and I will see you tomorrow. Just yell if you need me."

"You know I will."

She would yell if there was any trouble. John would be there. The boulevard shops had hired him five years ago to oversee their security. Officer Temple had been an institution on the police force before his retirement. John always said he had to retire because he'd ran so much his legs had extended their warranty. John was the boulevard's protector; he was her protector.

Monday was looking up. The list was already shorter and Lily had a luncheon date tomorrow. She was going to eat a burger and have a real Coke, not a diet one. This could be the beginning of a good week.

Lily stopped in the middle of the shop and looked around. Accomplishing so much, crisis averted and happy thoughts were leaving a lump in her stomach. When things were going well it usually meant that something big was about to happen, usually nothing good.

"Oh Lord, I don't need any more problems this week than the ones I already have."

Chapter Two

1. Pick up flowers.
2. Process flowers.
3. Make sure Abby knows her schedule AGAIN!

Wednesday morning, Lily headed to the wholesaler across the river. It was a sunny day with not a cloud in the sky, absolutely stunning as she drove through the Kansas City downtown area. At nine in the morning everyone was already at the law offices and in court. There was never a show at the Sprint Center that early unless the Big XII basketball championships were being held there. Chaos was always created with shuttles, press vans and thousands of fans walking from parking garages, but that was in March. Today there was no traffic at all. City Hall had something going on, Lily thought, as she saw the television vans and their mammoth satellites posted on the west side of Oak Street. She'd watch the news tonight to see what was going on. As she drove across the bridge she smelled the pungent aroma from the water treatment facility. It smelled like bad potato chips. That scent would stay with her until she entered the larger flower cooler and took a whiff of freesia and lilies.

With a beautiful blue sky above her and the sun beside her, this was going to be another great day. Neal would definitely have every flower she needed, except those roses. He had to have those tomorrow. He had to. That was what he did week after week. He had been in the business since he began driving deliveries at age sixteen. He had been a young man with long hair and the start of a mustache. He cut the hair but kept the facial hair.

Lily first met Neal when she was a little girl helping her mom in the shop one day. She'd heard the knock at the back door and her mother had said to open it. She did and there he was, this teenager with two boxes of flowers in his arms. Lily never forgot him, nor that diamond he had in his ear. He was the first man she ever saw who had a piercing of any kind.

By the next time she saw Neal she was the owner of the flower shop and was looking for a new wholesaler. There he was, mustache and earring all. Of course, he was older now but he was still that hard working teenager. Originally he wasn't her sales rep.

"I hate when that happens and it's always on the weddings when I have a difficult bride."

"I know, I know," Neal said in a sympathetic tone. He put his arm around her as if he were her older brother. "They'll be here. I promise. This girl will have her hydrangeas…"

"And roses!"

"And roses, Lily. Don't worry. Now, I'm going to pack this all up and we'll have you on your way. I'll call in the morning to confirm they are coming. Then I'll call you as soon as we get them loaded and headed your way."

He knew her idiosyncrasies. They weren't pretty but they were all Lily's. As she had told Neal's former boss last year, "I put myself out for my clients every weekend. I have to be perfect for every wedding. I am the one who is responsible for not ruining my bride's special day. So work with me." Neal did work with her.

It was nearly four Thursday afternoon when the Federal Express van pulled up in front of the flower shop. Lily had already called Neal three times and had always heard "they are coming" before she hung up in disgust. In her mind she understood but there were times like these when she really wanted to look for another job. Could she work part-time somewhere? Seriously, when did she have time for anything else besides this place?

But she had tried to have a relationship and a career. It had worked for awhile. In all actuality it had been his career that kept getting in the way. She had met him in a church. Of course she had. Where else did she go? Ministers were not easy to date, she soon discovered. You ended up dating his entire congregation, well maybe not all but several hundred of the busybodies who just had to know everything that was going on in the pastor's life. They nearly exhausted themselves searching for everything on the Catholic woman dating their precious 'god boy'. But that was in the past.

"Finally. Abby, the hydrangeas and roses are here!" Lily yelled as she signed for the flowers. The delivery had come directly from the airport because of the late hour. She noticed the wholesaler's address had been scratched out with her's added so it meant Neal hadn't even seen them.

The first box was filled with the garden roses. Perfect, they were absolutely perfect. "We need to get these in water," she said as she handed them off to Abby.

Then Lily opened the box of hydrangeas. Her heart sunk.

"Oh God." What else could she say? Abby came running to look inside the box.

"Oh God," was repeated by both women, one a prayer of petition, the other an exclamation. Inside the box lay thirty white hydrangeas, shriveled brown blooms on each stem.

"What happened to them?" Abby asked. "They have ice packs, solution packets on them. Have you ever seen anything like this?"

She looked at her boss but she already knew the answer. Lily just shook her head. Tears were filling her eyes. She rushed to the front desk and searched for her phone, searching for the emergency number of Neal's boss. She called.

"Bill, we have a huge problem. I just received my flowers. Well, the roses are fine but every last one of the hydrangeas are dead and I need them for a wedding on Saturday. I *have* to have those flowers."

She heard Bill saying all the right words, that they would be there tomorrow afternoon. Would that be good enough? Well, it was going to have to be good enough. What else could she do? It wasn't time to call the bride, yet. He would have them here by tomorrow night and she would just work all night long if necessary. Fortunately she only needed them at the reception. But how would she sleep tonight?

"What do you want me to do with these?" Abby was holding several limp, dead stems.

Lily wiped the tears from her face. "We trash them. Just save the ice packs and get those in the freezer. We can use them on future weddings. Flowers go in the trash and the box in the recycling bin out back. That's all we can do with them. Oh, and take a photo of them first so they can see what they looked like when we got them."

"Yes, boss." Abby disappeared out the back door.

Well, the bad thing had happened. Now the rest of the weekend would go off without a hitch, especially if her hydrangeas arrived in time. Lily collapsed in her desk chair.

What part-time job could she get? Maybe it was time for a different career. She hadn't been a florist all her adult life. She had other skills. She could begin again.

"Oh God," she said prayerfully.

Abby and Lily worked for a few more hours until it was dark. They would come in early tomorrow and begin again. On her way home Lily received a call from Bill explaining that he had contacted the grower and they were already preparing the flowers for an overnight trip to Kansas City. They had no idea what happened in transit. She could only imagine how much the shipping fees alone were costing Bill and the growers. She was assured that if they couldn't get them in, he was already searching the open market to get what she needed. With that news, she calmed down enough to eat a late dinner and go to bed, sleeping a few hours before her alarm rang.

By the time she reached the store she had said a full rosary of prayers. Her stomach was churning more than usual. Weddings were definitely ulcer makers. She kept reciting "everything will work out".

At noon a delivery truck was outside the shop's door once more. A signature, a snip of the heavy tape around the box and an opening of the lid displayed thirty perfect stems of white hydrangeas. Crisis, again, was averted and another happy bride would be guaranteed.

1. Breakfast
2. Pack extra shoes in car
3. Load up and be at church at eleven
4. Leave church by noon
5. Arrive at the hotel
6. Make sure Abby is at shop for pickup wedding and at other delivery
7. Finish reception and drop by Clinton wedding on Ward Parkway
8. Collapse

Chapter Three

The weather was absolutely perfect for this wedding, Lily thought as she and Abby loaded up the van.

"Don't forget the extra scissors." Her command sounded louder than usual in the quiet alley behind the shop. "Did you hear me? I didn't mean to yell."

She faintly heard the phone ringing. Abby had apparently left her to reach it. Good, the command hadn't been heard at all. She continued to load boxes. Mary Lee, this first bride of the day had selected pink. Pink. There were some nights Lily dreamt in pink. She wasn't quite sure why but most of her pleasant dreams had a lovely hue of pink stroked over each vision.

Were there not other colors? Not only for her dreams but for most weddings. Last year it had been purple. Every bridal guru in America had assured every gullible soon-to-be Mrs. that purple and all shades purple was the go-to color of all weddings chic. Or you just couldn't get married! Hmmm, the Kansas State alumni were fine with purple, but the University of Kansas soon-to-be-weds hated the complete idea. Over and over, Lily had heard, "Isn't there a shade of purple that isn't really purple? My fiancé went to KU. He's a Jayhawk and he just won't allow purple in the wedding." Rock Chalk all the way, except there was NO shade of purple that wasn't purple. What were they studying in Lawrence, Kansas?

Abby soon returned with the extra scissors—she had heard—and another box. "Here's for the pews and I already packed the bows."

"Thanks, honey. So who was on the phone?"

"Well, it was kind of weird. Neal just called to tell us they had a break-in overnight so if we need anything today they're going to be shut down. The police are swarming the place. I told him we were good."

Lily continued to check the van. "What did they take? Flowers?" She laughed out loud. "I mean do they have a crazy bride that went over budget?"

"He says that's what they don't understand. Apparently they took nothing. The place was tossed but the expensive equipment is still there. That's why they don't understand why the police are going nuts, dusting for prints, looking through packing slips and searching in their computers." Abby went back into the shop for one more box.

Lily couldn't think about all that craziness right now, she had her own. "Abby, I need the order. Let's go over it one more time."

"I know, I know!" Abby yelled as she ran to the back table. "I checked everything over but I know you have to do it yourself. Oh, and I packed extra hydrangeas for the aisle and a few roses…just in case."

"Thank you." Lily appreciated Abby not voicing her entire opinion which would have included a detailed list of her boss's OCD behavior. On the other hand, Lily preferred to describe herself as thorough. You could never be too thorough when working with brides, their mothers and weddings in general. It shouldn't be in your vocabulary to just "go with it".

She looked carefully over the order and nodded her head. "It looks like we have everything. So I will see you later. You have all the phone numbers for that pick up wedding but they should be here in about thirty minutes. The red garden roses are perfect for later. I already looked over the bouquets. I'll see you at the church as soon as I've finished down at the hotel."

"Have a good wedding. Oh and I brought a dress to wear. You said it was a small but classy wedding, right?"

Lily nodded as she got into the van. "Great, yes, we don't have anything at the reception so once I get there you can go on." She knew Abby had a date that night with a new guy she'd met over at the coffee place near the university. Actually she had known him in grade school but everyone did change, didn't they?

With the drive down Broadway uneventful and the decorating quiet and uninterrupted by anyone in the wedding party, Lily walked over to the bride's room to show off the bouquets. They were classic round style with hot pink roses and white spring fillers. As she unwrapped each individual creation the bridesmaids were all making different delightful noises, from "ooh" to "ah" and even the occasional "wow". The best comment was "I've never had a great bouquet like this when I've been in other weddings."

The bride peeked her veiled head from around the bathroom door of the suite and smiled. "Is mine here?"

"Nope. I forgot yours." Lily quickly swept out a large gathering of all hot pink roses, each bloom sprouting a crystal as big as a one carat diamond. Too bad the crystals weren't real.

She was sure the screams could be heard on the street

outside. "I love it. Mom, look. Look at my bouquet. It's exactly what I wanted." She grabbed the flowers out of Lily's hands. "Oh it's so heavy. I didn't expect that. Thank you, thank you. I love it."

She kept repeating her praises as she handed the bouquet off to one of her bridesmaids and gave Lily a big hug.

"I'm so happy you like it."

"It's," the bride looked around the room at the other flowers. "So much more than I thought it would be. You have made my day."

"No, you've made my day," Lily responded. "I'm so happy you love them. I thought they looked great too. It's one of the prettiest weddings so far this year."

"I'm one of the best weddings! That's what I wanted!" And now the woman who was to be married in less than an hour was turning into a giddy teenager who was getting revenge on her playmates. Time to go.

"I'm headed down to the reception to decorate. You have a fantastic day and a better married life."

The bride and her mother were jumping up and down and just threw a nodding look to Lily. They were now in the wedding zone, similar to the old television series, "The Twilight Zone", but not as deadly, or at least not as deadly to those who did their bidding and did it well. God help the cake decorator who put the wrong design on the cake or the hotel that didn't have the suite ready or even the photographer who made the bride sweat. The wedding zone was filled only with happy thoughts by the bride and her mother, sometimes her father and some of her attendants. There was always the one girl who stayed in the corner texting her boyfriend, mad that he couldn't make the trip or that the bride wouldn't let him sit at the head table with her.

They had been going out for three months, why couldn't he? But it was the bride's wedding. When she got married she would be better to her friends. Lily shut the door to the room and saw the one girl in the corner, texting. She wasn't smiling. Lily smiled knowingly.

The hotel delivery and set-up was easy enough with balls of hot pink roses staged from table to table. The head table was adorned with the now infamous white hydrangeas. White and hot pink shouted out from the reception room. It was striking, but all that pink reminded Lily of the movie *Steel Magnolias.* Thankfully, there was no blush or bashful shades to add to the show or to look like a liquid treatment for an upset stomach.

Lily made her way down Ward Parkway, probably the most beautiful drive in all of Kansas City. It's tree-lined, six lanes divided by a grassy median was laden with fountains and ambled past some of the biggest and best houses in the city. You couldn't just gawk unless you were a passenger. Most of the speeds on the Parkway exceeded the civilized world's expectations of safety especially as you rounded Meyer Circle. Notorious over the years for countless accidents and deaths, the Circle boasted one of the city's many fountains in the center. The street path had been shaved here and there and now the house on the southwest corner hadn't had a car fly into its front room in years. It took only fifteen minutes for her to reach Abby and their other wedding. She found her unwrapping the bridesmaids' bouquets as Lily entered.

"The bride already took a look at them and she loved them…especially the garden roses!"

Lily heaved a sigh of relief. Ms. Difficult has melted. "Good. I'll take them back to her in a second and then you can get on your way."

"You know they have a coordinator here and she'll probably take over for you. You could have all night off."

"Great," Lily muttered. What could or would she do? She could go back to the shop and clean or she could stay home and clean. Which, oh which, choice should she make?

"Did you lock up everything at the shop, Abs?"

"Yes, of course. You know that call from Neal really weirded me out. I mean, why would someone break in there and not take anything?"

Lily shook her head. When she was driving from reception to church she had been wondering the same thing. "I'm with you. Then the police there? I wonder why they were swarming the place…is that what Neal said?"

Abby looked up from the bouquets. "He said they were crazy like bees. Not one thing missing but he said it seemed like there were at least ten officers, even some detectives. Men in suits. What do you think they were looking for?"

"The police or the robbers?" Lily asked out loud. She cared about what was going on but she really cared if her wholesaler would be open on Monday and would they get their shipments on time for her three weddings next weekend. She hated to make it all about her but it was all about her business. There were never times that mistakes could be made when dealing with wedding flowers. You had to be one hundred percent, no, one hundred and ten percent perfect every time. Disappointment was not an option.

"I've been thinking that maybe the robbers burglarized the wrong business. I mean who robs a flower wholesaler?"

Abby had everything ready for the bride and all the corsages and boutonnieres were laid out on the foyer table. "What are you going to do tonight?"

"Well, I could clean the shop or my house. Yep, that's my life."

"Oh for heaven's sake. Go do something. Get out. You've been moping enough already."

Lily glared at her assistant. "I have not been moping. I was dumped, sort of…well, I was supposed to be getting married and now I'm not."

It would be two years at the end of this year. Abby had heard it all before and had lived through the 'dumping campaign by god boy'. Lily's boyfriend of three years had been a minister from a small church and had suddenly decided that he just couldn't continue in their relationship. They had talked about marriage, been planning a wedding and one day he called up and said he had taken a church assignment in Alabama. He was leaving on Monday. He apparently had no room in the car, or even an airplane ticket for Lily. At the same time, Lily's father was in the final stages of cancer. The minister wasn't even there for the poor man in the final breaths of life.

Abby pointed her finger at her boss. "When a man comes along I want you to go out and have a good time. You deserve someone special with special talents and good looks. Not that looks are important, your minister was cute but nothing special and you fell in love with him. I just think you can have feelings for handsome men too. Why not?"

Lily had heard all this before and it was growing tedious. Why did she let Abby go on? Perhaps it was easier than trying to shut her up.

"You have someone in mind or somewhere I should go to find this specimen?"

"You'll know him when you see him. Maybe he will just walk into the shop one day, who knows?" Abby knew it wasn't that easy for her to meet someone and she went to college with thousands of men. Her Jeremy was the first guy she had dated in six months.

"So we are back to the question of the night…clean shop or house?"

Abby smiled as Lily changed the subject. "I'll come in Monday and clean. Why don't you take the weekend off and come in later Monday? I know we have the weddings this week but take some time, some down time before we get crazy busy."

Lily sat down in the back pew and looked toward the simple cross of the church. "So I'm cleaning the house."

1. Go to shop
2. Call Neal and check on flowers for this week
3. Call the brides, reception, cake coordinator
4. Emails...respond!
5. Work on upcoming orders

Chapter Four

Monday came soon enough. Abby had followed true to form and was just arriving at the shop at eleven in the morning when Lily was unlocking the door. She wouldn't even say anything to her. She was a good worker but Abby needed to gain a little in the maturity department. Who was Lily kidding, herself? The girl needed to grow up a lot. In the Schmidt household there were no excuses for tardiness; there were no excuses for anything. Her responsibility gene was responsible for her life path and how she strode down it.

Abby and Lily exchanged knowing looks and went into the shop. The phone was ringing when they entered. Abby ran for it.

"Lily, it's Neal. He wants to talk to you." She handed her the phone.

Great, just great. Something was wrong. Lily's mind moved into overdrive with thoughts of no roses this week and she needed so many, over one hundred in a coral shade.

She cradled the phone, took a deep breath and tried to add a smile to her voice. "How are you? Everything all right?"

"Yes. Just wanted to tell you that everything is coming in and we will be good for your pick up on Wednesday. We are up and running but we did have a big mess to clean up. I think the police made more of a mess than the jerks who broke in."

"So, did you find out what they were looking for?" As Lily listened to Neal she saw Abby beginning to dump buckets and clean out the back room. Good girl. "They really didn't take anything?"

"No, they just got into our computers and apparently they went through our packing slips."

Neal and she agreed that it was the funniest thing they had ever heard and that she would see him Wednesday. As she hung up she knew it was time to get to work.

After two hours of emails and messages, Lily began to outline her schedule for Saturday. Great, they were working with one of the most difficult wedding coordinators in the city. It wasn't that she was nasty; she didn't exactly work. Right, that's what you could say about her. She was all marshmallow fluff and no exterior chocolate bunny. She appeared to be working but more times than Lily could add up, the coordinator had added hours of more work to the florist or the cake decorator's schedule. There were a growing list of churches who didn't allow her to do anything in their facility. She made two major caterers so mad they demanded that any client who had employed her either kept her away from them or they didn't take the wedding or event.

"Abby, we've got Gretchen on the Hayden wedding," she yelled to the back room.

"Are you kidding me? I thought she was going to New York City to be some big deal."

"No such luck. I already warned the mom but they are in love with her. I've said nothing more but I did add a little more to our service charge."

Abby stopped sweeping. "Not enough! I'm sure you didn't charge enough!"

The bell on the front door stopped their loud conversation. It was a man in a suit. They didn't see many of them in a flower shop. He probably had the wrong business.

Lily popped her head up from the desk and smiled. "Hello. Welcome. How can we help you today?"

He had his head down as he entered but as soon as he heard her it raised. Definitely, they had never seen anyone like him come into the shop. He had just a regular grey suit on but other than that nothing was regular about him. His almost military short hair cut allowed his green eyes to arrive before you saw the rest of his face, at least to Lily. On second look, his suit was the only thing that didn't look military. She knew what military look liked with her own brother recently retiring from the Army and living near Washington D.C. She stood up to walk toward him and saw the well polished shoes, the tight tie, the starched, pressed shirt. His dark brown hair was in place but he did have a little stubble, just a bit. Maybe his shaver wasn't his usual. Did he have to borrow one from someone or was he staying in a hotel? Then he smiled. She heard Abby behind her saying something like "hello gorgeous".

"I'm new to the area and I was just walking around." He pointed to the display in the window featuring silk peonies, the china and real hydrangea and azalea plants. "Love the window. It works; it brought me in."

"Great, happy you liked it," Lily said as calmly as she could. "So do you need some flowers today? We mostly do weddings and events but we have some cut flowers." She paused and then went for the question that her subconscious was begging her to ask. "Maybe for you wife or girlfriend?" *Tacky, Lily, but you couldn't help yourself.*

He shook his head, looking slightly embarrassed. Of course he was. She had made him. "No and no, just wanted to check out the local businesses," he answered coyly. "But who knows? Some day I might need wedding flowers."

"Uh huh." Grab hold of yourself, idiot, Lily was telling herself. You have been around nice looking men before. One of your best friends is a handsome guy, named one of the bachelors of the year in Kansas City. Why are you babbling? Check that, why can't you speak?

"So, this is your shop?"

Abby punched her in the back to answer. "Ow, I mean yes. It's a family business that began in the 1900's. So do you live here in the neighborhood?"

His smile suddenly disappeared. Lily noticed him fidgeting with one of her photo books on the table. "Right now I'm living out of a hotel room. Soon though…"

Ah hah! She was right. He had to use one of those disposable hotel razors. Those things never gave a close shave unless you were using it on your legs. Then you ended up with small cuts all over. Edward Scissorhands couldn't have done a better hatchet job.

"Well we're here." Lord, she was an idiot. We're here, for what? We're here, take me out?
We're here in case you want a good laugh at an idiot!

"So, do you bring in a lot of hydrangeas? They were my mom's favorite flower."

"Hydrangeas? Yes, we just had a wedding, a rather large

one, with hydrangeas on Saturday. I have some photos on my phone if you want to see." Lord, would her idiocy ever end? She still grabbed her phone and showed it to him. She was committed, or rather she should be committed.

By now Abby was standing next to her, equal to the insanity, with her broom like Cinderella, smiling at the poor man like she had never seen the male species before this Monday. She was humming "So This Is Love".

A sensation rolled up Lily's back and it wasn't love. Lily could tell he was lying, but it was nice of him to say he would love to see the tiny camera photos.

She came nearer, barely coming to his shoulders. He was over six feet tall but that she was used to. Her former boyfriend had been just under that height.

"Here's the church, this is her bouquet. This girl really liked color. Now here are the hydrangeas on the aisle," she said as she flipped along. He was pretending to really look but she could see him gaze up now and then, looking around the store. Quickly, he even managed a smile to Abby. "This is the reception. We did the pinks on the tables, see? Then on the head table we did all white hydrangeas. Your mother would've liked that."

He stopped looking and gazed directly into her face. "My mother?"

"Your mother. You said hydrangeas were her favorite flowers."

He smiled and suddenly she felt a hand midway up her back as if to distract her. It was working. "Right. Sorry. Yes, she would have absolutely loved these flowers. You do great work." He pulled his hand from her quickly and stepped away.

"We have really fresh flowers," she answered. She was feeling something but now her giddiness was turning to suspicion. He didn't remember for one minute that his mom loved hydrangeas? "In fact this week we had a problem with a shipment. We had to throw them all out and they had to Fed Ex a box in from South America."

"Wow. South America? Amazing," he was looking around again, clearly looking all the way past Abby to the back door. "Well, it was lovely meeting you both."

He was turning to leave.

"I'm Lily, that's Abby and your name is?"

"Oh sorry. How rude. I'm Dev Pierce. Hopefully I'll see you both around when I'm settled.
Have a good day."

His hand was on the door and he was out of their shop and placing his sunglasses on before Lily got all of her "you too" out.

"Do you think he'll be back? He was cute."

Abby was speaking but Lily wasn't answering. She was getting one of those feelings, usually reserved when she just "knew" that a member of the family was dying. It was prickly, she was getting a little nauseous, and she was thinking that, yes, he would be back. She wasn't certain that was a good thing. He had the looks, the name of a romance hero, the smile...he was too good to be true. He had secrets, probably too many to count. Too much of anything, especially a good thing, Lily had learned was never good.

Even though there was a sinking feeling in Lily's stomach, the day was going pretty well since the visit from the mysterious stranger. He had been lying and it wouldn't really matter but after the wholesaler's break-in, something just wasn't right about his little visit into her shop. He had been looking around the store for something and it wasn't his mother's favorite flower!

Just shake it off.

If she had flowers come in on time this week everything would be back on course. Abby was content sprucing up the front displays. She'd been a good worker today. It was Lily's time to take a turn cleaning.

"Abby, I'm going to the back."

There were tons of boxes from this weekend that needed to go to the recycling bin behind the store. Lily made another mental note to add to her list. Saturday, she had unpacked the van at her house and left several of the boxes in the garage, with three or four other boxes. She was getting quite a pile. She needed to get those back to the shop tomorrow and see if there was anything in them to clean out. Tuesday mornings there was a company that picked up all the cardboard so hopefully she'd get them here before they arrived.

Grabbing a couple of boxes, she opened the back door to throw them in. All she saw in the alley were flower boxes and stems of dead hydrangeas from last week's chaos. They were strewn everywhere, thrown in a complete mess where delivery trucks usually drove.

"What the heck? I don't have time for this."

She began to pick up the boxes and stack them where she always did. Then, one by one, she picked up the dead, brown hydrangeas.

"I hate hydrangeas. I hate whoever did this," she yelled out to no one in particular. The other shop keepers already thought she was a little off, this outburst wouldn't change their opinions. In fact, it would solidify them. Stem after stem there was not one flower with a preservative packet wrapped at the bottom. Had Abby suddenly become the dumbest girl on the block and tried to save them? They couldn't be used for anything or another time with a flower. What was going on? Had Abby put them in the freezer with the ice packs?

Lily stacked the stems by the doorstep. Once she'd finished cleaning, she grabbed the hydrangeas and brought them inside to count...one, two, three...twenty, twenty-one...twenty- nine, thirty. They were all there, all of the dead hydrangeas from the box and not one stem had a solution packet attached.

By the time Abby entered the back area, Lily was just sitting there looking at the dead and decaying stems.

"What on earth are you doing? You going to save them for some dead flower delivery joke?"

She looked up at Abby and stared for awhile. "Did you freeze the solution packets from the dead hydrangeas last week?" Lily knew she didn't but she wouldn't mind the answer being yes.

Abby laughed out loud. "Of course not, silly. I froze the ice blocks but not those. I left them on and in the box and just threw them all out Friday when I left the shop."

It was confirmed Abby wasn't the dumbest girl on the block; she ignored the dead flower delivery comment.

"I went back to the dumpster and all of these stems were

laying in the alley and not a one of them had a packet on."

"So?"

Lily looked at Abby as though she'd suddenly grown two heads. Really? Was she the only one finding something peculiar with the entire situation? Her stomach was churning. There were voices in her head yelling that line from a very old television sci-fi show, "Danger, danger, Will Robinson".

"Abby, someone was in our dumpster sometime this weekend, going through these dead hydrangeas. I went straight home Saturday and didn't even bring the van back. You went on your date. Neither one of us came in Sunday. Someone was looking for something and it was in those packets. By the way, I need a ride home tonight."

Abby nodded affirmatively. "No problem." She tilted her head as thought she was deep in thought solving the world's problems. "That's so silly about those packets. It's not like you can use them again."

Frustration was the only consequence of continuing this conversation with Abby. "Never mind. Just go back to doing what you're doing."

Lily just kept looking at the dead flowers as Abby left her alone. What in the blazes was going on around here? This was not normal. Her stomach was doing flip flops. She was afraid and she didn't know why. She did know that all her weird feelings of uncertainty centered around those hydrangeas.

Chapter Five

1. Finish up calls, emails and schedules for this weekend
2. Meet with new client
3. Abby comes in after her last morning class
4. Make sure I have all the vases ready to go
5. Stop thinking about weird preservative packets and handsome stranger
6. Call Neal to make sure we are good for the pickup tomorrow
7. Forgot boxes at house again... bring tomorrow!

It was already warm by nine in the morning and that only meant one thing in Kansas City on Memorial Day weekend…humidity hell. Lily was already sweating and she was just taking the short walk from the parking lot to the front door. The front door.

She stopped short on the sidewalk and saw the open door swinging on its hinges. Holy crap.
Don't go in, just call the police. Grabbing her cell, that's exactly what she did. As she told the 911 operator about the break-in she scanned inside to see how bad the damage was. There wasn't any that she could see. No broken glass, no stolen vases or flowers. The showroom refrigerator's door was open and she could see their personal fridge was wide open. Someone broke in to steal some ice cubes and an old ham sandwich?

Two officers pulled up within minutes. It wasn't a joke but they probably really had been at the doughnut shop up the street.

"You the owner?"

"Yes, Lily Schmidt. I called 911. The door was wide open when I arrived this morning."

One officer shook his head. "You really should have a security system."

Really? That's what you thought? "I do."

"Then you should've put it on. They work, you know."

Really? I get the one officer jerk face on patrol? "I turned it on before I left. If you check the pad over there you will see it was last programmed at 6:11 when I left last night."

The other officer, the quiet one, examined the pad, pressing one key and then another. "She's right. It was set at 6:11, then at 1:20 this morning it was disabled and then on again at 2:01 but they left the door wide open? Someone knew your code, ma'am."

"I'm the only one. I change it regularly anytime I have to have my assistant do it. I *do* trust her but changing it just keeps me feeling safer. I don't know who else would even remotely know this code. This is just crazy." Lily shook her head as she followed the police inside the store.

The policeman still rolling his eyes at Lily checked the refrigerator area and saw the mess on the floor. "I'm assuming you didn't leave it like this?"

"Of course not." *Are you kidding me?* Lily clenched her fists in anger. She was on her last nerve.

The other officer looked around by the register, at the computer still setting on the desk, the phone system. "Someone was targeting something in here. Did you have anything significant in the refrigerator?"

"Seriously, just some food items and freezer blocks we use on the flowers." Lily searched around the floor. The blocks were all gone.

"What ma'am?"

"The stupid freezer blocks. There's not one on the floor." She looked inside the freezer. "There's not one left." Now she was shaking her head in disbelief. What the heck was going on here? Why would some idiot steal those?

The senior officer looked at her blankly. "You're telling me that someone broke in to steal some ice blocks he could've bought in the camping section at Walmart? Were they special in some way? Did you hide money in them or something?"

Lily just shook her head as a couple of tears were forming in her eyes. She mumbled out loud, "They're just freezer blocks. We use them to keep the flowers cool. When they defrost they look like limp bags of mush. That's all they are. Sometimes we do buy them at Walmart." She bit her lip. *Don't cry over stupid things,* but she was having a difficult time keeping the tears at bay. What was going on?

"It was probably some prank just to upset you," the nicer cop assured. "No big deal. It's going to be fine."

He could see her tears. *Crap, don't cry in front of the police over spilled, or gone freezer blocks.* Ironically, she wanted one right now to place on the top of her throbbing head. This week was going to be calm and normal? That went right out with the OPEN door!

Officer Grumpy then heard his monitor. He was already stepping out of the store leaving the younger one to comfort her.

"Look, there really isn't anything you can do over this but go ahead and go to the station and fill out a report. Change your codes, maybe talk to your security company about an update. We're pretty much done here and it sounds like we have to go. Here's my card with my number if you need anything else. You have someone who could come be with you?"

Lily nodded yes but she knew Abby wouldn't be in until later. She was on her own, always.

He headed out the door. She stood there just looking at the ham sandwich on the floor. Oh and there was a hard boiled egg over by the shelves. Not much to clean up or throw away except to salvage her confidence. She moved to the front door and pulled it shut, locking it soundly. The "closed" sign was staying on until Abby appeared.

She stared blankly at the door's lock. Freezer blocks were stolen, preservative packets were picked out of the trash, a break-in, a mysterious stranger who was a terrible liar but an excellent distractor all added up to one scared florist who had chaos in a usually orderly world. Wait, add a break-in at the wholesaler and nothing stolen but someone was looking for flowers that had been shipped in from South America?

Lily stepped away from the door, landing up against the wall. She slumped down until she was sitting on the floor staring at the now inedible ham sandwich, oh, and the egg. Something was terribly wrong in her little corner of the world. She loved mysteries. *Columbo*, *Murder, She Wrote*...she could have them looped for hours on the mystery and murder channel but she didn't want to be part of one. Besides, didn't they usually involve a murder? Crap, a murder.

There hadn't been one…yet.

By the time Lily's consultation ended she wasn't even thinking about a break-in or any other mystery. She was concentrating on the wedding season. It was nearly seven but with the days getting longer she was calmed knowing she wouldn't have to leave the shop in the dark.

The couple had been nice enough. They were in their thirties and paying for the wedding on their own. That was becoming increasingly the norm with couples waiting to marry and intent on making it their unique ceremony, not something their parents planned for them. As they were still in front of her window she saw the mysterious stranger pass by. He smiled at the couple and started to open her door.

"I'm actually closed. Besides, I don't have a flower in the store, not even a hydrangea."

He didn't say anything, just stared at her. He really had been lying. He didn't even remember the deception. His mother's favorite flower was *not* a hydrangea. He probably didn't even have a mother.

Stop being ridiculous, Lily.

"I don't need flowers, but thank you," he calmly said. "I didn't want to miss you so I've been waiting until your customers left."

Lily's heart and stomach sank at the same time. Her bad feeling was back. This didn't sound good. If she screamed, who would hear her? Big John was gone for the day. She began to walk backward, nearer her desk where a pair of scissors laid on the corner. They would be her only protection. She held eye contact with him as he reached into his pocket. That's when she noticed he was in a suit with tie even on this hot day. Oh God. She reached for the corner of the desk.

He pulled out a badge. She still held her instrument of defense in her right hand as he stepped a little closer.

"Ms. Schmidt, I'm agent Devlin Pierce with the Department of Justice, DEA. I heard about your unusual burglary today and I'd like to talk to you about it. If you have the time," he said allowing the last few words to linger in the air.

He had a bit of an accent but Lily couldn't place it. She dealt with a lot of people and had traveled to more states than she hadn't but his pattern of speech was so subtle. There was just a hint of where he came from. His eyes were so pretty, just that perfect shade of green and his eyelashes so long, almost like her youngest nephew's in Maryland. That kid could bat those lashes and get you to buy anything on the video game aisle.

Lily needed to focus, it could mean her life one way or another.

"May I see your badge?" She extended her left hand out, still touching the scissors. He nodded and placed it in her hand. She had to use both hands to hold it, leaving her guard down. It looked like him; it looked official but she had never seen a federal badge. He seemed sincere but it could all be a ruse. For what? To return to the scene of the crime because he wanted the ham sandwich residing in the trash? Or maybe he wanted to heist tissue paper this time?

Come on Lily, get hold of yourself. He was real.

She read the badge number. He pulled out two more

pieces of identification. He hadn't taken a bad photo. Even his driver's license photo was good and his middle initial was "A". Ok, he seemed legitimate. She handed the items back to him and slid her weapon under a binder.

"Let's sit down at the table up front."

He wanted her to walk in front of him but she insisted he go first. If things went wrong she could stab him in the back. She needed her weapon of doom.

God, stop thinking like this. Too many television shows. He did chivalrously pull the chair out for her and she made a concession to sit down first. Lily slid her portfolios of happy brides and grooms over to one side. The little table for consultations made him appear even larger than when he stood. His knees were knocking up against the edge.

"So I need you to recount what's been going on around here. I know about your flower wholesaler's break-in and now your's. Anything else?"

She thought about it for a second. "Well, the weirdest thing happened…"

She began the story of the preservative packets. He pulled out a small note pad and began to write a few lines. He wasn't laughing. He was taking everything seriously, not like Officer Jerk Face.

She ended with, "Do you think this is all linked together?"

He looked up at her and put the pad down on the table. "Well, yes."

Her mouth must have gaped open since he smiled slightly, not nicely; well it was nice, but more humorously, at her.

Ah hah! Her stomach and its weird feeling had proved her correct one more time.

"I knew it. I knew it. Oh Lord, you don't know how much better you just made me feel."

"All right," now he was actually laughing. "I've never had anyone be happy about their involvement in a burglary but whatever makes you happy."

Now Lily was laughing. "I bet you haven't. Sorry, it's just that I've felt that something was wrong. Things weren't adding up but it still doesn't make any sense to me. What the heck is going on…if you can tell me."

He nodded and put the pad and pen away. He leaned over, nearer to her with his hands folded in front of him. She could barely smell a touch of cologne. He smelled fresh, maybe hotel soap…good hotel soap? She noticed he recently had a haircut, just a little of his neck had a different tan line and at this time of the day he had that stubble again. He had used the hotel shaver again. It looked like he had a mustache when his face tanned, the coloring under his nose lighter than the rest of his face, oh except for the chin. He'd had a beard and longer hair? Hmmm. Lily made a note to herself…stop watching those mysteries. She and Jessica Fletcher would have to part ways.

"I've been tracking Cartel shipments through Miami and by mistake you received that box."

She cocked her head to the left. "What? How?"

"We think someone at the airport didn't pick up a shipment of drugs that was being smuggled into the States through flower boxes. They were shipped from Miami to your wholesaler and your wholesaler delivered them to you;

your dead hydrangeas, the ones with the packets that were stolen out of your dumpster. They apparently came back for the ice blocks. We're pretty sure they were packed with heroin too."

Lily blinked a couple of times. "Drugs? Here? In Kansas City? In my shop?"

"Yes, it's not that unusual, just the way they did it, and of course, their mistake. If they hadn't messed up you wouldn't have been involved in any way."

They should have made a list, was her first thought. All this insanity was because someone in the Cartel made a mistake. Now she was just plain mad at incompetency creating chaos in her life.

"So now that's it, right?"

His face showed no emotion. "We think they may have missed something, maybe something with the box. We think you or your wholesaler may unwittingly still have it. We aren't sure. So," he let that word linger on the air for awhile. "We have begun surveillance on your wholesaler and now, given the activity you've had, for you."

"Surveillance of what? What more do they want? They came back and got the ice blocks. I have a business to run, and you don't seem to understand that I have weddings to do this weekend. This is my work, my job," she stopped right before she said her life. What else did she have?

He sat back and placed his hands on the edge of the table.

"I totally understand. We won't get in your way at all. We just need to watch for a few days," the agent pushed. "And, we need to keep you safe. We want to make sure the

Cartel understands that you had nothing to do with this."

"Of course I didn't!" Lily yelled out. "How absolutely absurd. This whole thing is nuts."

"I agree. You've been caught up in a terrible mistake, that's all. Nothing more. Your salesman is aware of what has happened. Their business understands what we need to do. We just need to make sure the Cartel is done with this entire episode. We have contacts but it may take a few weeks for us to call them off."

Lily shut her mouth tightly, biting the side so she wouldn't cry. She should be overjoyed that, at least, she would be safe and they were concerned about her safety. She'd be safer than her security system and Big John's well-meaning patrols.

"Ok, so what do I need to do?"

"Nothing, absolutely nothing," he answered quickly as he leaned in again. "I'll be here now and then for the next few days and we will have your shop under surveillance. We may add an extra camera but no one will notice. I promise. We do not want to interrupt your business in any shape or form," he said calmly. "Especially during your busiest season. I promise."

She believed him, as unbelievable as it was. She utterly believed him. His eyes were consoling in some way and that gnawing feeling in her stomach was gone summarily. She caught a flash from his right hand and noticed a ring. It was a college ring of some kind, rather large. On his left hand there was no wedding band.

"You don't need wedding flowers, do you?"

Oh goodness Lily, what are you doing?

He laughed out loud. "No, I don't."

"Oh, already married?"

Again, why are you trying to interrogate the DEA agent?

"No, never. Easier that way."

She was, for some reason, happy and then again sad. He was single but it sounded like he preferred to stay that way. What was happening in her pea brain? *An attractive man comes into your store, into your world, and you want to latch onto him immediately?*

"So," he continued. "I am going to help you lock up, see you out and I'll be back tomorrow. Over night we will be installing the equipment, and no, we don't need your code. Your security company is working with us to give us everything we need. I will meet you back at nine tomorrow morning with the new code to open the store. You may tell your assistant, Abby, isn't it?"

Lily's head was reeling. "How about the police and our retired officer who does security for the boulevard shops?"

"No one else. This is an independent mission. The police will not be brought in, and do not tell anyone, even your officer friend."

Lily figured Agent Pierce had done his homework with background checks on everyone including Big John. She took in a deep breath. Steady, girl. This could be an adventure, a little excitement. She didn't want too much excitement. Abby would be thrilled to hear all of it, including the part where Agent Eyes was to be their companion for a few days.

"And as far as anyone knows, I'm your relative?" He was asking her more than telling her.

"I don't know. Everyone knows my family around town. Well, we've been here for a long time. They know my sister lives in Virginia; my brother is in Maryland and our parents have passed away. We can think of something when we need to, can't we?"

He nodded. "Now, let's get you home. I'll follow behind you to make sure you get in your house and then we will begin tomorrow."

Lily could pretty much control any emergency but she was darn sure she couldn't control this situation, or the agent sitting across from her. He'd be here for a few days, clean this mess up, make sure everyone was safe and then he'd be gone.

It would be like a visit to Disney World for a few days and you hadn't received your final bill yet; lots of good times, rides galore and a price tag that might scare you to death.

Chapter Six

True to his word, Agent Devlin A. Pierce was waiting by the shop's door when Lily arrived.

She almost didn't recognize him without his suit but the jeans and a nice polo shirt was a welcome sight. He looked more, more obtainable? Likable? Less government like? Lily was ruminating in her brain all the descriptions as she approached.

"You ready for the new code?"

"Yes, sir," she said as she saluted. That was stupid. Why salute the man for letting you into your own store?

"No need for the salute. I'm not your commander; I'm your security." He punched in only three numbers and opened the door.

"You are going to notice a slight buzzing sound now when someone comes in through this door. There's a louder one on the back door. Also, we are going to change the code every night when we leave. It's built into the system."

Those were upgrades she could never afford with her current provider. The whole Cartel mistake might work out in her advantage.

"So are you going to tell me the code or write it down so I can memorize it and then eat the paper?" She laughed and then slightly snorted with her own amusement.

He wasn't amused. "It's simpler than that. Today we

start with 1-2-3, tomorrow 4-5-6 and so forth. Then we start over when we get to 20, if we have to."

He would be staying only a few days?

"I know you know it's my busy season, but I forgot to tell you that this is one of my busiest weekends. I have to buy flowers today and then Thursday and Friday I'll be working here almost night and day, then Saturday we deliver the weddings. There will be some long hours. Don't want you to get bored."

As they walked into the shop, Lily headed straight for her desk. The agent climbed up on it and was tinkering with something on the wall.

"I won't get bored and no problem with the hours. I'm working and when I'm sent somewhere it's usually 24/7. I'll stay out of your way as much as possible." He jumped down right in front of her.

Lily looked up and wondered what she had gotten herself into, not just this whole Cartel fiasco but the thoughts she kept having about Agent Pierce. Her thoughts were lingering on his eyes, his face, his shoulders…Crud, for all she knew, despite the nice badge he could be the Cartel, infiltrating the entire DEA!

The door buzzed and a man in a grey suit entered. He nodded to the agent and held his hand out to Lily.

"Ms. Schmidt, I'm FBI Agent Tom Fullerton and we're assisting the DEA with the surveillance." He looked to Agent Pierce. "The view is great. We've got a clear view of the back alley and the back room. Those cameras are working. This one is looking good." He pointed to the wall above Pierce.

"Ms. Schmidt we really appreciate your assistance. We realize that this is a huge inconvenience. Agent Pierce will stay out of your way as much as he can and we all will do our best to keep you safe and to get this over with as soon as possible."

Lily liked this agent immediately. He was seasoned, confident and he looked like an FBI agent - whatever an FBI agent was supposed to look like in Lily World. She could see Agent Fullerton's badge latched onto his belt buckle with the big letters FBI. Well, if Agent Pierce was a member of the Cartel then his disguise was pretty good and he seemed to be very comfortable with Fullerton. Lily decided to have complete faith.

"Now, Ms. Schmidt if you need anything Agent Pierce is in charge. We are just assisting. Thanks again and here's my card if you need anything or you can't get him." Lily grabbed it and looked at the address. She'd call her friend at one of the local television stations to check it out but then she'd have to lie to her about why. Crud. Undercover work was not honest.

"See you, Dev. Great catching up with you last night." He was almost out the door.

"You too, Tom. That was something seeing George Brett. I'll call you if I'm still here next week, maybe do that sushi place on the Plaza?"

"Sounds good." He was already on the sidewalk. Lily's face must've shown some degree of astonishment.

"What?" Pierce asked. "I have to eat."

"George Brett? What does he have to do with all of this?"

"We ate at his restaurant. He happened to be there. Tom's

brother had been on the Royals' farm club in Omaha, he sat down, we talked."

She just nodded and looked at him. "Great. Well, um, I need to buy flowers. Abby will be here any minute and I'm off." She grabbed the file folder off her desk and headed toward the front of the store.

"And I'm going with you."

She turned back around to look at him. "Um, no. I'll be fine."

He smiled. "Um, yes. I'm going with you."

He smiled. What a smile. Lily took it in. He had almost perfect teeth except for one little tooth on the bottom that was off just a bit. She'd been wrong when she said he was the mysterious handsome stranger…in jeans and a shirt he was attractive, yes, but he was cute. Devilish cute, like a little boy caught stealing a warm cookie.

"We had a deal, Ms. Schmidt. Remember?"

She nodded and turned away from him to look through her file. She had a country club area wedding this weekend. What was she going to to do with *him*? If he insisted on being her constant companion then she hoped, sort of, that everything was solved before Saturday.

Producing a large wedding was nerve wrecking, adding a high maintenance client with an over- the-top coordinator was insanity, and piling on a DEA agent who was there to solve a case and protect her was the perfect definition of a world gone mad.

"Fine. When Abby gets in the door, we make sure she has coffee. If she doesn't have coffee, she will need to get some. You do not want to see Abby without coffee."

He came up beside Lily and looked down at her. "We also need to bring her up to speed on what is going on and introduce your new employee."

"My employee?"

"Me," he said proudly patting himself on the chest. "By the way, what is an Abby without coffee?"

"Ah, Abby without coffee is, well, to put it nicely: Frankenstein. The monster Frankenstein, not from the Mel Brooks' movie. Got it?"

"Got it. Coffee. Abby must have."

She smiled. "Mel Brooks, not Yoda."

Bubbling, happy in love Abby, with coffee in hand strode into the shop. She pulled up short as she looked at Lily and then the man.

"Well, hello stranger." Her lyrical greeting was reminiscent of the old Hollywood actress Mae West and her sultry salutations.

Lily just shook her head. Oh Lord, he was going to be a distraction in so many ways. He already was for her but if the agent wasn't careful this college sweetheart would forget her latest Jeremy and fixate on his very prominent dimples when he smiled. Now Lily was doing it again.

"Abby, sit down. We need to talk to you."

"Yes, mommy," she laughed as she sat down. "Do you and daddy have something to tell me? I knew there was something up between you two when he came in." She was laughing full out as she looked at their blank faces. Lily now had her hands on her hips and was very serious.

Abby stopped laughing. "Oh, geez, you are either firing me or someone died."

"Not yet, and not yet." Lily was not amused by anything right now. "This is Agent Pierce with the DEA. Our burglaries of those stupid packets and the ice blocks have something to do with a drug shipment. He," she stopped to motion to him, "is here to surveil and to keep us safe for a few days until they make sure we *are* safe. He'll be around, that's all. Also, we have added security including cameras so don't do something stupid while you're working."

"Like pick my nose or something?" She still wasn't taking this seriously.

"Like something," Agent Pierce finally said. "This is serious. We want to make sure you and your boss are safe so just do what you do and I'll do what I need to do. We can go into everything after we get back." He was not smiling and there were no dimples showing. He seemed to emphasize the word 'need' and Abby finally stopped joking around. She took a drink of coffee and nodded affirmatively.

"So," Lily interjected. "We are off to buy flowers as usual. We've got those vases back there that need to be set out and then the to-do list is by the back phone. Just get as much done as you can. Then after we process the flowers we'll call for pizza. I'd like to get as much done today as possible. We have the Ward Parkway wedding this weekend. And we have Gretchen."

"What's a Gretchen?" Agent Pierce asked quickly. "Anything I need to be concerned about?" Abby and Lily shared a knowing look between them.

"You should be very afraid," Abby answered seriously. "Very afraid."

"I never knew so much went into just flowers for a wedding," Agent Pierce admitted on the ride back to the shop. "You have to do all that matching stuff every weekend?"

"Sometimes. This weekend the one client is very, very particular so it's mandatory. Most of the time it is easier but not with this one. Brides and moms are very special people. Something happens to most women when they're planning a wedding. It's some unexplained phenomenon that is just in a female's DNA. DNA…your expertise?"

He chuckled. "DNA, huh? Well, Neal seems nice. Very nice people down there. It's a shame this has happened to all of you."

That was nice of him. Yes, it was a shame and a nuisance, one she didn't need…ever. Certainly not this weekend nor any weekend. She had been just plodding along nicely if not quietly boring. Life hadn't been the same lately. Now it wasn't the same at all.

The car was quiet when he finally asked, "What's this processing thing you do with Abby when you get back?"

"Well, it's our word for it but basically we unpack all the flowers, cut and hydrate them, making sure they get clean water with some solution to keep them fresher longer. Some flowers get refrigeration and others need to sit out and open their blooms."

"So, I can be useful. I'll unload the van, you all do your processing thing. I can also use a phone and order a pizza."

She smiled at him while they waited for the red light to change. "Can you now? That does take talent not to mention, what kind of pizza were you ordering, Agent Pierce?"

"Well, Ms. Schmidt, I'm going to order what you all want. I learned a long time ago to just eat whatever was in front of me."

The light was green and she looked ahead. "Disciplining mother?"

"No, actually it was a corp cadet."

"Huh?"

"West Point. You needed to eat what was in front of you or you'd starve between the hours, the classes, the physical exertion. I learned it after two weeks there. I never thought I was a picky eater and because of that cadet, Cadet Phillip S. Branford, I am not to this day. Well, him and MRE's." He saw her confusion and it begged for more explanation. "Meals-ready-to-eat, you know, those packaged meals the Army hands out to you in the field? Didn't you see them on TV during coverage of the war after 9/11?"

It finally dawned on her. "Oh, yah. Like rations during World War II. Sorry, my brain went silent for a bit. So, you were in the Army? You were in Afghanistan or Iraq?"

He was silent for a few seconds. "Well, yes, yes and yes. That's all Ms. Schmidt."

And the door of open conversation was shut soundly. The sharing was dismissed with the uttering of her label. The silence was deafening for a few minutes.

"What is this Ms. Schmidt stuff? It is way too formal. Everyone calls me Lily. Since you will be unpacking my van you've sort of become an employee. Besides, if anyone hears you they are going to know something is up. They won't know what but they'll think it is a little weird."

"Ok, Lily. I suppose if I'm your employee then you should just call me Dev."

"Not Devlin?"

"Either is fine. We should drop the agent moniker as well, just in case someone is listening."

And he was back at work again and not only had a door shut once in this conversation, but now all the windows were being closed. The draft of information flowing had been too much for him. He was on the job, and she was the job. He remembered that but why couldn't Lily keep that in mind? He wasn't a date; he was an agent working on a drug case. He wasn't someone who had popped into her life to save her from the world she had created for herself. He was there to save her from a world that was existing around her. She had to remind herself that he was on the clock and when the clock chimed midnight in her fantasy world he wouldn't be there to grab her shoe or keep her from falling.

Chapter Seven

Saturday came way too soon for Lily. This week was proving a little overwhelming and it was all because her schedule had been compromised. All this criminal hubbub was just too much. If she wasn't thinking about it while she worked on arrangements, she was looking at it, at him… Devlin Pierce. He tried to blend in by making sure Abby and she were fed, that the phone was answered and that every customer who came in the shop in the last few days were welcomed and handled. He could handle people with that boyish smile she saw now and then. It seemed like his eyes sparkled especially when he spoke to women.

He wasn't Heathcliff but he could brood. His brow furrowed and those sparkling eyes went dark, almost hazel in color. She caught him with all smiles when Mrs. Notte and her grandson picked up her usual bouquet (Mrs. Notte announced he was a great addition to the shop's ambience.) but when he turned to retrieve the arrangement out of the cooler his face had completely transformed. Dark secrets were revealed on his face but she could only imagine what they were. Lily also noticed the usually well mannered and totally sophisticated garden- party-loving Mrs. Notte checking out the agent's physique. Her grandson, Garrett, preferred to slump in one of her chairs and look around the store. He was an odd one, a trust fund baby who had nothing better to do than jet set all over the world. Mrs. Notte had told her he had just returned from Argentina.

Her octogenarian client was now watching Dev walk away from her to go to the cooler. She was admiring the back of his jeans. Lily almost laughed out loud when the lady was nearly caught as Dev brought the arrangement to her too quickly. She had managed to pretend she was searching in her purse for something. Whew, that was a close one! She started to study him as he interacted with the now giggling elderly customer. Lily had noticed the perfect shoulders before but now she saw the the lovely tapering of his torso and strong muscled legs. Could a man be lovely? He could when his eyes sparkled, it had nothing to do with the body. She shook her head and went back to work. Enough. He will do his job and then he'll be gone to God knows where. Besides, she had her own job to do.

By Saturday morning she was in wedding mode and devoid of Devlin Pierce's charms. He was just another set of hands helping to load the van.

"No, that arrangement doesn't go with us. We're only using the hydrangeas." Dev looked at Lily, looked down at the flowers in his hands and then back at Lily.

"Ok," he muttered. Abby magically showed up behind him and grabbed the flowers out of his hands.

"She means these white ones. These are hydrangeas." She passed a box full of white blooms his way. "You'll catch on, newbie."

She giggled as she walked away but winked at Lily.

"Oh, Abby, go grab boxes out of my car. We can use them to pack the bouquets, boutonnieres and corsages. I've been meaning to bring them. My keys are by the phone."

"I've got your keys right here." Abby was on her way to the side parking lot.

"I sincerely doubt I will ever catch on, " Dev acknowledged. "You all have more names for more flowers than I will ever remember or ever care about remembering."

He loaded the box into the van and went off to catch up with Abby to help with her load. He could just picture the scintillating conversation in a Georgetown bar with his coworkers one night…

"Yes, those hydrangeas are just gorgeous, don't you think? I wonder if they're from South America." His female colleagues would swoon and the guys would wonder what had happened to him in Kansas City. What could happen to you in Kansas City?

And why were they giggling about the whole hydrangea thing anyway? Dev knew something was up between Lily and Abby and it was at his expense. What had he done? He had picked up the wrong arrangement. He didn't know what hydrangeas were…he stopped in the parking lot and held his head down. Damn, he was losing his touch. A good agent remembers his lines and he suddenly recalled his lie when he had first entered the shop. A good agent didn't have to deal with a wedding florist, one who seemingly remembered conversations verbatim and made incessant OCD-leaning lists. Lily had known there was something up with him from the very beginning when he lied about hydrangeas being his mother's favorite flowers. He was more adept in a cave or a desert in the Middle East dealing with terrorists than in a flower shop in the middle of America.

Abby and he carried back the boxes. Abby began to fill them with more flowers. Lily was looking at her order and going over it one more time. Yep, she was definitely OCD. Dev had that right. Did the woman ever just look at anything one time? She was constantly writing down this, taking a note there, checking and double checking. She could produce a piece of artwork with her post-it notes alone. He continued to step back and watch as bouquet after bouquet was unwrapped, checked, rewrapped and packed into the boxes.

Dev had seen this week's list. She had added "try to do a wedding with HIM". Did she think he was an imbecile? He wasn't always an agent or a soldier. He'd worked all through high school, first as a sacker at the local grocery store, junior year at McDonald's and senior year at Corman's Law Office. He wasn't some privileged pretty boy who had his entire life plotted out and paid for with his grandparents' money. His middle class family worked only hourly paid jobs. His mother wept, actually sobbed as he walked across the stage to receive his degree.

He was the first one in their family to do so. And when he threw his hat up in the air in celebration at West Point his mother was worried to tears that he might not find it! You never find it, the local kids pick those up. It was the American dream as far as they were all concerned. Their son had graduated from West Point. It seemed so long ago with so many memories growing between that happy day and now.

They should see him delivering flowers. They'd be so proud! They packed the last boxes into the front of the van and when Lily said they were ready to go he jumped into the passenger seat and buckled up. Hopefully he would make his family proud.

"It smells like a funeral home in here," he complained. Lily was placing her sunglasses on but he still knew she was glaring.

"It's supposed to. They are flowers." She began driving down the alley and on to the large wedding.

"When we get there, if you'll just start bringing in the flowers that would be great. Begin with the last three boxes we put in the front part of the van. That's their personal flowers. I'll keep them near me. The rest, we will separate according to rooms once we unload everything. I don't want dead flowers out in a hot van."

He laughed out loud. "I believe dead hydrangeas created this whole mess and gave you a new employee."

She paid attention to the road but smiled. "Yes, I suppose so but we don't want or need them today. Oh and don't try to be anything but a delivery guy today, please. This is a large home wedding, city known client who is difficult enough without having to explain you."

Dev began to complain, at what he didn't really know, but maybe it was her tone. Again, he wasn't an imbecile.

"Ms. Schmidt, I do know how to act around people. First, my mother taught me skills and then I have taken a few training courses."

"We are talking people, Agent Pierce. We are talking about a bride, her mother, her father, her wedding coordinator. Oh just wait. I can't wait to hear your assessment on Gretchen." Lily laughed out loud. "I can't wait to see you try to boss her around, so just take your lead from me and please, please don't deviate or try to get cute. Gretchen is a force of nature or black magic. None of us have figured it out yet."

He grinned and allowed his silence to say everything until he couldn't hold it in any longer.

"I'm always cute. At least, that's what Abby thinks, oh

and that nice Mrs. Notte."

"Mrs. Notte is probably delusional. Her chauffeur drives her to the store usually. Her grandson wants her committed so he can have control over her money and her credit card is monitored by her son in Bermuda because she can't keep track of anything. So don't hang your hat on her opinion. As far as Abby, well, she's young. Let's leave it at that."

"And you are immune completely, right?"

She didn't dare look at his smug face. Had he caught her studying him? What an egotist, a bore, a narcissist…what were some other words to describe him? She pretended to look out the window at some tree.

He laughed out loud in the silence. "I shut you up? I actually did it. I didn't know it could be done."

She knew her face was completely red with embarrassment. "You did not. I just don't know how to answer your absurd question. It's just that…"

He continued to laugh. He was beginning to enjoy delivering flowers.

"Just what, Lily?"

"I'm just saying that Mrs. Notte is Mrs. Notte and Abby's views of life and love are quite limited." She tried to keep her voice level but it almost sounded like stammering.

Dev stopped laughing abruptly. He wouldn't attempt a witty comeback at least not until they finished for the day. He stared out the window at the houses, the trees, the fountains on the parkway, anything to avoid eye contact with the "boss". He was a well educated man but in one sentence he had learned to never poke this bear again and if he did he might very well pull back a bloody stump. Or he could jeopardize his real job and the reason why he was even with her. Obviously she thought that one must be delusional or limited to find him attractive. She had her secrets too, it was obvious. Apparently her views of life and love were more expansive than he had thought. Who had hurt her?

It seemed like an eternity of silence until the van pulled into the long driveway and past the wrought iron gates. He was amazed at everything about this area. The drive was as long as the entrance to his subdivision back home and the house itself mimicked a huge plantation house on the James River with its white columns to greet all visitors.

"Nice house."

"Yes and nice wedding. Like I said before, we will get everything in and then I'll start showing you what goes where. We have a lot to do and they need to be happy, no, overjoyed."

"I'm at your service," he smiled, trying to be as professional as possible since his last mistake.

"Cute, at your service, very cute."

"Cute?" he asked and let it linger in the air. He just couldn't resist. Lily pretended not to hear him and completed the drive.

They began to unload as a swarm of women surrounded them. They were all talking at once in a high pitch only dolphins could hear. He speculated that the one with the veil stuck into the back of her head was no doubt the bride and the worried woman to her side was her mother.

The rest of the younger women looked like the girls he

usually saw in the bars in Alexandria, Virginia. They were young professionals on a path to debt or marrying up.

"They are so pretty. Do you work for Lily? Who are you? Is my bouquet there? Where does this go?" How could she listen to this all the time? He just put his head down and let the boss do her magic. As far as he was concerned he was deaf and dumb, not seeing, hearing or saying any evil.

Lily was now in her element with no thoughts of burglaries, the Cartel or even an attractive DEA agent. Calmly she told them they needed to unload all the flowers and get them out of the heat and then she would bring them their bouquets. She smiled nicely at her customers and agreed that the flowers were especially lovely this week. She wondered how they were doing and if they were excited. She mentioned it was a beautiful, rain free day with "look at these amazing, magical blue skies", just like she had promised her very worried bride.

Dev kept making his trips inside and then back out. He was actually beginning to sweat like he would during a mild workout. She did this every weekend? Lily was sweating too but looked more like a water fowl, calm at top and constant motion below. She just never stopped.

When they both reached the doorway, Dev blocked her, placing his hands barely on her shoulders.

"Why don't you just stay in here? You can talk to them and start to do your thing and I can do the grunt work. Give me the keys and I'll move the van when I'm done."

She nodded appreciatively and handed him the keys from her pocket. She was grateful she didn't have to go back out into that humidity. She watched him go back out before turning to the flowers she needed. She was feeling a little overheated but the hottest parts of her body were her shoulders. They were on fire. "Laying on of the hands" would never quite have the same connotation. But he had barely touched her and it wasn't just his touch; his green eyes were sparkling. At her. His concern for her welfare seemed genuine. He was looking at her, not as a subject in an investigation or even as a pretend boss. Her imagination was running wild.

"Shake it off," she murmured out loud. She had a wedding to do. Dev made a few more trips in, announced he had checked the van once and then twice to make sure everything was in and now was moving the van. A few minutes later he was at her side removing box lids. She was checking her paperwork when Gretchen Malloy came around the corner and stopped in her tracks.

"Well, hello. Whose little boy are you?"

Lily looked up and noticed Gretchen's view. She might throw up. But she couldn't. She did have some sort of regurgitation in her mouth and could taste her breakfast cereal. The woman's voice was like silk, usually it was like sand paper.

Dev said nothing, preferring to smile and to follow his boss's instructions.

"Hi Gretchen," Lily finally answered. "We're going to set up the inside first because of the heat and we'll do the outside last. The girls' bouquets are over there so just give me an hour to get things organized and then you can ask me about anything you need."

Dev could tell Lily was talking through her teeth, her mouth so tight he could see her jaw muscle. Obviously these two women tolerated each other professionally but they definitely didn't go out together and get a coffee on a day off. The older woman was full of pretense. She reminded him of a male peacock with color galore and knowing it. Her hair color was an outrageous shade of platinum and her face had layers of pasted makeup, more than her years could support. Her dress was print and stuck to every inch of her body. Black Louboutin shoes finished her look, the red bottoms visible as she hit the last step. They clashed with her dress. He knew those pricey gems from a relationship a few years back. They both realized it was over before it started. She had been all country club and he was the caddy shack. It was as simple as that.

He felt protective of his pretend boss immediately as the other woman snaked her way to his side. She was looking down at Lily, figuratively and in reality.

She looped her arm around his. "Lily, you do what you need to do, dear, and I'll just talk to your new man." She seemed to emphasize the last word.

Lily really did think she would throw up and if she did, she hoped to projectile right on Gretchen's pretty shoes. How the heck did the woman work in those stilettos? Lily just kept her head down knowing full well that her comfy shoes, her little black dress and light jacket, her haircut and color, her jewelry not to mention her entire body didn't add up to the price tag of those shoes. Hmm, wasn't there a witch who had a house fall on her and a little girl took her shoes? Where was the water bucket?

But Lily was in charge of her own business. Dev stood completely still as he glared down at Gretchen's touch. Was he in shock or was he going to body slam her? Lily couldn't take a chance on the latter.

She moved to loop her own arm around his other.

"I need to show my helper where the arrangements go so if you'll excuse, Gretchen, we have to get working. We can't just stand around and look pretty."

Dev felt a rush of relief. He had felt like a Christian being played with by the lion. Lily pulled him away from Gretchen's grip.

"That woman is a piece of work," he whispered when they were far enough away from her.

Lily shook her head. "You have no idea. We tried to warn you but you really must experience her for yourself. Later, I'll buy you a beer and tell you about the time she was so drunk at a reception that she grabbed the DJ's microphone and propositioned him."

"Really? Wow, this could be fun."

Lily still had her arm in through his and she tightened her grip. "No fun for you, mister. You are working, remember?"

"Yes, ma'am. Show me what I need to do."

Chapter Eight

For the next two hours, arrangements were placed, garlands were attached, flowers were pinned on and given out to the delight of everyone in the house. Lily always thought that wedding flowers were like Christmas morning presents…you knew you were going to get a gift that was brightly wrapped but you had no idea what it was or what it looked like. Dev just stood back watching Lily go. The work was her. He knew what that felt like. She was pleased when they were pleased. She smiled when they smiled. She was mirroring their emotions. Then she turned around and the smile and joy had vanished. He saw glimpses of the real Lily, the Lily that had sudden sadness color her face. What was causing that? Had it been some life or love experience that she supposedly had more of than Abby that created pain on a canvas of joy?

Obviously Lily was tired. He hadn't realized how physical creating wedding beauty could be. She carried box after box, stood for hours assembling and then she went out and delivered the result, creating an atmosphere of calm and happiness. She was really a force of nature.

Luckily, she was so in her world that she didn't notice him watching her. Advantage for him, for now. He liked studying her not for the investigation but for information. She was prey, but not for killing, he truly enjoyed watching her, watching what made Lily, Lily. Then his training checked in and he could feel eyes watching him. Behind him he could feel that coordinator's searing watchfulness.

He could also see her in the mirror on the opposite wall. She seemed fixated on him, well actually she was staring at his derriere. Really, this woman needed to be spayed or given some hormone treatment for overage sexpots. He looked away when he saw her moisten her lips. He just shook his head. Lily would get him out of this safely.

"So, boss, what else?"

His boss looked up, catching the view of Gretchen Malloy salivating, eyes fixed on every woman's favorite part of Agent Pierce's body.

"We are done. We are out of here."

"Thank God," he whispered.

Gretchen stepped in between them. "So, Lily, I need a few of the boxes for later when I take a few things down."

"I know you usually need them so I already left them in the garage. I stacked them in the corner. You will see them when you walk in."

"Um, so, Lily you never told me who this piece of dynamite is. Is he another one of your relatives or one of Abby's boyfriends?" Her voice dripped with sarcasm. She was totally insinuating that he couldn't possibly be her's. Of course, he couldn't possibly BE her's!

"Well, actually," Lily began but before she could even begin, Agent Pierce interrupted.

"We've been dating for a few months now so I thought I would help today." He was nonchalant, convincing with a lie this time and simply distracting to Lily as he moved to her side and slipped his arm through her's to hold her hand. Devlin Pierce had never touched anyone in an investigation like this, even when he'd been under deep cover. But this felt natural and besides he was fighting for Lily's honor. He was loving the look on the coordinator's face.

Gretchen Malloy was in complete shock and Lily smiled at the priceless look. So Agent Pierce could deceive effectively. His comment and her reaction was worth every cent of sarcasm and degradation, every dollar of inconvenience that she had ever experienced from that woman. She would definitely buy him a beer.

Finally, Gretchen released a breath and just uttered one word, "well". And then she repeated it again and again. Finally she looked back as she walked toward the garage and with a wave of her hand, dismissed them from her sight. She said it was nice to meet him and good for you Lily.

Gretchen Malloy was in shock. She never thought the girl had it in her. She opened the garage door and immediately saw the boxes stacked in the corner. They had been used for the bouquets and personal flowers. She grabbed a couple and moved them nearer her parked car. She turned her ankle a bit and the boxes toppled from her hands. A lid flew off landing near her trunk.

Inside were two ice blocks long forgotten beneath the colorful tissue paper. Gretchen grabbed them. She wasn't about to call Lily and her man back in. She'd keep them and use them on future weddings if she needed to but she had another purpose for them in mind.

"I'll use them this summer," she said out loud.

Lily and Agent Pierce walked silently to the van and closed the doors before they both convulsed into laughter.

"Did you see her face?" Dev couldn't breathe. "Oh that

was more fun than I've had in a long time, to take down someone in one sentence. I wasn't even nasty. She deserved so much more. Why do you take that crap off of her?"

"Oh," Lily laughed, wiping the happy tears from her eyes. "You have to. We live in a social media world and she could kill my business in one blog if I said or did something out of place to her. Or if she even perceived it. But that WAS fun. One sentence, who would have thought?"

There was a silence in the van again but this time it was comfortable. Lily felt normal with him. Some magical door had opened again or maybe it was just a window but either way there was a nice energy flowing between them. And it felt so good to really laugh again. Times had been tough and she really needed this today.

"I suppose I really, really owe you a beer now."

Dev smiled. "Well, if that's the case, I'm pretty sure I owe you a date."

She faced him at the stop light and her smile faded. He had to fix this immediately.

"Since we are dating and all," he quickly added.

Her face softened and he saw a little of the sadness return that had vanished oh so briefly. "Yah, since we're dating and have been for a few months. Good one."

He supposed he had to turn it into a joke, just like she was doing. And the silence returned, replaced by the air conditioner humming. Then tension had returned and neither one of them felt any comfort in either.

Once back at the shop, they unloaded the van quietly, each avoiding touching the other by accident. Cheery Abby watched the somber duo.

"Who died?"

Dev looked up quickly. "What are you talking about? Something happen?"

"No. You'd think someone died as quiet as you two are. Did Gretchen do something? Was she a real B-I-T-C-H today?" She spelled out the offensive word.

Lily shook her head and continued to unload the remainder of the boxes into the storage room.

Dev handed her a box. "Well, that woman is a trip. I don't know how you two deal with someone like that. Let's just say she was interesting and I'm thinking it is safer being on a firing line than doing weddings."

"Wow, you really did have a baptism of fire working your first wedding with Gretchen and in one of the biggest houses in Kansas City. Good job. You survived," Abby patted him softly on the back. "The rest of the day went well…" Abby continued talking as she worked.

Lily continued to do her clean up and picked up a few words here and there of Abby and Dev's banter. She'd been warm all the way home, even with the air conditioning turned to high, and the warmth was focused on her arm and hand. Oh Lord, him again. She had to get hold of her feelings. Usually she was pretty good shielding the world from what she was really thinking. She told her sister only occasionally some of her thoughts but it was safe. Her sister was miles away and the phone was her barrier wall. If she only knew all her thoughts or the very dire ones her sister would move heaven and hell to get to her. If she only knew.

"Lily, Lily," Abby repeated when she didn't answer. "I'm going to head out if you you don't need me anymore?"

"Sure, sure. Thanks for all your work here today and I'll see you Tuesday, right?" She came forward from the room to stand with her two employees.

"Yes, Tuesday right after class. Another week of June weddings! Can't wait. See you then." She looked over at Dev. "Will you still be here?"

"Not sure. We'll see how the weekend goes." Noncommittal had never sounded so good.

"Well if something does happen I want to know all the gory details!" Abby grabbed her purse and quickly left the store when she saw her boyfriend's car out front.

Dev leaned up against a worktable with hands in his pockets. "So, boss, now what do you do?"

She didn't even look at him but went into the shop to retrieve her bag and other purse from the desk.

"Now, I turn off the lights, set the alarm, or you do, and then I go home." He followed behind her and headed for the front door.

"But then what?"

"I'll get something to eat," she answered as she left the building, waiting for him to set the alarm. "Then I'll watch some TV and go to bed early. It's been a long week and next week won't be any easier, except no Gretchen."

"Thank God for that." He was smiling at her. "Let's go get that beer and let's get some food to go with it. I really don't feel like dressing up enough for some of the restaurants around the hotel."

She wasn't waiting for him as she walked to the car but she could feel him following her footsteps.

"My car is right over here."

"Nope, I'll drive. I know where I'm going, you don't." She was already placing her bags in the back of the car. "In fact, I'll follow you to the hotel and we can drop your car there."

"No, Lily. I'll follow you to your house and we will leave my car there. Remember, I'm supposed to keep you safe. Besides, I want to make sure that the police detail is in place.

Police detail? She thought they weren't involved. When did that happen? This was really beginning to sound like a bad Telemundo soap opera complete with the Cartel stalking the florist.

"Really?" she muttered. "What next? Oh God, I don't want to know."

He'd reached his car. "I'm following you. That's it."

She was too tired to fight him. When they reached her house she was looking down the street at the cars parked on either side. Was anyone out of place? She noticed a black sedan parked across from her driveway. One person was behind the wheel. Could the police be any more obvious? Didn't they ever watch "Murder, She Wrote"?

By the time they reached one of Lily's favorite Mexican restaurants, the lunch crowd was gone and it was too early for the suburban Saturday night dinner bunch. She had discovered on the way over that Agent Pierce enjoyed salsa, chips and the occasional margarita. He wasn't much for the "girly" drinks but loved a good Dunkel, a German beer and a shot of southern bourbon. But since he was on duty, he wouldn't be drinking anything tonight. She had her very own government designated driver.

For someone who claimed to love Mexican food, he was studying the menu like it was a college exam. She dug into her chips and salsa after ordering the super sized margarita on the rocks with salt. The server brought it to the table and she was taking her first sip by the time she saw his face again, menu down on the table.

"Did you find what you were looking for?"

He eyed her large libation, his left brow raised. "Is that big enough for you?"

She licked the salt rim. "Yep. Just right. It was a long day. Heck it was a long week."

"Salsa is good, so are the chips," he grabbed two chips at a time. "I couldn't believe all the physical work…the boxes, the lifting, the walking, the standing in one place. I had no idea doing weddings were this much work."

"Some are easier and then you have one like today. Add on your friend Gretchen," Lily couldn't help smiling as she watched him squirm a bit, "and you have the perfect storm." She took another sip. "I'm just happy it all went well. And I'll be paying for dinner. You worked very hard today, sir. Also, I'm pretty sure Gretchen dodged a sexual harassment suit."

He smiled at that. "I can't let you pay."

"Yes, you can. It really is the least I can do for your help."

He was opening his mouth to argue his point but thankfully the server showed up. Lily ordered her usual enchilada and tamale combo and her "DD" for the night ordered the grande burrito with queso sauce. He asked the waitress if it was good.

"It's one of our most ordered items," she answered with a subtle little smile forming as she took his menu. "Your first time here?"

Lord, was she flirting? Lily was getting tired of every woman hitting on her, on her…on her nothing. He was nothing to her, just the agent assigned to watch over her for a little while and then he would be gone, back to wherever he came from.

He was continuing a lovely conversation with the young lady while Lily dug into her drink and more chips. She looked up at the girl and handed her the basket.

"We need more chips, please. Thanks." Maybe that would make her leave.

"Did we need more chips?" Dev asked as the woman trotted away.

"Yes, we always need more chips. You can't have too many chips." She was beginning to feel the tequila. The sound of the word "chips" felt funny on her lips. Oh right, she hadn't eaten anything since breakfast and had drank very little water today. He was smiling at her as she raised her head from the birdbath margarita.

"So you will be drinking, I mean driving us back to my house."

"You think? You need to slow down, sport."

Sport? What was she, his pet now?

"I'm good, at least, I'll be good when I get some food." She thought about the term and it dawned on her. They were becoming buddies. Oh joy, she just loved being buddies with men. That's a path she didn't care to go down, again.

"So where do you live when you're not traveling?"

"Well, I have a townhouse in Virginia, near DC but I'm seldom there anymore. I grew up in the area."

"I love that area of the country. My brother and his family are in Maryland and my sister is in Virginia. Hate the traffic but love the history, the old houses. The way you travel around you must think Kansas City is pretty boring."

He shook his head. "No, not at all. Beautiful city and the people are nice too. Your highway traffic is crazy in its own right."

"It's not just the highways. Believe me it's nutty everywhere. It was pretty quiet today but we didn't have to deliver to several places or go downtown. I think there's some festival going on near the Sprint Center this weekend. During the summer there's either a festival or some race. They run all over the place from the Plaza, Ward Parkway, Corporate Woods, and Broadway. I sometimes hate runners."

She wasn't slurring her words but words were just flowing from her mouth. Humored by the "tequila Lily" he studied her face with amusement. She had a nice face and very few wrinkles. He knew her profile, age, birthdate and her background but that never truly told you everything about someone, especially someone like her. She was a unique one. There was some hidden chapter in her past. Yet, she was an open book for everyone to read at other times. You seldom had that in one person, at least the people he knew as friends. Everyone had their secrets but usually he didn't want to know what they were. Her's seemed to be life experiences that she internally took in as flaws to her personality. Lord, he was trying to read someone who was drinking lots of tequila. He needed to turn off for just a little while.

But he was used to working 24/7. In the field, in war, he was always present in the moment and now that he was back on U.S. soil for awhile, he needed to settle down, take a breath occasionally. Even though he was technically working he needed to do that right now. He'd lost track of the conversation. Hopefully she wasn't expecting him to listen to her. What did she say? Something about a mouse in the bride's shoe?

"What?"

"It was in her shoe. Yep, just sitting there in her shoe. Sure hope our food gets here. I should've eaten something while we were in the car, a snack bar, banana or something."

"But, what, how did the mouse get in her shoe?" Dev really did want to know at this point.

"I told you. It was in the freight district in that venue that went bankrupt. They had mice, big ones with the prettiest little brown eyes, no wait, maybe they were rats. Can't remember."

He laughed out loud. That food needed to get there now. Thankfully, the server was placing their plates in front of them. As she walked away, Lily was still thanking her for her generosity.

During the meal she began to sober up. The lengthy sentences became shorter, albeit still pithy. However, she was still talking about the rodents.

"I'm so glad we don't have to go back down there ever again or at least until someone else opens it up again. Hopefully the city will inspect it and make the new owner do some extensive renovations to come up to city code."

"Well, I have to admit something, Lily," Dev began. "I'm not usually surprised or out of my element but today…" He shook his head.

"I know. Weddings are just their own monster. Even the simple ones are a circus sometimes. Today we kind of threw you in among the piranhas."

"I might have had a better chance dealing with them than that wedding coordinator." She laughed out loud at his blunt uncomfortableness.

"You mean you are telling me you have never, ever run into someone like her?" He looked up as if he was thinking rather intently.

"Hmm, let me think. Terrorists, machetes, hand grenades, land mines…Gretchen. Nope, I have never run into someone like her. I have this idea."

She leaned closer across the table as if he was going to tell her some military secret. "Yes?"

"I think we should send her to fight ISIS. Maybe they'd all stop thinking about those virgins."

She snorted out loud and then Dev laughed at her. It was one natural enjoyable moment for the first time since all this craziness began.

"I can just see her," Lily stammered as tears began to run down her cheeks. "She'd have the hijab on but her platinum hair would be pink by that time and under the robes she'd be wearing some tight little outfit and lots of gold necklaces. Her eye shadow would form cat's eyes. She'd be wearing those shoes."

Dev could see the sight in his mind. "You forgot the whip. She'd probably have a whip in one hand and a cocktail in the other."

An eruption of laughter made their table the loudest in the restaurant. Officially they had bonded over Gretchen. She would make sure Abby knew about the whip AND the cocktail. Sadly, Lily would never look at Gretchen the same way and she'd have to watch her demeanor from now on…she didn't need to die laughing every time she saw the woman.

As the end of dinner approached she did manage to grab the check even though she had a disgruntled dinner companion. It was the least she could do for him after the day he'd had. She was pretty sure weddings and how to work them were not in the manual of any government entity. He'd learned some things on the fly and he had helped her out.

The check was paid and she dug in her purse. She handed her keys across the table.

"I could drive but you're here and I might as well use you." She knew as soon as the words came out of her mouth that his one brow was going to raise and darned if it didn't. His eyes sparkled, that was just a bonus for her mistake.

"Use me? Interesting, Ms. Schmidt."

She was already warm from the hot humid day, the alcohol and now her goof. She envisioned that her face was probably a new un-named shade of red.

"I'm sorry, I didn't mean anything…"

"I know. Just had to mess with you a little. Been a long day. Let's get you home." By the time he pulled into her garage, Lily was done in. He walked her inside.

"So, you know that car will be out there tonight and tomorrow. They have been told they are working with the FBI. They are to keep their eyes on you and report any suspicious activity. I'll check in and find out what we know and touch base with you tomorrow. I don't believe you are in any danger but we like to be safe."

She nodded and understood. She didn't believe she was in any sort of danger either but she didn't mind the precautions really.

He turned to go and stopped at the front door. "You see anything out of place in the house before I go? Check your rooms before I leave."

Lily turned on every light in the house, including her bedroom and the guest room. She didn't see anything out of place. Everything looked just as messy as when she left it in the tornado state this morning. She checked every room quickly, looking for whatever. She really didn't know. If anyone was hiding they were doing a darn fine job in her little closet surrounded by her clothes and shoes stuffed in there.

She came back to where he was standing. "If it had been clean I would have know something was wrong."

He smiled. "So, one more thing. Where's a good Catholic church?"

She smiled. It was as though he were asking where a good place to get an oil change was. "Well, we passed my church on the way back here. Do you remember? They have services there seven-thirty, nine, ten-thirty, noon and there's one in the evening. Can't remember."

"I can make one of those and yes, I remember the church. I'll check in tomorrow. Have a good night, you deserve it."

He was already down the walkway and to his car when she closed the door. She leaned against it and sighed. Lord, it had been a day. It was time for a bath and then early to bed. It would make no difference that the sun hadn't begun to set. Lily giggled out loud.

"Gretchen with a whip and a cocktail."

Chapter Nine

No matter what happened on Saturday, how late or early she got to bed and how much sleep she had actually gotten, Lily Schmidt went to Mass at seven-thirty on Sunday morning. If she didn't go early she wouldn't go. It had always been that way since becoming an adult. She had some schedule to her life and her only normalcy was Mass on Sunday morning. During the winter the schedule deviated a bit if she had a Saturday afternoon off and she could attend at night. Then there were those occasional ice storms when she didn't venture outside, preferring to luxuriate in her flannel pajamas under the covers until she was so hungry she had to get out of bed. No one was going to make her breakfast in an ice storm.

She sat in her pew at the back of church. There were the usual parishioners but it looked like summer had already taken its toll on attendance. Many people were enjoying the lake this weekend too. Last week it had been the same. She was in her own little world in church. The quiet that was usually so deafening in her home was soothing to her here. She tried to talk to God but mostly she listened or at least attempted to listen. "Practicing Catholic" was a good term for her; she hoped that the more she practiced the better she would get at her religion.

There was always that diversion of the cute baby, the toddler smiling at everyone and showing them his cookie. She wanted that cookie. She always stopped and picked up something for breakfast as soon as services were finished.

Lily was listening to her already grumbling stomach and wondering what would be on the menu today. If she stopped for a sit-down breakfast then she'd stop at the grocery store later. She was out of milk, bread and she didn't think she had any eggs. She stared at the toddler waving his coveted cookie. She needed cookies if she was going to live through June. Lord, sorry for making lists in my head before Mass. Was that a sin? Making lists was an obnoxious behavior, at least Abby saw it that way. She didn't like post-it notes either. Neither one was a sin, Lily decided. If anything, they were useful indiscretions. Nothing to report to God or in any confessional. It was the way she operated with her useful tools even if other people, including her siblings, thought they were sources of deviant behavior. They didn't appreciate her organizational skills or the glory of them.

She decided she'd just pick something up, maybe a bagel. She'd go to the store later. She needed lettuce too, maybe some vegetables. She stopped making her list and wondered if the patrol cop had followed her to church. She hadn't noticed but at this time in the morning she didn't notice much. She was pooped. Maybe he didn't since she was out in public? Who knew. She was already weary of all this. Closing her eyes, Lily tried to listen to God again. Someone had sat next to her on the left. Why do that when the entire pew to the right of her was empty?

The lector was announcing the reading and the beginning of Mass when she opened her eyes. She focused straight ahead, sometimes on the toddler now taunting her with that cookie, until she opened the readings for today. After the beginning prayers she sat down with the rest of the congregation. Lily slightly looked to her left and saw a large college ring on the man next to her. It looked like…

She turned her head completely to see Agent Pierce smiling back at her. "Hi," he whispered. "Didn't know if I'd make it."

She whispered hello in response and stuck her head into the missal. Listening to the first reading was near impossible, concentrating on the second *was* impossible. She stood automatically for the gospel. She couldn't even remember her grocery list at this point but she could smell the light cologne he was wearing. Placing her head down to supposedly follow what was being read from the pulpit, Lily could see he had dark loafers on with lightweight slacks. He had his hands placed on the pew in front of them. She hadn't noticed how tan his hands were and there was not even a light line near his ring. Apparently he didn't wear the ring all the time. Did he spend a lot of time at the beach?

Thankfully, they were able to sit down. Listening to the priest's homily would take more focus than she had today. Agent Pierce was sitting next to her at Mass. What the heck? Was this standard operating procedure for the DEA? It was as much as her lists were a sin.

Lily was doing quite well with her unexpected guest through the main part of the Mass. He had reached for the kneeler for her and they'd knelt side by side. She smiled slightly at him. Wouldn't want him to think that she meant to ignore him.

When they stood for the "Our Father", terror came upon her, not the Holy Spirit. Lord, the next part of the service was the sign of peace when you reached over to the person next to you and wished them peace. How ironic was that to wish an agent with the department of justice, peace? But you also showed them a sign of peace…a handshake, a nod to your neighbors in the pews in front of you, a kiss. She'd have to shake his hand. She'd have to pretend to suddenly be comfortable with him when all through Mass she had felt like ants were crawling up and down her skin.

Get a grip, Lily.

As Devlin Pierce casually extended his right hand, Lily turned too quickly. His hand struck her left breast. There was no recovery. Both of them were laughing as a few people turned to look in their direction.

"Sorry," he whispered as he grabbed her hand and shook lightly.

"It's ok, I mean," Lily stammered. *Shut up, Lily, just shut up.*

Oh good, it was time to kneel again. Church would be over soon, thank you Lord.

When it was time for communion, he raised the kneeler for them once more. She knew he was behind her but she could also feel him there. His touch was warm again on her hand. She wasn't burning up but she could feel where his hand had touched hers. She would not even think about what her left breast was feeling. And in church, Lily Schmidt!

She had never been so happy to get out of Sunday Mass. They were walking side by side out to the parking lot.

"So, breakfast?"

"You heard my stomach, didn't you? Sorry about that. I was going to pick up something."

"I saw a coffee place on my way here, a couple of blocks that way." He pointed in the direction. "You want to grab something?"

She should say no, right? Why? She was hungry? He probably didn't know anyone else in town except that FBI agent, so why not?

"Meet you there."

1. What was it about Agent Pierce?
2. Why was she warm whenever he barely touched her?
3. Would her world ever become normal again... had it just been a few days of chaos?
4. Do laundry today.
5. Mow the lawn.
6. Go to bed early.

Chapter Ten

Lily was making her list in her head while she drove to the coffee shop, only he didn't pull into the coffee shop. She parked next to his car.

"I thought we were going for coffee? This is a very nice restaurant." He seemed to be walking faster than usual.

"Do they have breakfast?"

"Yes, but it's a little pricier." She hated to be cheap but she really wasn't in the mood to spend over twenty dollars on an organic omelet.

"Fine. I'm paying. Come on," he motioned to her. "I'm really hungry."

She cocked her head to the right and rolled her eyes. She followed anyway.

She'd only eaten there one other time last year when her sister had been visiting. They'd gone after church and drank mimosas until it was time for lunch. She would not be drinking today.

The coffee was very good and the complimentary orange juice was a nice treat. They were seated out on the patio under a huge black umbrella. Agent Pierce ordered a very large breakfast but Lily just ordered a mini omelet with toast.

It was silence between them again.

"It's going to be hot today. You can already feel it,

but this is nice. Nice breeze." Lily attempted to begin a conversation.

He nodded.

He was watching a family with two toddlers cross the parking lot.

"Do you like kids?" Oh my gosh, she did not just ask that. What was wrong with her? Had she lost all social conversation skills?

"That little guy has been hitting his sister and no one sees him doing it." He was laughing at the sight. "Um, kids, yes, I do like kids. How about you?"

"I love my nephews and nieces but they're too far away to spoil all the time. I don't see too many children in my work unless they are flower girls or ring bearers."

He took a sip of coffee and looked right at her. His eyes weren't sparkling and seemed darker than she had seen. He was shifting uncomfortably in his chair.

"So, I need to tell you a couple of things," he began seriously. "We are still trying to gain some sort of contact with the Cartel to call them off. We know the ones responsible and we actually know their contact in the Miami Airport. Sad to say they have several so it's a hot mess."

"What does that mean for me?" Lily fidgeted with the paper napkin ring. It didn't sound good.

"Well, you are stuck with me for a few more days. We don't want to watch you all the time but they now know you are under our protection. They just want their drugs, not you."

"Comforting. When will all this be over?"

Their food came interrupting the access to the information she needed most.

"Soon," he answered quickly while the server placed their plates on the table. "Soon."

Small talk took over the conversation in between bites. She had been starving but you'd thought he'd been on a ten-mile hike the way he attacked his food.

"So did you get flowers on your last birthday? I mean, do you give flowers to a florist?" Agent Pierce was scraping off half the butter on his toast.

"Never have had flowers delivered to me."

"On your last birthday or on any birthday?"

"Never any time."

He dropped his knife and fork. "Never, ever?"

"Nope."

"What the heck? So what does a significant other send to the florist girlfriend? This is fascinating."

"Um, well, balloons. But my family, well, the cookie cake was probably the best, delivered by one of the local bakeries." Lily smiled thinking about that birthday. It had been a good one before everyone moved away, some permanently with death.

"I didn't notice any flowers in your house last night."

"Kind of like that old story…the shoemaker's children have no shoes. Besides, I get tired of seeing them. The house is my refuge sometimes." She'd finished her breakfast and was now focused on her coffee.

"This was good," he announced as he finished the last

bite. "I love having breakfast out but back home I'm usually alone so I just pop into one the coffee shops. This was a real treat."

"So this isn't a usual Sunday morning for you?"

He smiled. "Definitely not. I live near Alexandria and I usually go for an early run, then the coffee shop, grab a newspaper, sit on the doorstep and read it. Then I'll shower and figure out what I'm doing for the day. When I'm not working, I'm sort of lost. I'm trying to…" his voice trailed off.

Lily completely understood what he was saying. She had her work and that was it.

Occasionally she would meet with girlfriends but most of them were married with families or divorced and looking for that exciting someone.

The server brought the bill and before Lily could protest, his credit card was in the man's hand.

"You really didn't need to do that."

"I wanted to do it. Besides, I would've gone for a run, found a coffee shop, you know," he laughed.

"Same old, same old. Happy to have saved you from it."

"So boss, what do we have on the agenda this week?"

Lily leaned across the table with a very serious look on her face. He leaned in too as if she had the most important information since the Bible.

"Weddings. More weddings."

Chapter Eleven

1. Work on orders
2. Check on timing for Loose Park wedding
3. Finish schedules for Abby
4. Make sure Abby's friend Bea can help at the shop
5. Purchase new ice blocks!

This Monday was no different than any Monday in June. Lily had a substantial amount of cleanup work to do today and she didn't have the distraction of shoppers coming into the store. Today, Abby was not coming into work; Lily liked the quiet of working alone. She loved Abby but too much sunshine actually did give a person a sunburn. Abby was the sun and Lily was a pale white girl who melted in the heat. She preferred the shadows, the corner of a room where her back could be supported by a thick wall and she could just watch what happened around her.

That's another reason why she detested this Cartel insanity. She just wanted to be left alone.

But did she? Amazingly, there was no Agent Pierce greeting her today. She carefully keyed in the code sequence de jour. Lily took a deep breath as she walked into a quiet shop, one void of any burglary damage. So far so good.

She was startled by the front door buzzer. Lily turned quickly, her keys still in her hand, to see Big John's smiling face. His hands were filled with two coffee cups.

"How's my little girl?"

She released her breath, relaxing the grip on the keys. "One of those coffees better be for me."

"You know it is," he answered as he handed the cup over. "I thought I better check in since the store is closed today. I heard about your problems."

She took a quick drink and motioned for him to take a seat opposite her at the table. "You heard about that?"

"Yes, some of my former buddies on the force heard about your break-in from some patrol cops. They told me to keep my eyes open."

Good, one more set of eyes couldn't hurt. It was normal to sit down and talk to John early on a Monday morning but he was earlier than usual today. But she really needed to just have normal, the sooner the better.

"How's your wife?"

"Well, that's why I'm here early. She has a doctor's appointment this afternoon and I want to go with her. She's having trouble with her hip again."

John's wife had a bad spill in December. The hip was healing through the winter and with physical therapy she was almost up to par. Lily had heard she'd spent time with her daughter in Florida in the spring and a little of that sunshine could do any body good. But John seemed worried and that worried Lily. He was such a gentle soul and he and his wife seemed to have a heavenly marriage. They'd been together for nearly forty years. They had survived a lot, even the death of their oldest son. A death of a child had to be devastating but to make it even worse, if possible, he had been killed by the police. John had still been on the force at the time.

His son had been involved in drugs and was caught at the wrong place, with the wrong people, at the wrong time. No wonder he had retired within a year after the incident.

They had their daughter but she had moved away years ago. Currently, she lived somewhere on the east coast of Florida with John's only granddaughter. Of course, he had shared everything about that little girl. His smile was from ear to ear whenever he even mentioned her.

"I'm sorry she's going through that," Lily said softly. "How did she hurt it again?"

John looked down at his coffee cup. "She fell. That's all. She just fell." He looked up at Lily seriously. "Everyone needs to be careful. You just don't know when you're going to get hurt."

Lily saw an emptiness she had never seen. That man loved his wife so much that it looked like he was taking on her pain. The look sent a shiver down her back…you know the one… someone is walking on your grave feeling.

She'd never been so grateful to hear that dang buzzer at the entrance. Both of them jolted to standing positions as Agent Pierce entered. He looked at John and then Lily, adding a smile in her direction.

"Hi, Babe."

Lily gulped the sip of coffee down. She had done everything not to spew it out all over the table. Babe? John looked at Lily and then at the man in the doorway.

"Something you forgot to tell me, little girl?" John cocked his head in confusion.

"Well, I really haven't had time, you know weddings and all, but this is, this is,"she was stammering.

Agent Pierce extended his hand out to John. "I'm Dev. Lily and I have been going out. We started months ago online…her sister knew a friend of mine, you know how that goes."

John smiled and then looked back at Lily.

"Well, well. Miss Lily, look what you have found."

She scrunched her shoulders as if she'd been caught with her hand in the cookie jar. Her eyes had widened at the story that was being laid on her friend.

"So you know Lily's sister?"

"No, my friend in Virginia knows Elizabeth. I think their kids go to school together, one of the girls."

"Ah, yes. Well that makes sense. So you two started talking online?"

"Yes. I had just gotten out of the military and I was trying to restart my life. We hit it off on Skype. Then I ended up with a business that does some work in Kansas City and I took the opportunity to see where our relationship might head."

Lily watched in amazement. The man who couldn't tell a lie to save his soul when he was with her was a real piece of work. Pretty soon John was suggesting where he should go for the best ribs, Dev was mentioning the local beer he enjoyed. Lily finally sat down and finished her coffee, watching them as though they were actors on a movie screen.

Dev was relaxed and charming. Heck, she started to believe they were in a relationship.

She was believing every little detail. He knew her sister via a friend of his? Did he really know her? Oh Lord, this was getting terribly confusing. So much for an ordinary day. She heard John call her name and she was shocked out of her stupor of fantasy.

"Lily," he began. "I think you've found yourself a good one. You deserve someone like this. Well, I better get going. You take care and Dev, it was certainly good to meet you."

John grabbed Dev's hand in his. "Now, make sure my little girl stays safe. Don't you be hurting her."

"No sir. I'll make sure Lily is not hurt by anything or anyone."

Lily smiled but deep down she thought there was some kind of secret messaging going back and forth between these two alpha males. She suddenly felt like territory that each dog was claiming.

John was waving back at her as he left the store.

She stood with only Agent Pierce in the shop. Her hands were placed defiantly on her hips.

She stared at him as if he had grown an extra head.

"What?" Dev knew that look. His mother used to have the same stance when he came home late from baseball practice.

"You can lie and you do it quite well, Agent Pierce."

He smiled coyly, tilting his head to the left. "Not lying, Ms. Schmidt, playacting. When it's necessary, I can do it very well." He straightened his head and stared into her eyes.

"This isn't a game, Ms. Schmidt. I know you don't like lying to your friends but it is necessary, at least for now. You need to get over your naivety."

Now she was mad. "Excuse me? Naivety? I'm taking all of this very seriously and I want it over. NOW! Could you please just leave?"

"Are we having our first fight?" Dev casually retrieved his phone from his pants pocket and checked a text message.

"Arrrgghhh," Lily sputtered. She walked away from him to the back room and began to clean.

It was several minutes until Dev leaned up against the door to watch her. Her face was beet red and he could see her hands shake when she moved a couple glass vases to storage. She kept her head down as she worked around the room. He casually watched her, studied her again.

"Lily, I'm not really trying to make light of this situation. Listen, as soon as we have confirmation that you are not in danger, we will be gone and you can go back to your little life."

She stopped in her tracks, throwing a broom down on the floor. Dev straightened up. What had he said now?

"My little life? That's so kind of you big bad government agent." She came closer to him and looked up at his stoic face. There were no twinkling eyes, no smile. "You are a real jerk. I want you gone. I want you away from here. Can you just go sit out in your car? My little life is just too little to have you in it, so bloody well get out." She shoved her hands against his chest.

Dev backed away. He felt another text message through his pocket. It was probably Tom suggesting something as he watched this all unfold from the safety of his downtown office. He knew she was just upset but he was having doubts about what his next move should be. He never had this feeling in Iraq or Afghanistan or any of the other "stans" he had operated in.

He slowly walked backward, his hands extended out in an almost surrender movement. "I'm going. I'll be outside and around. I'll stop back in later with some lunch. I'll bring you something." Short, choppy sentences worked on small children and terrorists. He was hoping it worked on short angry women.

Quickly, without any more words or actions, he was gone and Lily was left alone standing in the middle of her shop, her world. She sat down in the middle of the floor with legs crossed, holding her head in her hands. Tears flowed down her face and began to puddle in front of her.

"It's my little world," she cried out loud. "Mine, not yours. And it's not that little. It's, it's…oh Lord help me."

Dev sat in the car in front of the shop. Tom had texted. He called him quickly. "What's she doing?"

"Well, Dev, she's sitting on the floor, crying, muttering. Oh, wait, she's getting up and going back to work."

Dev shook his head. "She uses work as her therapy. That's all she has right now that she can control and I'm taking away that control. She's not happy with this whole thing. We need to get this over for her as soon as possible."

Tom Fullerton laughed.

"What's so funny?"

"Well, do we need to get this over for you too?"

"Talk to you later." Dev placed his phone down on the seat next to him.

He strained to see inside the shop. He could watch via his phone through the security system but he wanted to give her some privacy. He shook his head.

What was it with her? He'd had other undercover work and he had excelled in most missions and cases but with her it was different. He liked her. She was very likable…all her clients loved her.

It was easier dealing with terrorists, at least you knew their motives and how they were going to treat you…they were going to kill you unless you killed them.

But her? What was the end game with her? And did he even want, or need to play?

It was noon before he entered the shop again. She looked at him from around the door of the backroom.

"I brought lunch and an apology for entering your life. Can we eat?"

Lily watched him skeptically as he laid down two bottles of water and two sandwiches from the deli around the corner. She walked slowly to the table and sat down without saying a word.

He was unwrapping the sandwich for her, placing a paper napkin on her lap.

"It's turkey, provolone, everything but peppers, no mayo

but I have mustard here." A mustard packet appeared in front of her face.

"Thank you." Lily took the packet. He'd ordered exactly what she would've ordered. Had he paid that much attention to last week's sandwiches? Of course he did. He was a spy.

"I made a joke that was very inappropriate and it will never happen again." He was calm.

Lily almost thought he sounded more detached than apologetic. He'd built some sort of a wall between them in the last few hours. She had no intention of breaking it down. Actually, she was more mad at herself and her little world than she was at him. She was just angry that he had realized that she did exist in her own bubble, with only her work to feed her needs. It was a sad thing to realize you were alone and your life depended on only making others happy, never enjoying that same joy.

"I'm sorry too," she blurted out. Why had she said that? There was an uncomfortable silence.

He finally looked over at her. "You have nothing to be sorry about. This has all been overwhelming for you and I am truly sorry that you are having to endure the uncertainty, the hovering, me. I was over the line and it won't happen again."

"No, I, well, it's just too much. I just don't like lying to my friends or even to my clients. They come in and out of my life and they deserve all the truth and integrity that I can offer. Not to mention the flowers."

He smiled. The eyes were twinkling. She saw the fine lines around his eyes from years of the same smile and too much sun. His dimples were more "dimply" if that was possible. He was cute. He was handsome. He was a DEA agent there to protect her.

Keep focused, Lily, for your own sake. He'll get everything closed out here and you will never see him again.

"Oh the flowers, I remember them," he joked. "So what do we have this week, boss?"

She outlined her mental list of things to do and places to be. Her week was back on track.

They were back on track. What track that was, Lily really didn't know but they were rolling again in the same direction.

Chapter Twelve

1. Check all bouquets this morning before loading
2. Ice blocks with all bouquets...it's going to be hot
3. Abby will deliver Thompson wedding
4. Make sure Bea knows what she's doing at shop
5. Bea needs to see the pickup items and needs the timing
6. Take water...the park will be hot

Loose Park was one of the prettiest locations in all of the Kansas City area. Lily had gone to high school just down the street and on those very few perfect spring days when students were let out a little early, they walked down to feed the ducks. A huge pond was the focal point of the park but the terraced greens allowed walkers, runners and picnickers the perfect spaces.

Brides thought the rose garden was the ideal location for their wedding. It was intimate except for the joggers, the runners, the walkers, the picnickers and the occasional loose dog on the run. It was accessible to everyone and was a pain for Lily.

Lily thought the rose garden was lovely and romantic but it was always a hassle finding the bridal party, walking the distance with boxes of flowers and enduring the usual heat. It was almost like a credo...have wedding in rose garden, must have blistering heat and humidity.

Today was to be no different. She had other reasons why she didn't want to be there but those were her's to keep.

"All right, so the bridal party is less than five minutes away," Lily said to Dev as they sat in the van waiting. She had the air conditioning on full blast but the sun coming in through the window was negating the cool.

"Then what?"

"Well, we'll meet them right over there in the circle drive. I'll pin on the boutonnieres and you can get in the boxes to hand out the bridesmaids' bouquets. Then we are done. We have nothing more to do at the reception since we did that this morning. I may check in with Abby but you can go on."

He looked at her, one brow raised. "Really? I can go on?"

She snorted. "I really forgot who I was talking to, I mean, I was really treating you like an employee. Sorry."

"Enough apologies for this week, please."

He really did want to put Monday's experience behind them. He still wasn't sure what was going on in her head sometimes but there was enough activity to run a large corporation. She was always thinking, planning, proposing and moving. The woman needed to just be for awhile. He wasn't sure she could do that for some reason.

"Oh, there they are." She pointed at the brightly colored red and green trolley. Sweating men in their black tuxes were coming down the stairs.

Lily and Dev packed up their boxes and met them under one of the awnings. Lily did her Lily thing, smiling, laughing, pinning on flowers, commiserating on the heat as

Dev unpacked bouquets and handed them out. She came over to make sure the girls knew how to hold them and to tell them how lovely they all looked. Lily took her photo of the bride and groom and wished them well. She motioned to him to grab the boxes and back to the van they went.

He noticed her shaking hands as she put the key into the ignition. "You ok?"

"Yes, sure."

"You sure?" He motioned to her hands. "You're shaking. You can't be cold so what's up?"

She sat back in the seat and stared straight ahead as she watched the bridal party move down into the garden.

"It's so pretty here but it has some bad memories for me."

He watched her face. The light and smiling Lily was replaced by pensive and brooding Lily.

Had it been a bad relationship? Had something happened here? His thoughts went dark to crime…maybe she had been mugged or attacked here? A good friend lost forever due to some criminal activity?

He sat in silence as he continued to watch her. She needed to tell him; he didn't need to interrogate her.

"My last wedding here, the last time I had to come here, I received the call my dad was dying."

A sledgehammer hit his heart. He knew that feeling. He knew that call. He knew you could do nothing, absolutely nothing. Just do your job.

"Did you make it in time?" he asked softly. He wanted her answer to be yes. His answer would've been no.

"No, he was gone by the time I got there. I didn't have Abby at the time. Some of my family was still helping, well, they were there and I had this wedding." She stopped talking and then let out an uncomfortable laugh.

"Funny, but it was a day exactly like today. But I was alone." She was realizing how heavy the conversation had become. She had to change it. "But that was before I had my trusty assistant boyfriend." She punched him on the arm and laughed again.

He smiled but he could see the hurt. They had something in common, something that wasn't that uncommon but it still hurt the same.

"Let's go see Abby, boss," he suggested. "I mean what am I going to do tonight? Clean my hotel room?"

"Funny, very funny."

Chapter Thirteen

1. Italian wedding week!
2. Make sure coral roses are really coral not orange.
3. Need Abby and Bea on Saturday.
4. Check with hotel on timing.
5. Check with bride's mother when they will be at the church.
6. Make sure all vases, bows, etc are done in advance.

Lily opened the shop Tuesday morning and nothing was different about anything. Oh joy!

Everything was normal. She waved at John as she entered the shop. He was standing across the street talking to Garrett Notte, Mrs. Notte's preppy grandson. Nothing unusual about that. John had known that boy since he was little. Mrs. Notte and her family had been well known in the Kansas City elite since the early 1920's and now Garrett was taking his own place as an up and comer.

A few minutes later she heard the front buzzer. She looked up from the desk counter to see Garrett standing there.

"I don't have anything for your grandmother this week, do I?" She was questioning and answering all in the same sentence. "I thought she was visiting your aunt in Hyannis."

"She is and no, she didn't have an order. I'm here for a different reason."

He seemed serious. She grabbed her infamous pair of scissors as she stood up and came to the front of the store. "What can I do for you?" she asked as she hid them behind her back.

"Your assistant, Abby, is she around?"

"Not yet, what did you want?" Lily tightened her hold around the instrument.

"I wanted to ask her out on a date."

Lily was totally relieved. He just wanted a date and she had thought he was a serial killer.

This would be the one time Agent Devlin Pierce was not hovering.

"Oh, Garrett, that's really nice. Um, you should ask her yourself but I will warn you she is dating someone right now that she's reconnected with, a guy she knew years ago but just found again."

"So, when will she be in?"

He was confident and undeterred. Good for him, Lily thought. She would just give up at that point.

"She'll be in after lunch today so you might want to come back then."

"I'll do that. Thank you." He gave a glance around the shop and turned to depart.

Well, that was weird, Lily thought but maybe it was just because he was uncomfortable asking her about Abby. She needed to go back to work and get some things done before Dev came in. In an hour, she received a text saying he was going to be later today. One part of her hoped that his mission, the case was solved and over and that the right person in the Cartel got the message that she had nothing here but flowers. The other part of her was less than hopeful and sad that when it was all over her rather large world now would diminish into a minuscule existence.

She came out of the back room when she heard the buzzer again and there stood the mother of the bride for this week's wedding.

"Lily." She already had her arms outstretched to go in for a large hug. Lily fell into her and smiled at the other woman beside her.

"Carol? How are you?" Lily asked from over the shoulder of the other.

"I'm great. Theresa said she had to come and bring you the check and fabric for Anna's bouquet so I thought I'd come with her to see you."

"She's always a tag along," Theresa teased. "How are we doing for this week?"

"Great, never better. Flowers will be in tomorrow and then I start in."

Lily had known these two clients for over ten years when she began doing family weddings for them. Carol Dimaio and Theresa Baldini had been childhood friends and then their children had been childhood friends so when you had one wedding, and if you did a good job, you had every wedding. She appreciated their loyalty and in return she was loyal to them. She'd do anything for these two women.

"Have a seat, if you two have time." All three pulled up chairs and started gossiping about what girl was getting married next, what former bride was pregnant and who had more grandchildren. It was like being with family, only they paid you!

“Theresa told me it didn’t work out with that minister you were dating,” Carol said as she touched Lily’s hand tenderly. “You know there’s someone out there, don’t you?”

Before Lily could answer, almost with pinpoint precision, Devlin Pierce arrived with her favorite mocha coffee in hand.

“I thought you could use this,” his voice trailed off as six sets of eyes took him in.

Then the supposed knowing eyes began to move. Carol looked at Theresa, Theresa looked at Carol, Carol looked at Lily, Theresa looked at Lily, Lily didn’t look at anyone but Dev and then Carol and Theresa smiled taking all of Devlin Pierce in their gazes.

“Well, hello,” they said in unison.

Dev smiled and handed the drink to Lily. “Hello.”

“Nice, Lily,” Theresa said as she nudged her slightly in the ribcage.

Carol stood up and stuck out her hand. “I’m Carol, one of Lily’s former clients and you are?” “Dev Pierce.”

“Dev Pierce, what?”

He looked over to Lily for guidance. She was not helping him one bit. Her arms were crossed in front of her chest and she was smiling at his uncomfortable behavior.

“Um, well, Lily and I are getting to know one another.”

She nodded at him. Nicely done, Agent Pierce. Not lying to her clients was a nod in the right direction.

“Are you two dating?” Theresa yelled over.

“Well, we are going out, yes.”

Oh this was fun, Lily thought but she had too much work to do today to allow this to continue.

"So Dev's sister's friend knows my sister back east and they kind of put us in touch with one another online. Dev's working here for a few months so we are enjoying the summer together."

Dev's eyes were twinkling, looking right at her. So, you can tell a little fib, Lily Schmidt.

Good on you.

"Nothing better than summer love," Theresa announced. "Well, Carol, we better get out of these lovebirds' space and get going on the rest of my errands. Lily, we'll see you Saturday at the church."

Carol shook hands with Dev one more time, waved at Lily as Theresa hugged her florist. "He's nice, very nice," she whispered. "I wouldn't mind those shoes at the bottom of my bed."

"Get out of here, lady. You have things to do," Lily directed. Lily watched them pass in front of her window. They were blowing kisses.

"They are crazy but wonderful. I love them to death."

"They love you. Apparently, a lot of people feel that way about you."

Did they? Lily's heart increased its beating. He was being charming again. She was acting foolish.

"That's nice and it keeps me in business."

"But it's not always an act. You truly care about those two," Dev said. "That's a rare talent you have Lily. You really care. That's also your downfall."

"Mmm, thank you, Dr. Phil."

"All right. I'm done. So what's on the agenda? Apparently, that woman's daughter's wedding is this week?"

"Yes, the third of her family. It's a big one and it's an Italian one."

"And that means?"

"Flowers, lots of flowers, and bling and cookies and bridesmaids."

"Good or a bad thing?" he asked for clarification.

"A little of both. Come on, I saved the filling of the buckets for you."

"Oh goody. Can't wait." It was going to be a long week for him. With no word back from their contacts, this mission was becoming a cloudy mess. Eventually he'd have to go back to DC, eventually they'd have to remove Lily's protection, eventually they'd have to give up on whatever was going on here.

Dev woke at the sound of his phone by his bed. He looked at the time, 2:04 am, and the caller id.

It was Tom.

"A rock was thrown through Lily's shop window. We've got it on surveillance but all you see is a hooded man, we're assuming it's a man."

"Jesus, why do that?" Dev was rubbing his eyes. She didn't need that today. It was Saturday and that big wedding.

"Not sure. How you want to play this?"

"Can we get the window fixed before she gets there this morning? Let's not even tell her and see what shakes out."

"Sure, Dev. We can get it done. It's just plain glass and no wording so, I'll do it. What time is she coming in?"

He had to think. What was her pattern? Had she told him?

"Um, she told me eight so I'm thinking she'll be there by six or seven."

"I'll get it done right now. I'll text you later."

"Thanks Tom. I appreciate it."

Dev laid back in bed and stared at the ceiling. The small green light of the smoke alarm was blinking in its usual intervals. Why throw a rock through her window? That wasn't professional or something any drug dealer from Miami or South America would do. That was minor league chaos just meant to scare her for no good reason. She couldn't produce drugs she didn't have, but someone thought she still had them. He was completely confused.

The Cartel's sophistication using flower shipments was genius. Who was going to check all those boxes, all those stems, preservative and ice packets one by one in customs? No one. At best, a box here and there was inspected. They just needed to grab the contact at the Miami Airport and to make darn sure the Cartel knew there was nothing here in Kansas City for them. Especially not Lily. This mission was more complicated than it needed to be and it all surrounded her for some reason. He didn't like it one bit.

Now he had to lie to her again. Well, not really lie. This would be a lie of omission. How had a drug case become a mission about one little florist?

Lily took Dev and Abby for a beer and appetizers in the hotel's bar after the set up of the reception was over. That was the least she could do. The three of them worked well as a team and she had needed every bit of help the entire day. With over forty guest tables to decorate there was more than enough work. Besides, they had a great system. Abby and Lily decorated as Dev delivered in more and more flowers. Nothing fazed him today but she noticed he didn't look at her very much. Of course, why would he? He was working two jobs right now, and she was both of them.

"So, did you know Garrett Notte was going to come in and ask me out?"

Dev almost spit out his beer. "What? That little preppy guy that comes in with his grandma?"

"Yep." Abby was laughing out loud. "Can you imagine me going out with him?"

Dev took the fifth and didn't answer. He still didn't have a true sense of Abby. Abby was just, well, Abby. She was happy, she was sad. She was flighty without a care in the world, but she was worried all the time about what her boyfriend thought.

"He came in and told me," Lily admitted. "I told him you had a steady but he was pretty confident he could ask you and you would say yes."

"Well, confident isn't the word. He was pushy. He wanted to hang out and you knew he had never used that term before. The boy doesn't know how to hang out."

Dev sat back in his chair and took another drink. What would a man, a boy like Garrett Notte want with a girl like Abby? Had he missed so much intelligence on interpersonal relationships while he was away in another part of the world?

"I know. I wanted to tell him that the two of you would have nothing in common, but I thought, well you never know." Lily had thought it was unusual but who was she to judge. She hadn't had a date in months, maybe over a year, or almost two? Oh Lord.

"Lily, how long have you known him?" Dev felt something was wrong. He didn't know what or why.

"Since he was little. I'd help mom in the shop and he would come in with his dad or grandmother. Their family is a pillar in the city."

"So he's known everyone on the block then?"

"Well, yes, I guess. I mean, I don't think he goes into the deli or the sports bar but he knows people and a lot of us know him. He's been gone for awhile but now he's here visiting his grandmother while his father is out of town."

He looked over at Abby. "I think you dodged a bullet with Mr. Stuffy. He might have been too controlling."

Abby and Lily did spit out their beer on hearing that comment.

"What did I say that was so funny?"

"Nothing, Mr. Stuffy. Absolutely nothing," Lily answered seriously.

Chapter Fourteen

1. Don't forget to check the yellow roses first thing tomorrow morning
2. Make sure Abby understands the delivery for Mrs. Baker at the lake
3. Call the reception venue one more time to make sure on access
4. Try to have a good time tonight despite...well, just despite

"I've gotta say this is becoming one of the most unusual missions I've ever been on." Devlin Pierce continued to look around Swope Park as they began their walk into the outside theater.

"I'm really a mission? Great." Lily still carried both tickets in her hand as security stopped them to look inside her purse. Right next to her was a federal agent who possibly had some small arms hidden on him somewhere but they were checking her Kate Spade purse. This was rich, albeit the humor was just inside her mind.

They were clicked through the turnstiles and two volunteers handed them the program for tonight, "Spamalot". Abby had bailed on her late this afternoon and Agent Pierce had readily volunteered for service. He was too quick to say yes and that bothered her for some reason. Did he know something about her security that she didn't? Or maybe it was as simple as not wanting to spend another dull night in his hotel room. That had to be getting old.

"You all have a good night and enjoy the show. Welcome to Starlight."

Dev seemed to be taking it all in but Lily wondered if he was scoping out "targets" or escape routes. After all, he was on a mission.

He leaned down to whisper into her ear. "I didn't mean the whole mission thing. It's a case of course and we just want you safe. Sorry if it sounded funnier than usual."

"Oh there was nothing funny about it." She looked down into her program. "This should be good tonight. Hope you like Monty Python."

She closed off to him a bit. If she only knew about the window and some of his other suspicions she wouldn't be talking to him at all. Lying was lying, even by omission. "Lily World" was difficult to live in with all its rigid rules. And he thought the Army was disciplined.

"Love Monty Python. Isn't this the one with the knight who refuses to die? Funny…he's not dead yet." Dev began laughing. "Pretty fountains. They have a restaurant here too?"

He was taking it all in. Kansas City continued to surprise him. He thought Virginia was green but for a city, the green space and fountains surpassed any of his thoughts of the midwestern town. Starlight Theatre had been around for years, situated in the largest and oldest park in the city. The outside theater was a family tradition for Lily. She had explained that a police friend of her dad's used to sneak her mom, sister and her in once the show had begun. Lily remembered where they used to sit and the very first and only time she saw Yul Brynner dance that fast waltz in "The King and I". She loved the buoyant hoop skirt of the female character's dress as it flew like large sheets of material strewn into the air. When they finally stopped dancing, the "Anna" character spun twice, finally toppling into a circular mass on the stage. Lily had been in love with bald headed men for only a few months after that. Then Bruce Willis came along and the crush was resurrected.

"The fountains and the restaurant are newer," Lily explained as he followed her. "There are other places to get food, you know nachos, popcorn and beer."

"Nachos and beer at the theater? I like this place."

"It is kind of like Royals' Stadium meets the Music Hall, I mean for your reference, the Kennedy Center. We don't have the bells that ring you to your seats after intermission though. They dim the lights here."

Lily continued to walk into the theater area. A few ushers asked her if she needed help to find her seats. She politely said no and asked them how their night was going.

Dev followed behind, watching her do her thing, her Lily thing. She walked with a purpose and exuded the energy of ownership. She was checking how they were and thanking them for volunteering. Did she know she had to pay for those seats? She was the guest not them. But he was learning tradition was very important to her. He also was discovering that she felt comfortable where her ghosts lived, where those loved ones had once been. That was so unlike him.

"The stage is pretty good size. Love those towers." He'd kept walking but she'd stopped in the front row of the area behind the orchestra seats.

"We're here," she said pointing at the seats. One of the volunteers laughed who was standing behind him.

"Never been here, have you? How are you, Lily?"

Dev followed back to her side as she pointed to seat number six. "No, he's never been here before. How are you, Margaret?"

"Fine, just fine. I was in Atlanta last week visiting my grandkids. How are the weddings going?"

"Pretty good. It's been hot though. We have an easy weekend and a little lighter schedule now that we're in the middle of summer. Thank heaven people are getting a clue and not getting married outside in this heat."

Dev actually felt entirely useless and invisible. He could've used these skills in the caves of Afghanistan. She seemed to know absolutely everyone. This was not a domain in his comfort level. It was way too friendly, too normal for his life. Too intimate. He continued to stand next to Lily but began to scope out the other concessions while looking over her head. A beer sounded good and so did the nachos. He could realistically eat his way through the show. He looked at the back of the seats as Lily was looking at photos on the woman's phone, probably the grandchildren. He spotted and zeroed in on his target, a barbecue sign. He hadn't eaten dinner so a sandwich would work. He'd have to run an extra mile tomorrow morning.

"Um, this is Devlin, Margaret," Lily poked him in the side to draw his attention. Exactly at that same time, she heard his stomach growl.

"Very nice to meet you," he said as he extended his hand.

The older woman eyed him up and down and smiled.

Then she looked over at Lily and winked.

"He's really hungry. Dev, why don't you go get yourself something."

He had her permission to fend for himself, forage through the snack bars and concession stands. He liked this part of Lily's world.

"What do you want?" he asked. He was already walking away.

"I'm good, maybe a diet drink?" He nodded and sprinted off.

"He's cute. Where did you find him?"

"Well, he just sort of walked into the shop one day." Lily was amusing herself. She wasn't lying, she couldn't do that to lovely Margaret. Lily had provided the flowers for her youngest daughter's wedding almost ten years ago. The original Lily had done the same for Margaret all those many years before. In a sense, they were family.

"Well, he's a keeper. You two look good together. Oops, I better go to work. See you, honey."

Lily knew she was blushing and she seemed to always be warm anytime Dev briefly touched her but it was hot out. There were even free water stands around the theater. She sat down and began to look through her program. Nancy and her husband Tom arrived and sat in the seats next to Dev's and Mr. Pearl and his son were already occupying their seats at the end of the row. The two season ticket holders next to her remained empty. Julie and John were always coming in at the very last second and they'd had that ritual for almost fifteen years now. As Starlight had been a family tradition for so many over the years, this row had created their own family, birthed in comedy, drama and music.

She was talking to Mr. Pearl when she saw Dev coming her way. He had a cardboard food carrier filled with a beer, what looked like a drink for her, french fries and some sort of sandwich. In his left hand he held a popcorn bucket, yes a bucket. He was smiling from ear to ear.

"For you madam." He handed the popcorn down to her as he sat down. She introduced him to everyone. He'd smile and continue to unwrap his sandwich.

"You got barbecue, didn't you?"

"I'm in Kansas City, aren't I?" He was already lifting the sandwich to his mouth. With the first bite, he locked his eyes as if in prayer or sublime pleasure. Lily laughed out loud.

She lifted the soda out of the carrier. "Mine?" He kept eating but managed a quick nod. Within a few bites the sandwich had vanished and he began his way way through the french fries.

"They just made these fries. Had to have them. You know I remember something from Afghanistan. There was this guy from Kansas City."

"A friend?"

"Well, he was there to do a job."

She continued to watch him in disbelief. The fries had almost evaporated into thin air and she'd only taken one sip from her drink. She hadn't touched the popcorn on the cement under their chairs.

"Army?"

"Well, yes, actually, he was a land mine specialist."

"Really?" She knew he was trained but land mines? It was a war but what did he do in it?

Obviously he was getting overpaid to make sure she was safe.

"Hello, hello, hello."

Julie and John had landed, yes landed. Julie was so sweet and huggable and then you had John who flew in from the west like a tornado in Kansas.

"And who is our new member of the family?" He looked right at Dev who had to place his beer down and wipe his face before standing to introduce himself.

"Devlin Pierce, nice to meet you sir."

"Devlin Pierce, sounds like James Bond, Lily. Where'd you get this character? Out of some romance novel?" John was laughing loudly but was shaking Dev's hand in friendship at the same time.

"We're dating," Dev answered quickly. He did it again. What was wrong with him? He knew.

He didn't want her to be the one to lie.

"Great, well we love Lily so don't screw this up, understand?" Dev smiled and Lily attempted poorly to become invisible as she slumped into the iron chair. John was threatening the DEA guy, rich.

Everyone sat down as more of the crowd rushed to their seats.

"Is that everyone now?" Dev whispered into her ear. She could smell the beer and barbecue on his breath.

"Pretty much. There are a few of my former clients out

here now and then but once the show begins you should be out of danger, at least until intermission."

The executive director of Starlight greeted everyone from the stage and then requested they rise for the singing of the national anthem. The orchestra began. The audience, most of them, came to attention or quiet. Lily eyed Dev with her peripheral vision and saw the ramrod straight body of the man next to her. His hand crisp and unshaken in a salute but quickly moved over his heart.

Luckily, Kansas City was the type of city that embraced patriotism. In this fly-over country it was common to salute the flag or place your hand over your heart, to attempt to sing the anthem's high notes and to respect service men and women. He would be welcome here. She doubted he could say the same for some of the other places he had visited. Oh, and they didn't have barbecue like Kansas City.

After they were in their seats, John and Lily began talking about the next musical. Nancy was asking Dev if it was his first time here. The music began and conversations ended.

"I love this beer," Dev whispered again in her ear.

"You've had beer before."

"But this is good. Boulevard, very good. In fact this is a good night, date." She shook her head at his attempt, yet feeble, at humor.

"So happy you could join me, Mr. Pierce."

"No problem, Ms. Schmidt."

They were shoulder to shoulder in the seats. She felt sorry for him and his containment but those broad shoulders of his just didn't fit in one seat. She was so warm and it wasn't just the temperature. Of course, her first row seats with the wide walkway between them and the orchestra area allowed him plenty of room for those long legs. It must be hell on a plane for him, Lily thought as he stretched them out.

During the first act, there were times she thought Dev was actually crying from laughter. He and John couldn't control it. Obviously, Monty Python had written everything with a man's humor and psyche in mind. There were some funny bits but these two were rolling while a few of the older women watched in wonderment. Lily's favorite part was the servant hitting coconuts to sound like horse's hooves. By intermission everyone was exhausted in one way or another.

The lights lifted and Mr. Pearl and his son were on their way home. Nancy and Tom were leaving too. Their little girl had early swim classes and the boys were leaving for camp. Dev stood up as soon as he could to stretch, meeting John in the walkway to talk. She and Julie remained seated talking about the next show and if they were renewing for next year. Of course they were; they couldn't break up the family.

Lily tried to talk to Julie and listen in to the men's discussion. She heard bits and pieces "great person", "Afghanistan", Washington DC", "works" and "Ft. Bragg". Julie was talking about her daughter and the new house.

Then she heard, "I thought that was you, dear man," come from liquid syrup lips. Lily looked up to see Gretchen behind Dev, placing her arms around his waist. John's eyes were wide as Dev grabbed one hand and turned to face her. Lily only hoped he didn't snap it off.

"Oh, hello." That's all he said as he returned Gretchen's hand to her side.

"So, Lily, you two really are dating? I know you said you were but you know a girl can dream," Gretchen drooled as she fluttered her eyelashes. How old was Gretchen now?

"And a girl can keep on dreaming," Dev said nonchalantly as he turned around to continue his conversation with John. Lily stifled a raucous laugh.

"Hello Gretchen," Lily said as blandly as possible. "Yes, we are here together."

Gretchen stood uncomfortably looking at Dev's back. "Well, I just wanted to say hello." She began to leave but then crouched down near Lily.

"Good for you, Lily. He is absolutely divine. Enjoy." And then she vanished in the sweat of the night like a bat that had lost its way in a cave. There were bats at Starlight in the towers but seldom did they ever come down, attack and visit. Tonight it had happened. Gretchen knew how to ruin a good night in heaven.

The lights lowered and the men took their seats.

"I almost hurt her. Wasn't expecting a sneak attack." She didn't think she would ever get used to these whispers in her ear.

"Wow, I bet you really are fun on a date." She looked right into his eyes and they were twinkling.

"I can be. Aren't I?"

She turned her head and looked forward to the stage. She wasn't going to answer him while he had that grin on his face. His cover was still intact; he was her boyfriend and by tomorrow afternoon half of the wedding world in the city would know it. She'd be lucky if she didn't have clients calling to congratulate her.

If he were her boyfriend and if they truly were dating, she would congratulate herself and get her own billboard on I-70 to tell all of Kansas City. A girl could dream.

Chapter Fifteen

"So, Abby, are you going tomorrow night? That was the show you weren't certain about." Lily continued to work on the arrangement in front of her. She needed it delivered in a couple of hours. Abby could deliver it and then head home or to Jeremy or to whatever they had planned tonight. After the consultation, Lily would just head home to pay bills and collapse.

Dev was working at his laptop but his concentration broke when he heard the question.

They'd had such a good time last week he wouldn't mind going again. It was better than the hotel room. Lord, if his Army buddies ever got hold of that kind of the intel about him he'd be throttled. Devlin Pierce enjoyed musicals, who knew? No one would if he had his way. Of course, Tom Fullerton did know. Dev had informed him where they were going last week. He was walking a fine line with Lily. Someone needed to watch her but it didn't have to be as close as the seat next to her, physically touching her through most of the night. It couldn't be helped…those chairs were too darn close.

He smiled when he heard Abby say she couldn't make it. She was helping her mom do some show in Overland Park, some women's empowerment group. He looked up and saw Lily handing the flowers to Abby.

"Here's the address and after you're done just head home. I'm good with my watchdog."

He smiled again. "I resemble that remark."

"Yes, you do," she laughed. "Just don't bark or scratch yourself inappropriately and you can stay inside."

"Night, Dev." Abby was out the door and the two of them were left staring at each other.

"So…"

"I can go." It was out of his mouth before he had thought. What was he thinking? "I mean if you need someone to go. I enjoyed it." Too much, he thought. "I mean it is better than sitting in the hotel room all night."

She came toward her desk to look at the information in her calendar.

"I know for a fact, Agent Pierce, you don't just sit around your hotel room. Hmmm, this bride coming in is a friend of one of my past girls. I loved that bride."

"Well, Ms. Schmidt, I don't know where you are getting your intel but I do sit nights alone in my room." The glove was dropped. Banter would soon ensue. He really enjoyed that about her. Most women didn't have that wit to take a simple statement and destruct and construct an argument worthy of Socrates.

"I've seen you out with my own eyes." Oops, she shouldn't have said that. It made her out to be some sort of a stalker or a spy hiding behind trees and bushes with sunglasses and trench coat despite the temperatures of summer.

"Ah hah! You've been spying on me!" After he turned the lid down on his computer he crossed his arms in front of him defiantly. "Where and when?"

"Well," she began to stammer and play with her stuffed R2D2 on her desk. She hit his "I talk" button and he let out his little R2D2 noise.

"Waiting, Ms. Schmidt." He wouldn't let her off the hook so easily. She finally looked up and sighed.

"All right. I was driving by the outdoor cafe on the Plaza Saturday night after the last wedding and you were there with someone." She paused. It was a woman. He had been there with a woman and she felt utterly stupid right now. He wasn't her boyfriend. Remember, Lily, he's a federal agent.

His arms relaxed in front of him. "My aunt. You saw my aunt. And by the way, did you have a policeman following you, young lady?"

"Yes, sir, I did." His aunt, well she was very young and very pretty.

"I can see it on your face. You don't believe it was my aunt."

"It's not my business." She hit R2D2 again.

He stood up and came toward her. "Don't hit that button again. You're the one who was spying on me."

She had to look up at him from this position. It was so hot in the shop. "I wasn't spying."

He smiled, his eyes twinkling. "You went around the block twice, Lily. The police officer must have been completely incensed." He had seen her go by and then drive around the corner and then again. He had pointed it out to his Aunt Patricia, the woman he was protecting was driving around in circles, well, around the block, twice.

"I was looking for a place we're delivering to next week. I kept missing the address."

Dev decided he'd let it go. She was actually lying and he had no idea why. Of course, he had no idea except for the unmitigated nosiness she displayed why she kept going around the block.

"Oh, well that makes sense." Now he was lying. They could go on like this for hours, days. "You saw me with my Aunt Patricia. She lives up north by the airport and we met for dinner. Saturday night. I hadn't seen her in almost three years so it was nice to catch up."

He knew she'd seen him and Lily thought he probably knew she was actually lying to his face about the delivery location. She could go on from here.

"She's very pretty. Did you have a nice visit?"

"Actually, a great time. Dinner was good and the conversation was even better. Her husband passed away when I was deployed so I never really was able to talk to her about what he went through with his cancer. He suffered for eighteen months and she was there every step of the way." His thoughts went very dark. He was never there for his family when cancer called them home, nor was he there for the suffering. He just drifted in and out of their lives and they were so happy to see him, to wish him well, so grateful he was safe at home. He didn't feel like he had a home, not now.

She noticed his brow furrowed and he looked down suddenly. He was surely thinking about something else, perhaps the death, the loss of family. Of being away.

"So, do you want to go with me to Starlight again?" If

she lightened the conversation maybe they could go on again.

His head bobbed up. "One condition. I'll buy you dinner before we go out. I was starving and ate like a maniac the last time. Sorry about that."

Lily passed by him, picking up his laptop from the table and offering it to him as she readied for her meeting.

"You were fine. I'm sorry I didn't think about you and food. You must have been starving. You know what, I will let you buy me dinner. I'm so tired of cooking."

"And I miss cooking," he said quickly.

She was surprised. "You cook? You like cooking?"

"Love it. It's my zen."

She laughed out loud at that word. Zen and Agent Pierce just weren't compatible words. "Now, you're just messing with me."

He placed the laptop in his bag and zipped it shut, moving it behind the desk.

"No, seriously. Cooking calms me down. I love how the fresh vegetables feel, the smell of a really good cut of beef, the spices. I began cooking in college. I didn't have too much time to do it but when I'd come home on break my mom and I would cook all day. The kitchen was our domain."

She really knew nothing about this man. She finished placing her materials and listened to the silence. Peeking from behind her eyelashes she could see the sadness of his face once more. It was intense grief. He had mentioned his mother and that feeling was overwhelming for him.

Lily guessed that his mother had passed away. She knew that look and she felt that sadness so many times. You never really got over your mother passing away but she had thought that relative feeling was exclusively for daughters but now she knew better. Seeing his face, her realization was that sons felt that way too.

Break the silence, Lily. "So how about we cut out of here early tomorrow and you can cook in my kitchen, something easy so we aren't late but something you like. You don't have to buy dinner but if you cook we'll both be happy. I will require help with the dishes. I hate doing dishes."

A thin smile crossed his lips. "Sounds like a good deal to me."

By the next afternoon, Lily was ready for a home cooked meal. She didn't really care what he made just so she didn't have to do it. Abby and she had worked like crazy people today so she could leave early. She'd dropped by an event space, purchased flowers, set up the production schedule for the rest of the week and left Abby with a few other jobs.

Lily left Dev alone in the kitchen once she showed him the spice cabinet. She couldn't wait to take a shower and find something cool to wear for the outside show. It was over ninety degrees again today and the weather channel just kept showing excessive heat warnings.

Everyone knew it already!

She took her time. After an hour of showering, finding something to wear and trying to do something with her frizzy hair, she opened her bedroom door to an aroma so wonderful she wanted to kiss him. Oh darn. She wanted to kiss him. Stop it, stop it. Get it together. He's here doing a job, remember? You are his mission. Repeat again and again.

Her last relationship had certainly done a number on her confidence. She was never a needy girl. If she made a date with a girlfriend she kept that date even if the star football player asked her out for the same night. Not that the said football player ever did that but that's what she hoped she would've done for a friend. She was not one who looked over at the other man's grass when she had her own to mow. Now she was just being silly.

She was still barefoot when she entered the kitchen. He'd thrown one of her floral aprons on and had changed into walking shorts and a casual shirt.

"It smells great in here and I'm so hungry."

He smiled at her and some of her doubts vanished. They were becoming good friends and that was it. That should be enough now and then. In your life there were times that you needed someone like him, not just for your protection but for your sanity. After her past relationship she needed to get back in the pool, but stay in the low end, oh heck, she needed to stay in the kiddie pool!

"After the work you've been doing you should be famished. I hope you like it."

She sat down at the table and looked at the place mats, dishes and silverware. Holy Moly, he'd set the table. She usually ate while watching television from her sofa most nights. The DVR was the greatest invention since microwaves and air-conditioning, all right behind indoor plumbing.

He placed a salad, one of those beautifully chopped ones in front of her and at his place.

"We can start with these."

She dug in. "Where did you get the dressing? It's great. Which one did you use?"

"I made my own."

Holy Moly, he knew the way to a girl's heart! The buzzer on the oven blared in her small kitchen.

He removed something from the oven, bringing it over to the table.

"I knew we didn't have much time and with the heat I didn't want anything too heavy. This is a French dish I like to make...baked chicken legs and thighs with vegetables, zucchini, pepper, onion and fresh tomatoes. Oh and basil with white wine."

He went back to the counter and grabbed green beans. "Can't get enough veggies in the summer."

Her mouth gaped open. She'd taken a shower, found a lightweight dress in her closet and tried to do something with her humidity hating hair. Devlin Pierce had produced a three course meal and it was French. She was such a slug. What other talents did this agent have? As soon as she thought it, her entire body became warm. She hadn't even touched him.

"Do your federal agent buddies know your secret cooking talents?" She took a bit of the haricot verts, just French green beans. The chicken leg and thigh was so good it melted in her mouth.

"Some. Tom knows I love food and I love to cook. His wife is a gourmet chef, studied in New York City in the early years of their marriage when he was assigned there. Some of my old Army buds know but I don't cook for just anybody off the street. It's not something you talk about when you're fighting the Taliban."

He was quiet again. When his thoughts wrapped too tightly in his mind, Lily always heard the anguish in the silence. His life experiences far outweighed anything she could possibly imagine. She'd only seen glimpses in some of his descriptions but she could only imagine and wonder. She wanted to make him feel better but in reality no one could probably do that, even a good therapist for PTSD.

"Ah crap, I forgot the wine." He began to rise from the table but she motioned him back down.

"No, at least let me buy you a drink once we get out there. I could use one after the last few days." The heat and last weekend's weddings really had stretched her energy and then on Sunday she'd delivered arrangements for a baby shower. Monday had been filled with appointments and funeral deliveries. She'd barely had time yesterday to catch up and begin the entire wedding cycle again.

Dev nodded. He'd let her do that. By the time they left, the dishes had been done and everything had been put away. The kitchen was in better shape than before he cooked. He was going to make someone a very fine wife!

She locked the front door and trailed behind him down the driveway. Her trusty dusty police detail had just pulled up, conspicuously across from her house. Dev waved at him as he opened the passenger car door.

"I can drive." She stopped short of the door.

"I know that but now that I know where I'm going, I'm driving, madam." His hand directed her in. She wasn't going to argue. It was nice having a car door opened, someone else driving, especially when she was so tired.

She'd eaten a wonderful dinner and she didn't have to cook. And he'd done the dishes. This night just couldn't get any better. Hopefully, Gretchen didn't have tickets for tonight's performance.

Once at Starlight they ordered drinks at one of the bars. Her vodka and tonic with a lime twist had never tasted so refreshing on such a warm night. Dev ordered his Boulevard beer, not adventuring out into the mayhem of liquor world. They sat at one of the many tables as he finally looked at the front of the program.

"I never asked what the show was, did I?" She sipped her drink and smiled.

"Nope."

"When did you think I would notice?"

She took another sip. "Sooner than this. You're not very perceptive, sir, and I believe you are losing your skills of observation. Perhaps the barbecue and beer of the city are clouding your talents."

He looked over his sunglasses with a glare that almost scared her to her toes. She didn't really feel scared or threatened. She felt smug, yes, smug. Paybacks for an earlier discussion when he'd caught her "observing" him at that cafe.

"Mama Mia? Really, Lily? Monty Python is one thing, but ABBA? Jesus." She pretended to be shocked at his exclamation.

"Oh my, Mr. Pierce does not appreciate the musical gift of the world that is ABBA? I would think that a culinary genius as yourself would be enlightened enough to enjoy this music given to the people of the world by these geniuses. You know, kind of like Monet respecting Degas.

Mutual admiration and all that."

He sat back in his chair pretending to read the program.

"Do you know any of the songs?" She was verbally poking him and having the best time doing it.

"Yes." He continued reading. "Are you kidding me? The show is about a girl who doesn't know who her father is and the mother thinks he's one of the three but she doesn't know for sure? They're on an island in Greece and Sofie is getting married and the men are coming to escort her down the aisle?"

"Pretty much. That's the plot."

"It's a wedding. Don't you get your fill of those things?"

She took a good slug of her drink. "Oh yah. No one knows how much and no one will. It's my job and I do it very well."

"The flowers or the bullshit?"

"Why, Mr. Pierce, you certainly have colorful vocabulary tonight." Her laughter filled the bar area.

"Do you need another one of those so I can find out what you really think?"

She nodded affirmatively as he got up to serve her. She liked having a manservant. But she wondered what this would cost her. She'd have to stop after this drink. She was loosening up a little too much and no good ever came from that. In her twenties she'd partied a little too much. She never wanted to go there again. That was the past and her life had turned into responsibilities and work ethics. There was no going back to carefree days of no house payments and sleeping until it was almost time for lunch.

One hand held her drink, in his other was another beer.

"Shall we go to your seats before you can't get down that steep walkway?"

She looked down at her feet. "Always wear shoes I can walk in here. I learned my lesson when I was ten. I had to wear my good shoes, my beautiful very shiny shoes. I slid all the way down to row A."

Now he was the one laughing out loud. "Did you bruise your…pride?"

She shook her head as she headed down to the seats. "Nope, my butt."

Lily continued walking but she could hear him laughing behind her. At times she was annoyed by this whole drug caper but tonight was not one of them. She was loving her time with him. Some day they would figure all this out and he would be gone. He was the puppy that followed her home and now she didn't want to give him up. His real owners would show up and she'd be alone again. Alone, not lonely. Sure, keep telling yourself that Lily.

The row was filled with her friends. John greeted Dev by name and they began to talk about something. Mr. Pearl had purchased kettle corn, her favorite. Even though she wasn't hungry she couldn't pass it up. Besides, Mr. Pearl enjoyed taunting her with the carnival delicacy. John and Dev sat down when they noticed the executive director on the stage.

John punched her in the arm. "I like him, really like him. Can we keep him?"

Lord, now they were having a bromance and she was in the middle like sticky peanut butter that you had wedged on the roof of your mouth. No jelly, just the sticky cheap brand of peanut butter you ate in college when you had no income. She took another sip of her drink and placed it in the cupholder.

"How long does this last?" she whispered to Dev.

"Well I don't know. I've never seen it."

She was whispering again. "I'm not talking about the show. I'm talking about my situation, this. You here with me, watching over me. You know I don't like doing this to my friends."

His eyes softened, the thin lines around the edges invisible now. "We are exhausting all our leads. Not much longer. While I'm with you so many people are doing their work behind the scenes and I am too. This is so much larger than just that box that was sent to you by mistake. I'm sorry about your friends, truly. You'll be able to explain that my job got in the way. No lying there."

Their friend, silence, sat between them. They stood for the National Anthem and she watched him from the corner of her eye. Thank heavens for peripheral vision. She was wiping a tear away as he stood at attention. She could only imagine what he looked like in uniform, protecting his country and now in this job, serving it. What kind of a man did that and volunteered to do it?

The executive director came out one more time and asked for Jill Nathan.

A spotlight found the young woman a few rows ahead of them in the orchestra area. "We have a delivery for you, Jill."

She looked around in confusion as one of the volunteers

brought her a bouquet of red roses. Dev looked at Lily but she had no idea what was going on.

"Jill, this show is about love," the voice from the stage explained. "Tonight this is a very special time for you."

A young man dressed in shirt and tie and two other sets of couples came over to her seat and then he knelt down on one knee.

Lily felt her stomach reel. Are you kidding me? First there's a wedding in this show, now the girl gets flowers delivered to her right in front of me and now a proposal? Lily realized the other couples were obviously family. Jill nodded enthusiastically and the couple kissed. She went off to thunderous applause, a new ring and a new beginning.

"You should have handed them your card," Dev joked.

She glared at him. "Some day, one day I'd love to get flowers. The ring is nice but I have nice jewelry, but the flowers, just once."

Dev shook his head. "I know you said you never received a flower delivery but it's so hard to believe."

Lily nodded. "Yep. You know I told you that but I forgot one delivery. When my dad died another florist sent me a plant. It does seem pathetic, doesn't it? Since I've owned the shop, anyone I've gone out with has thought it silly to send flowers to a florist. But just once."

Dev didn't know what to say, again. The look on her face was hopeful, yet regret erased the brightness in her eyes. Yet it could be the vodka. But romance was crap, especially right in front of your eyes.

When the overture began he nudged her again, his

attempt to lift her mood. “This better be good.”

She smiled. The brightness was back. “It’s ABBA music.”

They both smirked at each other. The lively cast began the first song “Honey, Honey” and then “Money, Money, Money” followed. By the time the male dancers were dressed in swim fins with rubber ducks around their waists, Dev was laughing and John and he were pointing at certain individual actors. She didn’t want to know why.

Intermission brought more conversation and thankfully no Gretchen, Queen of Inappropriate Seduction. Julie wanted to know more about how they had met. Lily told her about the meal he had prepared and she was completely jealous. John knew how to grill and that was the entire extent of his culinary skills. Nancy and her husband as well as Mr. Pearl and his son cut out early, leaving the two couples.

By the time the show finished and the cast came out to do an encore everyone was up from their seats. John and Julie said their goodbyes and headed to the exit but Dev was swaying along with Lily. His arm landed around her waist as he grabbed her hand to pull her into the walkway to dance. She was enjoying it so much for a little time she forgot the pretense and made believe it was reality. As people tried to pass them they broke apart.

He leaned down over the noise. “Should we get going?”

“We can take our time. No early morning for me, what about you?”

“Nope. Let’s enjoy this.”

She was. Finally the cast stopped singing and dancing and the curtain came down on one of the best nights she’d had in a long time.

He reached for her and it felt so natural to allow him to hold her hand as they moved through the crowd. There was a little tingling but the warmth she was feeling was not a heat wave. It was just the warmth of a man's hand holding her's. He was becoming a very special man who had been dropped into her life for this very special night.

Chapter Sixteen

1. Go to church
2. Groceries...need food
3. Laundry...need clothes
4. Mow...yuk

Lily had made her list for Sunday at the shop the other day. Devlin Pierce must have seen it.

She was pulling into the driveway with her groceries when his car pulled in behind her.

She grabbed one bag out of the backseat as he got out of the car.

"Hey stranger. Missed you at church. You just can't be away from me for more than twenty-four hours?" He was still wearing his dark Secret Service type sunglasses so she couldn't see his eyes, those eyes that gave away his mood every time. That's when she noticed her police detail was not in the usual spot.

"Oh, you're my caretaker for the day?"

"Yep. Saving money when we can." He continued to walk to her. "More bags?"

"Only one more and the milk."

"Got it."

It wasn't until they were in the kitchen that he removed the eyewear. He looked tired. She'd actually been surprised when he hadn't shown up at church. It had become so natural to have him in the pew beside her and then breakfast afterward. Part of her missed him when he wasn't around, the other part kept telling the first part that she needed to stop reading more into this "relationship" of sorts. He was doing his job.

She busied herself making sure all the groceries were put away. Apparently, he'd walked over to the church just off the Plaza this morning and had coffee at one of the many Starbucks around town.

"I'm here to mow your lawn. Where's the mower?"

She stood frozen in the middle of the kitchen. Now she really did want to kiss that handsome face. That's when she saw the Georgetown tee shirt and the faded blue jeans he wore.

"Don't toy with me Agent Pierce. This is nothing to make fun of. I mean, if you're serious I might just sit down and cry with joy."

His half smile made her smile. "Where's the mower before I change my mind?"

"Backyard in the shed. The key to the shed is in the drawer right there by the back door. Shouldn't need any gas. I filled it the last time I mowed."

He saluted her and went on. She could actually say she'd not been this happy in months, oh heck, maybe almost a year? She'd always dreamed of a man who would mow her lawn, one she didn't have to pay once he was finished. Oh, she'd have to do something for him. Maybe she could cook something?

She heard the mower running as she threw in her first load of laundry and scanned the refrigerator. Lily had just been at the store but it seemed like she had nothing to fix. No, wait. She had that roast, carrots and celery. Next she checked the kitchen island for the potatoes she'd bought last week. Yep, still good and ready to be used. What man didn't like pot roast? As she watched him go by the window, Lily figured he might be the one man in the world who didn't like it, oh him and Prince Charles? She just couldn't see his Royal Highness eating pot roast across the table from Camilla. "I say, Lovey, this pot roast is simply divine." Actually in Lily's mind he sounded more like Thurston Howell III from the old television show "Gilligan's Island".

She'd have to take a chance. She could throw it in, have it almost ready by the time she gave him a second beer for his efforts.

By the time he finished the back yard and now was in the front, the heat of the noon sun was beating down on him. Why had Dev volunteered to mow her lawn? He didn't even mow his own lawn. His HOA furnished all outside work and landscaping. Good thing, since he was traveling so much lately. They were having an election in Kansas City this coming November and if he didn't get this wrapped up soon he figured his time would count for residency. Actually, he didn't mind it but it was time to go home, to be done playing house.

As he mowed, he thought about Tom Fullerton's comment the other night over dinner. His wife and he had been so gracious to offer him the occasional home cooked meal. Dev had talked about Lily, maybe a little too much.

He saw Tom's wife wink at her husband in some all knowing fashion and that's when his friend had mentioned that Lily seemed to be good for Dev.

"Good for what?" Dev had laughed. "She's someone involved in the case I'm working."

"Is that all?" Tom's wife had asked as she cleared off the dishes. "You seem to really like being around her."

Tom watched his wife leave for the kitchen. "She has a point you know. I haven't seen you this happy in a long time, Dev. You've been down for awhile and now I've seen you laugh, kid around, enjoy life. That girl is good for you."

"I can't believe you're talking like this. You know I'm working."

Tom shook his head. "I know when you've gone undercover you're working but maybe you're at a ballgame with a suspect. Besides, when you have gone out with her its been after hours, on the weekend, and if you didn't watch her we'd have to be yelling for a security detail all the time. Actually, if we had to do that she probably wouldn't have any protection. You're saving us money, Dev. The taxpayers thank you."

"I haven't gone over any lines but sometimes they are getting blurred. We've, I've invented the cover story that I'm her boyfriend. I did that, not her. What the hell was I thinking?"

Tom's grin performed the work of a verbal answer.

"Not funny. I know what you're thinking, Tom Fullerton and she's not my type. I mean you remember the girl I was dating in DC, the one with the Louboutin stilettos? Does she even remotely look or act like Lily?"

"No," Tom answered quickly, "you've got me there. Lily is nothing like that girl. Lily is way better. Lily doesn't have the money, the family, the big house or country club. Frankly she definitely doesn't have the body of that skinny model type who barely ate anything. I'm not sure she even enjoyed food and you even said she didn't enjoy meeting anyone you knew. But Lily has that "something" factor. It's the feeling that she gives you when she's around. You want to be around her. I watch that security footage occasionally and the way she handles people is something to behold. Heck, the staff I have overseeing the surveillance bring popcorn. She's even entertaining when she's working like crazy. Dev, she's like a fire and you're a moth. You may get burned, boy, if you don't handle this correctly and honestly."

"I know. She hates lying to everyone even if it is to save her skin. On jobs, sometimes you don't play by all the rules in the book but I'm trying. I don't want her coming back on me because of anything I did during this whole process. I definitely don't want her hurt."

Tom laughed out loud and grabbed the remaining dishes off the table.

"I'm talking about you. She'll go on and survive when you leave and never come back, but you, you're going to leave and you will have left something here, part of yourself… the good Dev, the gentle warrior, the man I heard about rescuing a little girl in the middle of a mine field, the good friend who has picked me up in the middle of the night from Reagan airport when my flight was delayed, the man who did CPR at a pickup ballgame in Alexandria. You do nothing about this woman and I'm thinking you might regret it."

Dev continued to mow thinking about the other night.

That was more talk from Tom than he'd ever heard him spout. She would go on and he would leave. Distance would be his friend when it came to Lily but here he was mowing her damn lawn. He couldn't help himself. He'd made an effort to be without her, making sure he didn't go to church and to her Mass. He'd walked almost a mile to the church on the other side of the Plaza to prove that point. He'd walked back to get coffee and a breakfast sandwich, preferring to stay away from the now all too common Sunday brunches. He missed their conversations as they talked about nothing at all. He'd grab a newspaper on the way into whatever restaurant they were going to and pull the sports page to see how the Royals were doing. She told him on more than one occasion she thought people who read the entire newspaper in a dining establishment were rude, especially on a Sunday when others were waiting to eat.

The newspaper was immediately put away for later in his silent hotel room. Her admonishment was more a plea for attention in his mind but he felt guilty that day when he saw the line of people waiting to get in.

"See, small children are having to wait in the hot sun because of people reading the newspaper."

"Do you want to walk back to your house, Ms. Schmidt?"

She had playfully grabbed his car keys out of his hand and ran to his car. He'd picked her up that morning and they'd ridden together to church. Lily didn't run very fast, heck, she didn't run, Dev continued to think to himself. She said she hated skiing, ice and roller skating and couldn't play a team sport to save herself from masked bandits. The woman didn't have an athletic bone in her body but she liked sports. From some things she said, he knew she understood just about every sport except for cricket…who did?

He finished the yard, ending by the front door. He looked up to see her standing there with a bottle of his favorite beer, opened and the cold steam shooting from the top. He pulled his shirt up to wipe off his face.

Queen of Seduction Gretchen pulled up in front of Lily's house at the same time. She stared with wide eyes at Dev's partially bare chest with a little more than a modicum of disbelief.

"What? What's wrong? Did I kill some plant?"

Lily's face had quickly changed. "No, look behind you. Trouble is coming." Lily didn't finish the sentence…trouble is coming for a sweaty, half bare chested man with faded jeans.

Dev grabbed the beer and looked in the direction of her stare. "Jesus. What is she doing here?"

Gretchen was already negotiating the slightly inclined drive in her tall wedge shoes as she began waving. She had something in her hand.

"My, my, this is a treat to see the happy couple on a Sunday." Her syrupy tone made Lily instantly nauseous. "I've brought that ribbon for Friday's bride, you know, the Gail Tomkins wedding at that venue up north. She wants this wrapped on her bouquet only, Lily."

"I know, Gretchen. It's so kind of you to bring it on a Sunday." Dev almost spit out his beer, knowing by now that Lily was not being Lily.

"I know. I was driving in the area and I remembered you

had this little house here so I thought I'd save myself an extra trip. Hello boyfriend." Her target was now Dev.

"You're on your own, boyfriend," Lily whispered from the top step, dead even with his ear so he only heard.

"Nice to see you, ma'am." Gretchen frowned.

"Oh I'm way too young to be a ma'am. Dev, right?"

He nodded, kept his mouth shut by taking another drink. Thank God it was after noon on Sunday so he could go buy more beer. He was going to need a couple more.

"So, you two are just playing house today? Being domestic? How long, Lily, before we get to plan your little wedding?"

Dev gulped down the remainder of the bottle. *Need more beer now.*

"We're doing some work around the house, getting some things done since I have that Friday night wedding." Lily ignored the wedding comment. Besides, there was no way Gretchen would have anything to do with any wedding she might have. But she didn't have to worry about that, now did she?

There was an awkward silence as Gretchen surveyed the two of them in depth and Lily issued her own stare down. Dev felt like a lab rat and the python cage was just two feet away.

"I better get cleaned up. We've got things to do. Excuse me, ma'am." He handed his empty bottle to his "girlfriend" and escaped.

Lily laughed on the inside, his Virginian accent drawled long on the word Gretchen didn't want to hear. She grabbed the ribbon from her as Dev pushed the mower around them into the backyard.

"I don't know where or how you got him, Lily Schmidt but that man is a keeper. I've seen you two a few times now and whatever you're doing, keep doing it." Then she was gone like the Wicked Witch in the "Wizard of Oz", marching down the drive to her car and magically disappearing as quickly as she had arrived.

All I'm doing is being his job.

As she pulled away, Dev snuck through the house, hiding behind the open door. "Is she gone?" he whispered.

She giggled. The grown man who was probably packing while he mowed (again, where had he put that gun?) was frightened of one woman. Well, she understood; she was too.

"Yes, you idiot. She's gone." Lily entered the house, laughing at his fear. She knew scarier brides than Gretchen. "I owe you for the mowing. I'm making dinner but it won't be ready for another hour. I have more beer."

"Afternoon dinner on a Sunday? I haven't had that in so long." He hadn't since the last time his mother made it before he went away. She'd made pot roast, his favorite, and pecan pie.

She wasn't feeling well and she'd cooked just for him. His dad and brother had enjoyed the food too, but the menu had been planned with him in mind only. The four of the them had sat at the table for almost three hours that day, enjoying stories, the food and each other.

"I need to clean up a little. I've got some other clothes in the car so..."

"I'll get you a towel. You need a shower?"

"No, I just need to wash up and change, get this grass off of me. I need to work out tonight so I'll shower later."

They sounded like some old married couple, Dev thought as he walked out to the car. What had Tom said… moth to the flame? He could just get in his car and drive away right now, but he couldn't. He just couldn't.

As he cleaned up in the bathroom and changed clothes, Dev began to smell something baking. It smelled good. He thought she couldn't cook but this smelled great. It smelled like a memory…like pot roast. He just might regret this Sunday afternoon for the rest of his life.

After dinner, Dev sat on Lily's back porch, drinking his third beer of the day.

"So, if I were putting together a list for the rest of the night, I'd say one…drink some water.Two…change into workout clothes. Three…go down to the gym. Four…do my usual routine of treadmill, weights and heavy weights. Five…go back to room and shower. Six…check my computer for reports. Seven…plan my week."

"You are mocking me." Lily sat next to him, drinking her own beer. Even though it had been warm, a cool front was coming through dropping the Kansas City humidity way down.

"I'm not mocking, I'm learning from the professor. Nothing wrong about lists."

"Seriously, you really think that?"

"Yep." He looked at her after realizing her tone was now very serious. "What's wrong with your list making?"

She took a deep breath, followed by a sigh before she explained.

"My father said that I over organized my life and if I wasn't careful I was going to organize myself right out of life." He saw the pain on her face, her light hearted spirit changed by heavy memories.

"It's what makes you, you. If you didn't have your lists you wouldn't be as successful as you are, you'd forget stuff, Gretchen would eat you for lunch, brides couldn't get married, Abby would have to run the business…"

She wiped away a tear as she burst into laughter. "Ok, ok, I get it. Thank you. I appreciate that. Without my lists, I'd be a forgetful ninny."

"Oh, well now we're talking about Abby's boyfriend."

"You know you can be quite funny, Agent Pierce." They clinked their bottles together in an informal toast.

"And you can be quite relaxed when you want to be, Ms. Schmidt."

"Oh, I forgot dessert." She jumped up and went inside quickly, leaving Dev in the quiet.

Could the woman just sit down? He didn't need dessert, he was still full from dinner. The roast had almost tasted like his mother's, at least what he could remember of the dish. Lily had placed all the vegetables in with the roast. His mom used to make mashed potatoes. But he'd had two helpings along with a fresh salad and green beans. A home cooked meal had been more than enough payment for mowing.

"I hope you like this. It was my mom's favorite and

frankly it was on sale." His beer was empty anyway. She handed him the bowl.

"It's butter pecan. Do you like pecans? Some people do and some don't. I almost bought a pecan pie today but with it just being me, I don't need the calories of an entire pie and I would've eaten it, especially since I have to work with Gretchen this week."

She was rambling as he looked into the bowl of ice cream in disbelief. She was saying something about a pecan pie and he was staring at pecans. Even though the ice cream was cold, he suddenly felt very warm as if he was nearing a metaphorical fire. His wings were getting singed. Was this some cosmic joke? Were they really this good at role playing? If he didn't keep this under control he just might disintegrate…and to ashes you shall return.

Chapter Seventeen

1. Buy flowers.
2. Dev has meeting and will be gone after we return.
3. John is bringing lunch to the shop.
4. Abby out back on Thursday.

"So, here's the live feed from the shop. I have another agent watching full time today." Agent Fullerton looked at the small screen on his desk. "Good quality. What's she doing?"

"Processing the flowers, cutting them, getting them in water. She has this Friday wedding with that crazy coordinator."

Dev sat across the desk, leaning back in the chair. "Now, that woman is a real trip."

"Someone just came in with a bag." He turned the screen for Dev to see.

"That's John. He's bringing her lunch. They do that on a regular basis. I talked her into having him come there so she could still be under surveillance."

"She doesn't know, does she?" Tom grimaced as soon as he'd asked and saw Dev's face harden. "You want to play it this way?"

"Yes, for now. She knows she's being watched but she doesn't know about the hidden cameras and the microphones. She thinks John will protect her and she has me on speed dial just in case. She also thinks KCPD is patrolling the block today."

Tom shook his head. His friend truly was playing with fire in more than one way, and not metaphorically any longer.

"Dev, her with John?"

"It's normal for them to have lunch."

Tom turned the screen back around. "That's not what I asked."

"I'm more interested, and concerned with that hooded figure. He threw a rock. I've had reports that he paces in front of the store some nights like he's trying to figure out what he's going to do. I've also seen him a couple of times in the early morning hours, looking inside the van and in the garbage bin. He's looking for something and I'm worried he's getting desperate."

"Has he been at her house?"

"Not sure. I haven't seen him and the detail officers haven't but that doesn't mean he hasn't come from another direction, or in a vehicle. We don't have cameras there."

Tom grimaced again. "That was your choice, Dev. You didn't think you'd be here for months, remember?"

He shook his head. Dev had thought that this would be a simple clean up but obviously they'd missed something. That hooded figure was still searching for something and he/she truly thought Lily had it, whatever it was.

Tom turned and clicked the sound button on the feed.

"So my daughter and granddaughter are coming in from Miami, Lily."

Lily was starving. She took a bite, way too big, chewing and nodding at the same time. Finally she swallowed. "I bet your wife is thrilled."

"She is. This is a blessing."

"How's your daughter doing, ok now?" Lily knew his only remaining child had the little girl on her own and from what John didn't say had been through some tough times. He didn't go into many details but it had been touch and go for awhile. She thought he'd even traveled to Miami during one bad event. Even with her he shielded that part of his life.

"Oh, she's great." John stared down at the table. He stopped talking and was obviously thinking about something he'd rather not share.

"And your granddaughter?"

"She's wonderful." His broad smile filled his face and lit his eyes, a little moisture forming at their edges. "She dances ballet, well she's learning. She's the most graceful thing I've ever seen. We get these videos of her. Last week she was a blooming flower with pink petals and everything. You would've loved that, little girl."

"Yes, I think I would've. That sounds so cute. When my nieces were babies they had photo sessions where they put the child in a clay pot and decorated around them to make them look like flowers. The babies are so cute. It almost makes me want to have one."

Where on earth had that come from? Lily hadn't thought about children since her last relationship. She didn't think about a family on a daily basis at all, maybe yearly, all right, every New Year's Eve. When the damn ball dropped she thought she felt another egg die. An angel got their wings when a bell rang, her eggs died when a ball dropped.

"You got that new man. He'd be a good daddy. You two need to get going on that little project." He pushed her shoulder in jest.

That was a job she didn't think Agent Pierce would be the least interested in.

"Not sure yet. We just began so we have a long way to go." Yes, when the investigation ended so did their relationship, the real and the pretend.

"He's former Army, you can tell. It's the way he stands and he's called me "sir" more times than I can count when I've seen him. Just the other morning when he was bringing you coffee, he waved over to me and said, "good morning, sir". Nice to see manners, of course, you wouldn't have some bad guy, Lily. You deserve someone like him." He touched her hand softly. "I never did like that other guy. He seemed like bad news, like he was a fake always keeping secrets."

She laughed out loud. If he only knew about Agent Pierce. "John, he was a minister!"

"Well, you never know about people. Where I grew up in Alabama we had a preacher that used to hit his wife and kids. His own son finally shot him dead when he was preaching at the pulpit. So you never know. Army man might just be the one, Lily. You gotta give it time to see how it grows."

"It seems like I'm always waiting for some bud to open and some flower to bloom larger and now you're telling me I have to wait on a man to do it?"

"It's your garden and your shop, Lily. You're in charge of how those flowers are arranged."

"Well, I know one thing for sure," Lily said softly as she held one of his big paws in her hands. "I love my Big John."

He leaned over to hug her. "And I love my little girl, no matter what."

Tom hit the mute button. They'd heard enough. He looked up to see Dev's blank face. "Dev, I smell smoke."

"I don't."

"You sure? With what I just heard I think we have more information than you need but I think your wings are burning."

Devlin Pierce shut his eyes. He was desperate to finish this mission.

Chapter Eighteen

1. Finish off bouquets
2. Don't forget to wrap brides' bouquet in special ribbon
3. As soon as Abby arrives take off
4. Dev will be coming along

It was almost one in the afternoon when Dev and Lily arrived at the venue. The ceremony was taking place in front of a beautiful white gazebo surrounded by azaleas. The reception was located on the property in a large ballroom. Lily's van was filled with flowers of every shade of peach, coral, and salmon. She gave her orders to Dev who received "tall" duty. Thankfully, if she were going to have a DEA assistant, they had sent her a tall one who could attach the flower pieces at the top of the gazebo without a step ladder.

Lily began to prep the ballroom, placing arrangements on tables and adding candlelight. The bride and bridesmaids came down to see their bouquets. She had clapped and hugged Lily so tightly she couldn't breathe. Another happy bride would soon be in the books. She was walking by the large windows with the bride, talking about the special ribbon wrap when she saw the view by the gazebo.

Gretchen was talking to Dev as he was working. At least he had kept working. When Abby was the center of attention she usually stopped to carry on a conversation. The over zealous wedding coordinator was adorned in black leggings, tall heels and a tunic that was more revealing in a shocking pink color. Her tanned décolletage was the only focus of the outfit with an illusion blouse over a corseted top. How old was she?

It was time for the boss to check the assistant's work, now! She smiled at the bride and said she needed to go out. Her quick steps had her out by the other two in minutes.

"It looks good, honey." She drew the last word out so maybe Gretchen could get one more huge hint to back off. "Hi Gretchen. Ready for tonight?"

"Well of course, Lily. I was just telling Dev that the bride and groom are having their black lab serve as the ring bearer. Isn't that just the cutest thing to have your pup bring the rings?" She had her hand at Dev's upper arm, slightly squeezing his muscle.

"Cute, very cute. So, Dev, all done?" Lily stood next to him on the other side.

"Just about, baby." His smile, that she could only see, was all teeth. "Anything else need to go up?"

"No, it looks good. Gretchen, you need anything else? We need to continue the setup on the reception, oh and the bride has already seen the bouquet. Everything is good."

Lily grabbed him by the hand and away from the clutches of the evil seducer. "You can thank me later for that little rescue."

So that's what jealousy looks like, Dev thought to

himself. Actually, Gretchen had been pretty friendly today, not totally obnoxious except for her lack of respect for his personal space. Apparently, she was believing the boyfriend/girlfriend scenario just as much as Big John. Lily was still holding his hand as they entered the building.

"Oh, I'm sorry," she said as she finally broke the hold. "I got a little carried away."

"It's ok. I'm really starting to enjoy these setups, I mean the flowers." He nervously caught his mistake. How old was he, sixteen again?

It was then that a blood curdling scream filled the venue. Lily even saw Gretchen hasten from the outside. She could run in those heels. Dev was halfway up the stairs, taking three steps at a time before Lily even began to move. Was there another mouse in a shoe?

By the time Gretchen and she reached the bride's room, Dev was holding a dog by its collar and the bride was holding a small piece of chewed paper. Her makeup would have to be redone, two stripes of mascara lining her face down to her chin. The other women in the room were either laughing or crying, or both simultaneously.

Lily figured the dog had eaten the groom's note of love before they took their marriage vows but Dev's scowl made her think it was much more serious.

"For the love of God, what has happened in here and why is my bride crying?" Gretchen asked breathlessly as she placed her arm around the girl.

"This, this," she stammered holding the one inch wide piece of paper, "was our marriage license and Two Bit ate it. That mongrel ate my license. He said a dog would be great for us as a couple. He was so wrong." She kept pointing at the dog over and over. Two Bit laid at Dev's feet enjoying the stroking he was receiving. Lily assumed "he" was the groom.

Now Gretchen was crying and wailing. "And that is why you don't have some animal in your wedding. Well, you'll just have to get married without it and then on Monday you march yourself back down to the county offices and get another."

"I can't get married without a license. It wouldn't be legal." Her mother was now on the other side of the sobbing bride, agreeing with her daughter.

"Oh for heaven's sake, you two have lived together for two years."

Lily nearly fell over in a heap of laughter at Gretchen's faux pas. She couldn't look over at Dev. She could see his body shaking from laughter as he held the poor dog. Of course Gretchen was correct but to bellow it out for all to hear?

The mother of the bride pushed Gretchen away and demanded she leave the room. Lily motioned for Dev to come with her as they exited too. He thought he could see the poor dog pleading with his eyes to stay by his side. Two Bit needed protection. They ended up in the tight hallway with Gretchen.

"I mean, what's the big deal? You two virtually live together too, don't you? So what's a few days?"

Lily and Dev chose silence. She actually felt sorry for Gretchen. Of course, when she relayed the story to Abby, and Abby laughed so hard she peed her pants, her lovely little assistant would not be so kind to the shrew. Abby had been drowned in Gretchen's wake several times and had felt the burn of her words. She would have no forgiveness for Gretchen's fallibility.

"Um, Lily, I need to make a call. Maybe I can get this fixed but I need the bride and groom's names, addresses, etc. Any information we can get. Gretchen, could you find out when they got the license and which county?"

"Me? Go back in there after they treated me so rudely?" Gretchen was back to being Gretchen and Lily's compassion was waning.

"I'll go," Lily suggested to Dev. "What else do you need?"

"Anything they can remember...a judge's name, a clerk's name...I don't know what's on a marriage license in Missouri. Anything will be helpful."

Lily rushed in to see what she could do while Dev began calling someone. He went down the stairs, away from Gretchen. Soon, Lily was marching down next to him with as much info as she had written in the notes on her cell.

"Thanks, honey," he answered as he took the phone from her. "Yes, it was that county." He walked away as he continued to talk.

One way or another there was going to be a party so Lily continued to decorate. One of the ladies from the venue came in to visit as she worked. She liked her new assistant, too. Every woman in the world seemed to like her new assistant.

Dev entered the room and asked for the keys to the van.

"I'll be back as soon as I can with a license. What time is the wedding?"

"Five. The traffic is going to be a killer."

"I'll be ok. I drive in DC, remember, and other dangerous places. I'll be back in time or close to it."

Lily looked toward the venue's coordinator. "Go tell them that the license is coming. I don't know how he is getting this done on a Friday afternoon but it is coming."

It was four o'clock when Lily finished the last table decoration after several interruptions from a grateful bride, mother, father, sister, it seemed like the entire bridal party after awhile. The groom even hugged her. She just hoped Dev would get there on time so there wasn't another meltdown up in that bridal room. The groom had apparently begged forgiveness and the wedding would go on. The dog and Gretchen weren't fairing as well. The dog was now banned to the groom's dressing room and the illustrious wedding coordinator had been told to get off the premises. Somehow it had all become her fault. She should never have let them use a dog in the wedding and how dare she say what she said.

Lily could hear the final sentence from the bride's mother as Gretchen left.

"How dare you judge my daughter, you old hag!" Everyone at the event space heard her.

The bridal party had been calmed down enough so they could take some pre-wedding photos. Lily watched them from the window. She was worried about this bride. She wasn't really smiling in the photos. Lily knew that smile very well, she'd been doing the same thing all afternoon. One of the groomsmen brought Two Bit onto the lawn.

The groom went to get him, loving on him, kissing him on the head. He brought him on the leash over to the bride who stood stoically in front of the gazebo. The dog's head was about as low as it could possibly get.

Lily just shook her head. The poor animal didn't know what he was doing. She knew for sure they would be laughing about this fiasco on their anniversary. Maybe they'd even make some money off it on some bridal blog… the dog ate our license.

The groom was saying something to his bride and finally she leaned down and pet their dog. The little family formed a hug unit and the bride smiled true and real for the first time in the last few hours of conflict. All was forgiven, until the dog started to eat her bouquet. That dog was hungry.

The venue's coordinator suggested they all get inside since guests were coming. Dev had twenty-five minutes. She saw the van pull into the driveway and park on the side. An older gentleman got out of the passenger side and Dev came strolling up on his left side, helping him up the steps. She met them at the door.

"You made it. Did you get it?" Even Lily was wringing her hands over this one.

"I did and I got them a judge just in case. Lily Schmidt, Judge Paul Stanley."

"Thank you so much, your honor." His warm smile suddenly calmed her down. She only hoped he could do the same magic for this bride.

"I hate to do this to you, sir, but they're upstairs. It's over here." Dev assisted him up the stairs, slowly. The squeals after a few minutes assured Lily there would be a wedding and there would be a happy bride, a relieved groom and a dog that really needed to stay away from the bride's mother.

Dev came back down the stairs two at a time meeting her at the bottom.

"You have everything ready? Sorry I wasn't any help."

"You did enough. By the way, I do think they forgot the officiant."

Dev nodded. "I figured when I noticed one of the programs and there was no name for a minister or judge. Besides, he insisted he meet them, signing everything so it would be legal. They'll still have to file some items but this will get them by and he's thrilled to do something happy for a change. Oh, I need water for him and if there's a small snack. He's diabetic and he needs a little something."

"Got it." She rushed into the venue coordinator's office and within five minutes the judge had what he needed. Dev remained at the bottom of the stairs so he could help his friend make it down safely.

"Do I want to know how you know him?"

"Well, you can imagine but I also know him personally. I was at West Point with his youngest son. We also served together."

"That's wonderful," Lily muttered. She was so immensely proud of Dev. Her new found "friend" was a wonderful man, thoughtful, kind…

"I brought his son's body back from Afghanistan."

Dev was no longer with her. He was with his friend, this man's son. She could see the face of grief…he was accompanying him back to his father, back in a flag-draped box. His mood was miles away and years behind.

She touched his arm to say sorry but his attention had moved to his fragile friend. He was making his way down the stairs.

"I'm coming, sir." Slowly they made their way down. The judge still held a water bottle in his hand.

"Crisis averted, young lady," he said as he greeted her. "So I hear you are a very special woman, Ms. Schmidt."

She glanced at Agent Pierce who now looked slightly uncomfortable. "You did, did you? Well, that was very nice. Thank you so much for doing this."

"No problem. It's going to cost you. You'll have to wait with me until my wife can get here after the wedding to pick me up."

"That is no problem at all, sir. I'm just so grateful. Thank you so much for coming to the rescue."

He was cute and very unassuming. Little in stature, bent in age, the judge was more Lily's height. His smile lit her heart.

"Oh I'm just an old romantic, kind of like this guy here," the judge stuck a finger in Dev's ribcage. "So, we've got this all figured out now. Those two up there, don't know about them." He shook his head. "The dog ate the license and they forgot to get someone to marry them. The groom said he's an attorney? Hope he's never in my court."

"And she's an accountant." Lily and he shared the laugh, the judge hugging her at the end of their amusement.

He looked over to Dev. "I like her. She's a keeper, if you know what I mean and don't be telling me anything about you're just doing your job. It's ok. You never know when God drops a gold nugget down from heaven. You're supposed to pick it up and cherish it, no matter where it came from. Or the next time, He might drop a big rock."

Lily smirked and Dev followed behind him outside. She was in love with a little old judge.

She was a gold nugget from God. Darn and he said he was married! She watched Dev sit him down in a side chair as guests filled in the rows of seats. Lily helped the bridal group proceed down the aisle. All of this hubbub and confusion was for a fifteen-minute ceremony but this was just the beginning of it all for this couple. There'd be years of hubbub that wouldn't always be calmed by an agent who knew someone, saving the day just in the nick of time. As the guests began to flow into the reception, Lily joined the two men sitting in the empty front row. They were talking about baseball.

"I'm pretty sure I'm open next Saturday. I'll drive."

"Ah, sweet Lily. I like that name." The judge welcomed her with a smile and an outstretched hand. "And she'll come to."

She looked at Dev. "Where am I going?"

"A Royals' game next Saturday if you can. The game doesn't start until a little past seven."

"And my wife will so appreciate your presence. Maureen loves baseball but she doesn't like to talk about it, she just likes to watch. Personally, I think she's just ogling the men in their uniforms, especially her Royals. Her favorite color has always been blue."

"Pauley, what are you saying about me?"

All three of them watched the older woman walking across the grass, her hands on her hips.

Her smile became wider as she saw a familiar face.

"Devlin Pierce, is that you? Look at you. You look better now than you did in your uniform."

"See, I told you. She likes her men," the judge said as he winked at Lily.

Dev greeted her with a hug and a kiss. She held onto him like he was her life vest in a stormy sea. Maybe he had been at one time. Lily envied the grace of this couple. She wanted to some day, years from now, go chasing after her own husband, wondering what adventure he had gone on, and hopefully he would share the story or the experience with her.

"Maureen, dear, I performed a lovely wedding for a terribly beautiful, handsome couple. Not sure it's going to work out but I did my job. Bless their hearts."

She continued to hold Dev's hand as she sat down next to her husband. "Hello, dear." She kissed him on the cheek and held his right hand. "Why aren't they going to work out?"

"Well, they're a little confused about why they're getting married. Seems they are one of those power couples you read about, not sure who they're going to rule over but they're going to have power. But they can't control a dog. They have way too much already so there's no way for them to grow together. What'd we have? A hundred dollars?"

"Don't short change us, Paul. We had one hundred and fifteen dollars. I cashed out my savings account and mother thought you'd never amount to anything. Bless her soul."

She wasn't sure why she did it but since Dev was standing directly next to her, Lily reached over and held his hand. He didn't move, he didn't swat her hand away, in fact his body moved closer to her's until his right arm was touching her left one. They stood in absolute silence, perhaps in awe, watching the devoted couple. It was pure love, quiet and unassuming.

"Thanks for picking me up, dear." The judge kissed his wife's cheek. "Time to go home."

She helped lift him off the chair. "Seems like I'm always coming for you."

"I like you to feel wanted," he joked. "Well, Dev, my boy, you drop by the office next week if you can and we will coordinate this little outing. Club level seats are pretty nice so don't eat dinner before and yes, you will be driving. Ms. Schmidt, you will be joining us."

She took the command as a gentle directive. Maureen smiled at her.

"Wonderful, I'll have another woman with me. After all these years I just get too tired of talking to this man." Obviously, she was cajoling him. "Let's go home and get you a nice meal. I've made baked chicken."

They slowly crossed the yard, continuing their banter. "I want that," Lily said out loud.

"Me too." His answer lingered on the air until they decided they were starving.

It was almost nine in the evening by the time Lily had dropped off the van. Dev checked her detail coming on duty at her home while she parked her car in the garage and came into the house. The timer had already turned on the living room lamps. She kicked her shoes off, dropped her bags in the nearest chair and figured she better get the mail.

She was humming some song from the restaurant where they'd eaten as she opened the front door to grab the mail. Two steps out, she thought she heard something in the bushes on the side of the house. She'd heard reports that there was a raccoon rummaging through trash in the neighborhood. Maybe he was building a condo in her yard.

She was headed back in with her mail when she saw a figure from the left side, a hooded figure. He or she was coming toward her. Lily was frozen in time. Oh Lord, it had all come to this. She dropped the mail and opened the door but the figure was on her when she finally screamed. At the same time a woman police officer was running up the yard to her rescue.

The figure seemed confused, his head rotating to look at her and then the officer. He backed away and began running across the neighbors' yards.

"Are you ok, Ms. Schmidt?" The woman wasn't following him but coming to her aid.

Lily stood in shock, managing to nod her head. She'd been holding her breath, finally releasing it.

"What the bloody hell was that?" she asked the officer.

"That was why I'm here."

Dev received the call before he even made it back to the hotel. He'd turned the car around and began to speed back to her. It only took him minutes to arrive in Lily's driveway. He could see her sitting on the sofa with her police officer. There was another black and white parked out front with its lights on. He talked briefly with them and slowly made his way into the house.

As he entered, she immediately looked up at him, her tear-stained face silently asking him a question. He wouldn't know how to answer her. He motioned for the officer and he talked to her briefly before she departed. There wasn't anything more she could do at this point. He needed to be the one to explain, to protect and to take the wrath if need be.

He grabbed two beers out of the refrigerator, walked into the living room and held an opened one in front of Lily's face.

She grabbed the beer but didn't look at him as he sat directly across from her on the coffee table.

"Now you know why you had a protective detail. I'm so happy you're ok."

"When were you going to tell me that you knew someone was watching me? When, Agent Pierce? That police officer stayed with me. She didn't even try to go after the guy which means, and don't tell me I'm being ridiculous, that you want him out there. You're trying to catch him and you set me up. Do not deny it."

Dev winced at the pain he heard in her voice. Well, it was actually not as bad as he thought it was going to be but it hurt him all the same.

"I won't deny it."

She looked directly into his face and hit his upper arm with a balled-up fist. "Damn you."

She had a good punch, Dev thought. He'd take a shot on the arm over the look of betrayal any day.

"Lily, we are making progress…"

"Oh that's wonderful," she interrupted, the sarcasm dripping on each word. "What's the end game, me dead? This thing has gone on for months. We've become, we've become friends and now I'm figuring that this is all a game with you people. You don't care about me. You care about putting some Cartel away and getting those drugs."

"Lily, you're upset and you *are* being ridiculous."

Her eyes widened. "I cannot believe you just said that. Get out." Lily pointed at the door and grabbed the beer out of his hand.

She stood up for emphasis. "Get up and get out." He remained seated.

"No."

"What? This is still my house, isn't it?"

Dev looked up at her. "Sit down, give me my beer and let's talk this out." She stood her ground, one hand holding the beer, the other on her hip.

He was coldly staring at her. He could see her hands still shaking, her pale skin sporting goosebumps and tears in those wide eyes. But she was Lily and she could handle this. He knew she could.

"Lily, please sit down and give me a chance to explain what I can."

Slowly she moved to the sofa and sat down. She took a drink of the beer and held his gaze. "Explain," she demanded as she pushed the beer into his hand.

"Ok, well, you have had a protective detail on you, the police or me since the very beginning. We put in surveillance cameras in your shop because that's where the original crime took place and where we thought they would return to get whatever is missing that we don't have a clue about. It takes time to convince the bad guys that they need to move on and that's what we're doing. You're fine and you will be fine. I will not allow anything to happen to you, I promise."

She continued to examine his face, to read any false uttering. But could she? Did she even know when he was lying? He had been so bad at it that very first day but now lines were so blurred and she was so confused.

"You know I watch murder mysteries all the time," she announced. "I know when things aren't sounding right. Nothing about this sounds right, Dev, not even you."

He felt nauseous as though he'd been shot in the stomach, but the hole was in his heart.

What more could he tell her and keep the mission on track?

"Sometimes," he paused trying to find the right words, "lines get blurred like with you and me."

Lily was listening very intently. He had her full attention but her anger was still there.

"We are friends, Lily. I've come to respect you greatly and I do hope we stay in touch when this is all over."

Lily heard the word "respect" and her heart plummeted. But why? She always knew he was going to say this. What else could he say? That he'd fallen madly in love with her in these past months, that he wanted to whisk her away to some island to make love in the sun? What was wrong with her that she couldn't see what was right in front of her eyes?

"But," Dev continued, "I have a job to do. We are doing that job together, I know that. Without your help, your openness to allow me into your world, I couldn't get this done. And I will get this done, you will be fine and it will be over very soon. I'm so sorry about this scare but I really believe that's all this guy was trying to do was scare you. We can handle this, but we've got to do this together. I can't tell you everything. You have to trust me, Lily, please."

She had been holding her breath again. Slowly, she let the air out and took another drink of beer.

"You so owe me, Devlin Pierce."

He smiled shyly not realizing his eyes were twinkling. "I know, Lily Schmidt, I know."

Later, he made sure her bedroom windows were locked before she went to sleep. He grabbed a pillow from the other bedroom and camped out in the living room. It was before dawn when he heard another noise and scouted around the perimeter of the house. He waved at the officer in the car.

He came back into the house and smelled coffee. Everything looked normal and now with the fragrance of caffeine, everything seemed normal. But he was worried that nothing was normal in Lily's world. Everything had changed overnight, literally. He wasn't sure he could fix what was or wasn't going on between them.

She came around the corner in a robe and slippers. She held the coffee pot. "Coffee, right?"

He nodded. He could hear her humming "It's Been A Hard Day's Night".

"Well, I'm not serving you. I don't feel like it, yet," she yelled from the kitchen.

His friend was back. Maybe.

Devlin Pierce tried to get a run in everyday but some days the heat in the Heartland was just too much. This morning, a cool fall breeze was flowing as he ran around the Plaza. He'd already run a couple of miles as he headed for his favorite coffee shop on the corner but something caught his eye.

He hadn't seen postcards in the longest time and unless you were actually around one of the many tourist attractions in Washington DC, you seldom saw them anywhere. He stopped to see a rack of them, most featuring landmarks of Kansas City but the ones that caught his attention were of Christmas lights and the Plaza. His relatives in the area had always shared their tradition of coming down for the turning on of the lights on Thanksgiving night but somewhere in his brain he'd translated it into a tree lighting occasion on the square.

There would be a children's choir singing and the usual suspects such as the mayor and of course jolly St. Nick. If you were really lucky, your local councilman would show up.

But these cards held the beauty of something much larger. Strings upon strings of lights adorned the buildings for blocks. The multi colored structures blended well with the Spanish architecture. During this summer he must have jogged past this building countless times but this was the first time something had captured his attention and left him speechless. One card featured the lighting with the crowds of people in the shadows. He'd never known any tradition where the people gathered for an event of the people, not the National tree, nor a Governor's tree. Generations of families must've taken part in this ceremony year after year.

He didn't know if it seemed odd to him or familiar like returning home after a long deployment with everyone waiting there to greet you.

Lily had told him stories of her own family visits to the lighting. He could almost smell and taste the hot chocolate as she described how they stood on top of one of the parking garages one year with snow falling, cocoa in hand and the awe of the beginning of the Christmas season in Kansas City. He'd watched her face as she remembered and he swore she was glowing as bright as one of those bulbs. Her family had spent the day together doing the usual Thanksgiving day activities of feasting and football and then the younger members headed down to the Country Club Plaza to watch the lights welcome the Christmas season. By the end of the night they all ended up at a pizza place playing trivia games. He'd like to see the lights turn on with thousands of other people. He wouldn't mind seeing them with her beside him.

Yes, Kansas City might be a place he'd like to visit again.

He knew when he finally returned to Virginia and hit the door of his townhouse it would be empty. That thought kept creeping into his head more and more these days as the investigation was wrapping up. The other night's chaos only brought him one more step closer to flying away. For the first time in a long time, he didn't like the feeling one bit.

He headed for his coffee, a quick read of any newspaper laying around and then he needed to head back to the hotel, shower and make sure he was on time at the shop. This week Lily and he had moved on, even a few jokes were thrown back and forth. Today, at the end of this long wedding day, they had a baseball game to go to. Although he'd been with Tom and his wife a couple of nights this summer, he was looking forward to the companionship of the judge and his wife. And it would be the first time Lily would be included in his life circle. She'd be meeting people who really knew him and he wasn't sure how he felt about that. He'd have to take a chance.

Chapter Nineteen

1. Remain calm
2. Don't eat too slowly, but don't take large bites when eating
3. Smile a lot and try not to answer many questions
4. Have a good time, forget the other night...you're sitting on the Club level at the Royals' game

Lily's list making was carrying on in her brain as they all sat down with their food. The Judge and Dev were sitting together, leaving her with Maureen Stanley. It didn't take the woman long before the questions began. After the other night she'd be particularly careful in her answers.

"How long have the two of you known each other?" The game hadn't even started!

Lily was taking the first bite of a very large brat with sauerkraut, mustard and onions (she wouldn't be kissing anyone tonight). She chewed as quickly as she could.

"Not long, months."

She planned on being as vague as humanly possible.

"Hmm, I just wondered with him in Virginia and you owning a shop here." The older woman squinted her eyes and came closer to Lily's face, seemingly analyzing her every blink and pursing of lips.

"And how did you meet him?"

"He walked into my shop one day. Funny thing, he just kind of kept hanging around and boom, here we are." Lily's heart was beating faster. She didn't want to lie to people who seemed so important to Dev.

Maureen Stanley took a deep breath and sat back in her seat.

"Ah, I think I understand. He's here on an investigation. You're very good because frankly, I don't know if you are part of it all, covering for him or just being nice to an old lady. But you are very good, Lily. All right. I'll stop with the questions."

Thank God, Lily prayed. Maybe they could just enjoy the game now?

Dev came by them as he walked back to the snack bar. He touched her shoulder as he passed. He slid it slowly to touch the side of her neck. Without thinking, she turned into the slight caress.

"You need anything?"

She looked up at him. "No, I'm good, but thank you."

The judge's wife laughed out loud. "Oh, you are good. He doesn't even realize what he feels for you."

Lily placed her plate down on the table beside her. She really didn't want to be rude but what was this woman talking about? Devlin Pierce had made everything very clear, well sort of, to her the other night. They were friends, or at least he hoped they were.

"Honestly, Mrs. Stanley, I don't know what you're talking about. I'm just me and I don't understand how you came to that conclusion."

She grabbed Lily's hand and softly petted the top of it.

"Honey, that's the beauty of it. That's the way it should be. Let it take time and with your profession in mind, allow it to bloom, don't rush it, let it open up on its own. I mean let him open up but don't let him take too long or the boy will never be ready for delivery."

Lily's voice lowered. "What are you seeing that I'm not? I mean, I really like him, what he's allowed me to know and maybe that's all an act too. We're friends right now but I can't see us together. I mean, look at him." She motioned as he walked by.

"Oh he's got lots of scars, Lily and most of those are not pretty. I'm not talking the physical ones. Don't sell yourself short. Did you see how he touched your shoulder? Did you notice he wanted to make sure you were comfortable? He didn't want to just know if you needed a beer or some chips, he was making sure you were safe here with me. Oh, and that the two of you were ok."

Lily quickly understood. "Oh." There was no other answer for this wise woman beside her. Something was there between them but for something to be there both of them were going to have to embrace the unknown and it was always frightening jumping into a black hole. That's why she'd never done it. It was one thing to be hurt over and over by people you thought you were in love with but once they were gone and out of your life, you survived and you went on. She couldn't think of him gone now that he was here.

After the other night, she knew for sure that the case would soon be over. Her busy fall season would begin. Flowers would be delivered all over town every week until

Halloween and it would slow down a bit. The holidays would begin. She had weddings over Thanksgiving so she wouldn't be flying back east to visit her brother or her sister. She had cousins in town she could share a turkey with but with a wedding on Friday night that meant she'd have to leave early to work. Christmas and New Year's would be just around the corner. She had several events over the holidays so she wouldn't be with family again. The new year would bring Valentine's Day…she was tired just thinking about it. There was no room for anyone except her brides. Besides, he'd be gone as soon as it was all over. Soon.

"Lily, let's join them up there and enjoy tonight. What do you say?" Maureen patted her hand again. "Just enjoy the time you have."

Lily nodded, the lump in her throat forming to stop the tears from falling. The woman was a mind reader. She smiled slightly as they moved up beside the men. Dev looked down at her and mouthed "are you ok?" She nodded and began talking to her female companion about the catcher for the home team. They both thought he was cute.

Several innings later, Dev and the Judge had been invited into the press box. Lily had managed to put herself together again and wanted to know more, as delicately as she could, about the Stanleys' relationship with Devlin Pierce.

"Our son Michael and Devlin were at West Point together. He came a couple of times to Kansas City during break time, besides he has family here. An uncle, aunt, yes, his mother's sister lives here. The boys were the best of friends, anyway, they both deployed together a couple of times and it was the third rotation, a bad mission, something went very wrong. Michael was shot and Dev kept him alive until a chopper got them out of there. Dev brought him back to us. He insisted. He has stayed in touch ever since." She stopped abruptly, tightening her lips and clenching her fists.

"You know," Maureen continued, "the Army wasn't going to allow him to bring Michael home; he was too important for the work over there but Dev would've gone AWOL if he had to. I'm not sure how but he would've. I can still remember him standing at attention as the casket came out of the airplane." Her voice trailed off to another time.

"But then," she continued, "when his mother died, well, he couldn't get back in time. It was so very sad. I think he's still holding it in, never made peace with it. They were so close, Lily."

"That's awful." Lily now knew a secret about Devlin Pierce. Lily now knew she and the agent that protected her shared more than just friendship.

"He's a good guy, Lily. He has a good heart but he's been hurt and I bet you have too." She lightly touched Lily's leg. "Sorry, sorry, not going to talk about that. Um, our favorite player is up to bat."

They both smiled and at the same time said, "He has the nicest back end."

All the two men heard as they entered the room was hysterical laughter. Both women were in tears, assuring them that everything was perfectly fine.

It was nearing midnight before they headed back across the river after delivering the couple to their home north of the city. As they were coming across the bridge, a backup of traffic had developed.

"Is it a wreck? I see police lights." Lily was leaning out of her passenger window. "We could be sitting here for hours if that's the case."

"No early Mass for you," Dev joked. "No, it seems to be moving, slowly, but moving."

He leaned out and saw the police on the side. He knew exactly what it was on a Saturday night.

"It's a DUI check."

Suddenly she was afraid. Why? She'd only had a beer and she wasn't driving. "Are you all right?" she stammered.

"Of course. I'm more worried if they make me get out of the car."

Lily couldn't figure that one out. One more car and they'd be in the spotlight. Dev had already reached for the rental car registration and paperwork in the glove compartment. He'd also pulled out his driver's license. One officer motioned for him to pull forward.

His window already down, he handed out his information.

"Virginia?"

"Yes, officer. Visiting."

"Please step out of the vehicle."

She'd never seen Dev so quiet and official. He closed the car door and stood beside it as another officer moved a flashlight around the interior. She smiled but he just continued. She heard Dev say he wanted to speak to whoever was in charge. What was going on? He said he was fine.

A few minutes later another officer was standing in front of him.

"You want to explain, Mr. Pierce?"

"Your officer wanted to search me for some reason. I'm carrying. If you allow me to reach for my billfold I'll show you my permit and my badge."

"Your badge?"

"Yes, sir. I'm working undercover and I'd rather not have every cop in the world know."

"Get it out. You one of us?"

"No, I'm out of state, federal."

As soon as a badge was presented it was handed back immediately as he motioned for their car to be sent through.

They crossed the bridge and were soon on their way.

"I have been wondering, do you have a gun?" Lily had to ask after all these months.

"Yes."

"Elaborate please."

"No."

"Yes. Where do you have it? It'll make me feel safer and after the other night, you owe me, remember?"

He laughed out loud. "If I told you, I'd have to kill you. I have been waiting so long to use that line. I just had to keep you going."

She hit his shoulder, less than playfully for the second time in a week. "You still haven't told me where it is."

"On my leg."

"Crud, I thought it might be in the heel of your shoe."

"No, that's where my secret phone is."

She rolled her eyes. "You know Jessica Fletcher didn't need all that stuff to solve cases. That's why she's my hero."

"Heroes come in all shapes and sizes, Lily. Maxwell Smart is mine."

They were both laughing by now. They seemed to be the best together when they were laughing or eating. She wasn't sure where those two shared talents would land them but it was fun finding out. Until he left.

"Bucko, you might have to give up on Agent 86. No more telephone booths, so you're no Agent 86."

"And you, madam are no Agent 99." He was still laughing but she suddenly went quiet. "I mean, you're not tall enough. You'd have to be seven feet tall to loom over me."

"I can't be her or any woman with you." She wasn't sure if she had said it out loud or only in her thoughts but the car became very quiet the rest of the trip to her house.

He phoned ahead to the detail and her protection was sitting there as he walked her in, checked the house and walked back to the front door to go.

"I won't be at church tomorrow, early meeting but I'll check in. It was a good time tonight and I'm happy you got to know those two. They are wonderful people."

She was holding onto the door for support, tired and disgusted again on a Saturday night.

"We can agree on that. They are very special and they have something so special. All those years they've been together. Do you know they knew each other just one month before they were married? Can you imagine?"

"No, not really, not nowadays. Things are so different."

"Don't I know it." Another Saturday night and she wanted him out of her house and away from her. Her tone was clipped. She'd decided very quickly that laughing and eating was not enough!

He was stalling, trying to think of something witty to say to her, to make her like him again. It was important to him. She hadn't appreciated the kidding about their physical differences and her dislike of him in this moment was palpable.

"Lily, I wasn't making fun of you. I'm sorry if you thought I was." Her eyes were downcast as he apologized. He couldn't stand this. She was trying to close the door on him but his foot was wedged in the way.

He closed the distance between them to mere inches, touching her cheek and lifting it so he could see her water-filled eyes.

"I'm so sorry."

"I'm tired. Long day and night, long few months."

"I'm going to say it one more time," he was still holding her chin gently in his hand. "I'm so sorry if I hurt your feelings. It wasn't my intention." He paused slightly and lowered his head. "I guess I missed it by *that much*."

She threw her head back as she laughed into his face. He'd used an old gag line from the "Get Smart" television show and movie.

"Get out of here."

"You're throwing me out again on a Saturday night? We good now?" He wanted to make sure his joke, Maxwell Smart's coined phrase, had hit its mark.

"Yes, get out of here. I'll talk to you tomorrow." She was pushing his back out of her way. "Lock up behind me."

"Yes, mother."

As he bounded down the sidewalk, he glared back at her. "I mean it. Yell if you need anything. Goodnight."

His headlights were showing as she locked the door and turned to go to bed. It had been a long, informative day. Her feelings were in a tumult with no direction or appropriate path in the horizon.

As she entered her bedroom, she whispered out loud.

"I need you."

Chapter Twenty

1. Rest of flowers coming this morning
2. Make sure everything is ready for weekend
3. Check all schedules
4. Mrs. Notte coming in for orchid, no delivery now
5. Meet Big John for lunch at the bistro

Lily was rushing around this morning. She'd gone back to sleep after the alarm went off and just couldn't get moving today, and she had so much to do! She didn't make coffee, instead pulling through the local coffee shop drive thru. Not only did she need caffeine, she needed sugar and opted for a caramel macchiato, no sugar free.

She coded in the security numbers once she got to the door of the shop. Today it was 5-6-7.

She balanced her files and coffee in one hand. The red button still showed on the pad. She began the process over… 5-6-7 and still no green light. One more time and she'd be locked out for an hour until the security company or some tech from some government agency came.

She really didn't need this today. Those were the correct numbers. There was no doubt in her mind as she laid her folders, bag and coffee on the cement and reached inside her purse for her cell.

As she waited for someone on the other end of the line, she waved at Big John across the street. He smiled but kept walking. Wow, he was early today. Maybe he had something planned with his family since his daughter and granddaughter were still in town.

"Yes, I have a problem with my system. Lily Schmidt, yes, I'm that Lily Schmidt with the special problem." She hated being the one with the alphabet problem…FBI, DEA…oh and don't forget the most important Cartel. Next they asked her a series of security questions. Of course she had the right answers.

"Look, I put in the proper code for today 5-6-7 and the system isn't allowing me access. The button is still red and I've tried twice. Maybe we had an electrical outage overnight?"

She was grasping at any sort of a solution or answer to her difficulty. She looked through the shop's window to see if anything was thrown around but everything seemed to be in order. She wouldn't really be able to tell until she entered and had a good look around.

Lily punched in 8-9-10 and a green button showed immediately.

"Thank you, it's open now. I'll call you back immediately if I need anything else but please notify Agent Pierce."

She knew that something wasn't right with that code. Had someone been in the shop again?

But the security company hadn't said anything but try the next sequence. Maybe there had been a power outage. Gathering her things, she hurried into the shop, surveying as she hurried along. The phone was already ringing. After handling that call there was another and another. She appreciated the business but it was almost ten by now and her caramel macchiato was certainly cold. She'd need to micro zap it now. As she picked it up she saw the note she'd left last night before she'd closed the shop. It reminded her that Mrs. Notte's orchid she had ordered was ready for pickup and supposedly she was coming in at one. If Abby wasn't on time this morning, she'd have to cut her lunch date short and she really didn't want to do that. Big John was the only constant in her life and they hadn't had lunch alfresco in several weeks.

Actually, it was easier not to see Big John, to not lie to him about what had been going on. It was frightening to think that Abby was the only other person trusted with her secrets. It was equally amazing that Abby hadn't told a soul. Even Neal and the flower wholesale group didn't know the full extent of the subterfuge.

She took the top off her cup and saw the murky separated mess. It was a lost cause, one for the sink and trash. She moved to the back work area and heard the knock on the back door.

"Lily, it's Danny." She immediately opened to see her usual flower delivery man. Neal had sent him out early with the remainder of her flowers for Saturday's wedding. He was a welcome sight, normal and that's what she needed right now.

"Hey pretty lady, how's it going?"

"Better now that you're here and early."

He handed off two boxes, she signed the invoice and he was on his way. She began to cut the first bunch of flowers when she heard the buzzer on the front door. Thank God, the day was getting better and Abby was miraculously early.

"Boss, I'm here. I'm supposed to remind you that Mrs. Notte is coming in to pick up that plant."

"Yes, got it. She'll be in at one. I'm back here and I've got the rest of the flowers for Saturday. They'll all fit in the cooler."

Abby was humming some tune Lily couldn't place. Maybe it was Gavin DeGraw? She knew Abby had gone to his concert last week. But Lily didn't know his music very well. Or maybe it was Counting Crows? Abby had gone to that concert Sunday night. That girl sounded so carefree without a worry in the world, and her life was like that too. A concert one night, drinks with the girls another and stringing poor Jeremy along while doing it all.

She thought Abby really cared about the little idiot but in the past Abby had cared for a lot of little idiots, most of them were a lot like Jeremy. Wouldn't that be nice to have a string of boys, men who'd take her to the movies, concerts or dinners? Lily never really had that in her life, such a carefree lifestyle of noncommittal delight void of any responsibility. Nope, she'd come out of the womb with the responsibility gene and now the weight of the shop and her life were on her shoulders alone. She was living to work most of the time and her outings with Dev were her only time off. When she was with him she could almost give up the worrying, the wondering, the fear. Of course, they'd have a lovely time, an awkward goodbye at the door (now an unsure hug) and she'd walk inside her house to all those fears once more. Most people had blood in their veins but she had fear coursing through every part of her body, pooling in her brain and heart.

Finishing her work, she cleaned up and made sure all the flowers were cool and happy, ready for the work to come Thursday and Friday. She looked up at the clock to notice she had five minutes to meet Big John. After lunch she would call Dev and make sure he'd been notified about the goof up this morning. She had the nagging thought that someone had known the code system, had used the code in the middle of the night and the security company just wasn't telling her. She hoped she wasn't being used as bait again or she'd be telling the alphabet soup of government agents her own particular words with a couple of letters.

Truthfully, she wanted to talk to Dev. He hadn't been around the last couple of weeks.

Instead, she had her detail outside the house and Agent Fullerton had dropped by occasionally. He actually bought flowers for his wife, becoming a regular customer.

By the time she reached the corner of the block she saw Big John sitting at a table outside the bistro, two sandwiches and two drinks laid out in front of him.

"Sorry I'm a little late. This morning has been insane. First I turned off the alarm *and* went back to sleep which made me late, then I had a hard time with the security system and couldn't get into the shop so I had to call them, then the phone was ringing off the hook, the flowers came and I didn't even get to drink my blasted coffee." She was exhausted just telling the story of her morning.

He was laughing and then his face became serious. "Are you telling me you haven't had caffeine yet, little girl? The world is in danger! Spare your children."

"Very funny. What did you get me?" She was starving. She'd pay him back in the next couple of weeks with a longer lunch and maybe by then she could tell him about the Cartel caper. Hopefully, yes, she'd think it again, hopefully it would be over soon. She didn't mind the extra protection at night but the neighbors were beginning to wonder about her and what she "really" did for a living.

"I got you a turkey, no mayo on your wheat bread." He passed the sandwich toward her. "And an iced tea with no sugar. Now take a break and breath before you come undone."

"Sounds perfect. It's been a heck of a week and it's only Wednesday. Just one wedding Saturday and I'm looking forward to coming home after its over and just watching television." She paused. She was even speaking faster than normal. "I do need to take a breath, don't I?"

Reaching over to pat his large paw of a hand she added, "Thanks for caring, really. I appreciate you so much. You'll never know."

"No problem. I just want you to be great, not just good. By the way, haven't seen your boyfriend lately. You two didn't break up, did you?"

"Um, well, he's out of town for work."

"What does he do again?" John was staring right into her lying eyes.

Lord, she had to look right into his eyes and lie to an ex-cop, a protector, a friend.

"He works for an international company and they find people and put them where they need to be. Kind of a head hunter of sorts." What a pile of crap but she was beginning to amuse herself. He did find people and he did place them where those people needed to be, usually in jail.

She asked how his wife was. She was concerned about her health and injury.

"Well, we had her checked over and it wasn't good, little girl." She could see the anguish on John's face.

"From that fall?"

"She was hurting again, remember? They did some looking around and she has cancer, Lily.When she was in her late forties she had breast cancer but she was in remission so long we thought she'd beat it. They found a spot on her left lung and she's in chemo right now. Thank God my daughter and granddaughter are here right now."

Lily laid her sandwich down and stopped eating. She felt sick to her stomach as she saw the anguish on his gentle face.

"When do they have to go back to Florida?"

He smiled slightly. "I hope not for a long while. Its been tough, very tough. I'm under a lot of pressure. But you know what it's like."

She nodded and her thoughts turned to her mother and father. It was tough living through cancer or any disease. It was tough living through the uncertainty and then the vanishing act that death performed so well on the human race, on loved ones.

"So, didn't you have a mugging at your house or something a few months ago?"

Lily tried not to show her surprise. "How'd you hear about that?"

"Oh some of the patrol guys told me about it. I know it seems like you're a target at your house, your shop but things have been happening around the area. They think there's a burglary group hitting the smaller businesses and some of the residences. You know, some young thugs trying to make a name."

"They need to do it somewhere else," Lily muttered. "Let's talk about something else. I'm so done with all that." At least she could tell the truth about something.

Lily began to fill him in on Abby's romance with Jeremy and a few stories about some of the most recent weddings. He roared with laughter as she told him about the dog that ate the license.

"Oh my." He was crying he was laughing so hard. "You don't know how good it is to laugh."

For these minutes at lunch, she felt lighter than usual with Big John, with her friend. But she had to get back to business. Lily looked down to check the time. It was almost one but Abby would be there for Mrs. Notte. Hopefully the phaelanopsis plant would be what she wanted.

"You need to get back for Mrs. Notte and that orchid?"

"No, Abby's there. She'll take care of her. I hope she likes it." Lily took another sip of her tea and pushed back from the table.

"But you know how Mrs. Notte can be after all these years. Or if she sends her grandson to pick up I'm not sure how Abby will handle that…he's been trying to date her all this summer. They're both so picky so I better get back just in case. The way this day's gone you never know."

Big John stood up too and hugged her like he always did.

"You take care of yourself, little girl. I couldn't bear it if you got hurt."

She nuzzled her head against his large chest. She felt like she was saying goodbye to him forever.

"I will, you too. Tell your wife I'm thinking of her always." She blew him a kiss and turned away.

Her smile vanished, her breath quickened and her steps were rushed.

The only way he'd known about that orchid was if he'd seen her note sometime through the night…the note that was on her desk.

Chapter Twenty-One

With every step, Lily breathed in and out and uttered "Oh my God." It was said as a prayer. It was said in desperation. As she finally reached the door of the shop and entered, she felt sick to her stomach. The months of uncertainty had faded into the reality of betrayal. Her current condition was etched on her face.

"You sick?" Abby yelled as she ran toward her. "You look like death? What did you eat for lunch?"

Lily could hardly stand and began to quickly reach for the chair near the consultation table. Abby pulled it over and sat her down. Lily's vision was blurred, her breathing rapid. She really was violently ill. She pulled her phone out quickly and started to scan the contacts.

"Should I call 911? I'll do it, don't you do it. Are you having a heart attack? Have you been poisoned, I mean food poisoning? Can it hit that quickly? Oh please tell me what to do."

Abby's hand was waving frantically in front of Lily's face. She thought the little idiot would hit her phone before she could find the number. She continued scanning her phone.

Her eyes never left it as she started to direct Abby before her assistant hurt her or called 911. "Don't call 911. I'm calling for help right now. Lock the door right now. RIGHT NOW. We are closed."

Abby did as she was told and then like a misbehaving

puppy returned to Lily's side.

"Just sit, Abby. Don't do anything but sit down and let me be for a second, please. I have to think."

Abby sat but didn't understand. Her wide eyes were watching her boss's color return to her face but Lily was still visibly shaken. She'd never seen her like this, not through all of this craziness with the drugs and the Cartel, nor the FBI or Agent Pierce. Who was Lily calling?

And why were they suddenly closed at one in the afternoon?

Finally, Lily had found the number and was putting the phone to her ear. "Please, please pick up." It was a prayer not a request.

She heard the voice and realized it was a message. When she heard "leave a message and I'll get to you as soon as possible" her stomach flipped again but she had to get in touch with him.

"Agent Pierce, please call me immediately. This is life or death important, please," she begged as she looked up to see Abby's wide eyes filling with tears. "Dev, I think I'm in big trouble and I'm really scared. Not kidding. Oh and it's me, Lily."

She placed the phone in her lap and reached to grab Abby's hands in her's. "Abby, has Mrs. Notte picked up that plant yet?"

Abby nodded quickly. "Well, she didn't. Creepy Garrett did and he was really weird to me. He came in early while you were at lunch. Maybe he was weird because I refused to go out with him. I don't know but he's always just looking around. My skin crawls. Sometimes it looks like he's studying me. Weird."

Lily rolled her eyes. She really didn't care about how creepy Garrett Notte was. It was already determined that he was weird. It didn't matter. Nothing really mattered right now.

"Abby, we may have to stay here all night. I don't know what to do until we hear from Dev. I know who was involved in the burglaries and we may be in trouble but if you leave or I leave I think we might be in more trouble. Do you understand?"

Abby nodded and allowed more tears to flow down her cheeks. "Should I have Jeremy come over?" She gasped out loud. "It isn't Jeremy is it? I think I love him and if it's him I don't know what I'll do." She grabbed her chest as if she was in pain.

Melodramatics at this time of crisis? Really? Lily's patience, not that she had any right now, was vanishing quickly.

Lily shook her head. "No, you ninny. It's not Jeremy. That boy couldn't steal anything even if you left the door open and had a sign pointing the way to the money! Geez, Abby."

But who it was in reality defied every trust. Maybe having Jeremy here wouldn't be such a bad idea.

"Sorry, yes. Jeremy should come over but let's wait a little while. If anyone, I mean anyone, comes to that door to come in, I don't care if it's the Mayor, we are closed and we are doing massive cleaning. We had a water issue, left a faucet running while I was at lunch, got it?"

This was the time to lie and to do it well. "But I didn't."

Lily sighed. "I know you didn't but for our safety we can't let anyone in so we're going to tell them this story. Please Abby just trust me."

Abby nodded. Perhaps the gravity of the situation was dawning on her but Lily didn't want to tell her what she suspected. Trust, how ironic that it all came down to that.

Lily took in a deep breath and got up. "So, let's go to work. Let's get ahead on doing some of the bows we need for the next few weeks, inventorying vases, pulling some things for this weekend…" Now she was verbalizing her list and she felt in control but so desperately trying to stay in that safe condition.

She couldn't tell her helper what she suspected at least not until she talked to Dev and told him. Told him what? That she suspected a very dear friend was involved in a huge betrayal? Was somehow involved in placing her in a dangerous position and had probably orchestrated the chaos that had enveloped them since those damn hydrangeas had mistakenly ended up in her shop?

She looked at the cell phone as though it would magically ring if she just willed it to do so.

Please, Lord, don't let Dev be in the Middle East, she prayed silently.

Lily watched Abby go to the back room. "Abby, lock that back door too. Now."

About that time the shop's line rang and Lily jumped out of her seat and her skin. Abby ran to grab it and was talking to a client.

Who else was involved in this? Could she trust the police? Big John had been told by them about the incident at the house. She had to keep busy while she waited. She did what she did best and went to work. But she continued to pray while she did.

Two hours passed. A few people walked by the shop slowly, seeing the closed sign. Some pointed and some even tried the door. At four, Big John walked by and rattled the door. She looked up from the desk and waved. She could tell he was wondering why they were closed but she didn't leave the desk. She couldn't; her body was concrete, cementing her to her chair. Her legs were numb, her hands were shaking. She waved and smiled. It was probably the fake smile of all time. An Academy Award might be coming her way.

"We're working on a project, very time sensitive," she yelled without leaving her position.

"Oh there's John, should we let him in?" Abby asked as she waved too.

Lily turned in the chair and mouthed the word "no".

"Go back to work, now. Look like we are really busy, please Abby."

Poor Abby didn't have a clue and as she saw the fear on Lily's face she was beginning to understand. Not Big John?

He waved back and nodded his head. He was making his usual route down the boulevard.

He strolled away. He understood. Lily just hoped he didn't understand too much.

They made a list for Jeremy of what they would need for the night. One thing about Jeremy, he might not be the brightest bulb but he certainly loved Abby. He never questioned why they were camping out over at the shop nor why he was joining them. He was bringing provisions, some food and a few items for sleeping.

It was half past four when Lily's phone rang. She picked up immediately to say hello.

"Lily, what is it? What's happened?"

It was Dev. Relief flooded her but she couldn't get the words out. She was crying hysterically, handing the phone to Abby. She'd heard his voice and had lost what little control she had remaining.

"Um, Agent Pierce, Dev, this is Abby. Lily is having a meltdown right now. We have the store locked up. You know my boyfriend, Jeremy, well he's bringing some stuff over and we are all staying the night here. She's insisting that we're in some danger."

Lily listened as she tried to pull herself together. Dev must be talking since Abby was listening intently.

"Well, she had lunch with John, our security guy, remember him? Then she came in and made me lock up. She looked like she was sick and she wouldn't let me call 9-1-1. I think maybe something happened with Big John…" Abby stopped mid-sentence and handed the phone to Lily.

She took it and heard his voice again. "Lily, just listen. I'm going to call Agent Fullerton as soon as I hang up. Not sure why they haven't come by. They should be watching and notice that something isn't right. Fullerton is the only one you are going to allow in the store. Only him. I'm going to hang up now and call him and I'll call you right back to tell you how this is going down. You are going to be safe. I won't let anything happen to you. Now hang up and I'll call you in just a few minutes. It's almost over now. I promise. Now hang up."

She clicked at his direction. He was going to take care of her. She breathed out and wiped the tears from her face with her sleeve. Abby handed her a tissue.

"Lily, it's going to be ok. We can do this together."

She nodded. She did love Abby. She was a nut but she was her little nut. She hated that she was involved at all, but she hated she was involved too. It hurt so bad.

Within five minutes the phone rang again and this time Lily was able to talk.

"Lily, Fullerton is on his way. When he comes to the door, he'll look like one of your delivery guys. He's borrowing a truck from Fed Ex. We don't want anyone to get wise. But when he gets there he is going to tell you that the invoice is COD. You never pay that way so you'll know it's him. Just a precaution and it will make you feel better. Got it?"

"I'm here, I've got it. I'm fine now. It was just hearing your voice before and I'm just so tired and upset about all of this, Dev. Help me," she pleaded.

"Sweetheart, just hang in there. You've been a trooper through all of this and I have a feeling that it really is almost over. Fullerton is going to hand you an address for a hotel and he's going to be following you over there. You'll go in and there's a suite for you three. Jeremy needs to be protected too for the time being. Tom will just look like he's making a delivery to the hotel. You'll have someone assigned to you and they'll be taking you up to the room. They'll be outside your door all night until you hear from me or Fullerton. No one else, Lily. No one. You will be protected. Hang in there, now let me talk to Abby."

She hadn't gotten in one word but frankly she didn't know what to say. She needed to tell him about Big John. But did he know? Had he used her again? Why did he want to speak to Abby?

Abby said hello and giggled a little. She said "yes" and then she said "no" and "I understand" before handing the phone back to her. Lily's arms were crossed in exasperation. What was his game now?

"You really want to talk to me now?" she asked.

"Oh I knew you wouldn't like that," he said but she could hear him laughing. "You always have to be in control, well Abby can do some things too. She's a good kid. You don't need to know everything, Mrs. Fletcher."

"The police chief of Cabot Cove would not keep anything from Jessica Fletcher."

He laughed again. "You're probably right. That nitwit needed her to solve all those murders.So you are going to a luxury hotel on the government's dime so that should make you feel better. They have great robes too."

She listened to him ramble on about room service, ice cream, big screen television before blurting out, "Dev, I'm so scared and Big John."

There was a pause in speech before he answered deliberately. "I know. I'm so sorry you were ever involved in this. Lily you will be fine. You always are, no matter what. Remember?"

"I don't feel fine. We only have one wedding this weekend but…" her voice trailed off in thought. Her entire life, her career didn't seem very important right now for the first time in a very long while.

"You will get it done. You always do. We will make sure that bride is happy. Is it Saturday?"

"Yes."

"Then you have plenty of time. I'll have you right back on schedule by Thursday. Will that work?"

She thought for a moment as she pulled the order on the desk. "Yes, we can do it. It's not very large and I have my flowers but you know I need to start working tomorrow."

"Let's wait until tomorrow to worry about that. Let me do it, do the worrying for you. You have a nice night and then in the morning we will re-group and see where we go."

She'd never had anyone do the worrying for her. It was impossible for her to let go but she had to let him do his job and she just had to go to the bloody hotel.

"I don't know where you are but I wish you were here." Lily was calm as she admitted something out loud she hadn't admitted to herself.

There was silence and then quietly she heard, "You don't know how much I wish I were there right now." He paused. Perhaps it was time to say something out loud that had only been in his thoughts. "I wish I could hold you right now and make you feel safe. But I will make you safe no matter what. I promise. So, I'll try to talk to you later. Fullerton will be there soon."

He hung up. Her mouth was open to say something. She wasn't sure what she was going to say in response. She stared at the phone. He wished he could hold her. She wished that so much not just in this moment. She was in love with him. When had that happened and how could it happen? Her fear was overtaken with sadness. He wasn't in love with her. He was being kind and gentle and protective. Was he in love with her? Could he be, ever?

Her thoughts of the heart were interrupted by the loud banging of Jeremy at the door. She nearly jumped a foot out of the chair. He looked like a misguided boy scout with a Hello Kitty sleeping bag under his left arm and a pizza in his right hand. He was knocking with his foot, almost falling over onto the sidewalk in the process. He was off balance with a huge filled backpack hanging off his right shoulder.

"He is so cute. My knight in shining armor," Abby said as she ran for the door.

Lily could only laugh. If that was her knight in shining armor she would hate to see the court jester, but he was sweet. He kissed Abby fiercely as she shuttled him in, closing the door quickly and locking it once more.

"So, I got this call from the dude you were dating, Lily," he began, "and he says we're all going to some cushy hotel for the night? He told me to get my butt over here but I didn't know if you still needed the sleeping bag and stuff. I could only carry the pizza and my backpack but the rest is in the car."

Lily smiled. Dev had called Jeremy? Wow that must have been a phone call! He talked to the dude she was dating. She wondered if Dev told him who he really was. The probability was low if Agent Pierce wanted to continue the secrecy. Or maybe he did and Jeremy just thought that the DEA and the FBI were two new channels on Hulu.

Now there was a delivery man at the door with a flower

box in hand. He was from Federal Express. He knocked on the glass. Agent Tom Fullerton was here..

"I have a COD for Lily."

All three of the shop's inhabitants came to the door. Lily unlocked and opened for him. He handed her a slip to sign as he came into the shop.

"You need to sign this. Let's make it look good just in case someone is watching."

He completely understood her situation. His hat covered most of his face but Lily recognized him. Her now weekly customer had almost become a friend like most of her clients always did.

"Thanks so much. We've been waiting for this package." She played along. Just in case.

"So, you are going to process this in the back room just like you ladies would do and I'm going to leave," he directed as he looked up from the box. "Then I want you three to leave just like you've finished your day. Jeremy, you drive your car with Abby, and Lily you head out in yours. You're going to the Intercontinental on the Plaza, so just go your usual route. I'll be following."

Jeremy muttered "sweet" as Lily glared at him.

"This isn't a vacation." She took the box from the agent. "I just check in under my name?"

"Yes. Let's just make this as normal as possible. If anyone asks you about the hotel, they are comping you a night for a job you're doing for them."

"But," she stopped. Fullerton turned around to look at her. "But they have their own florist. They wouldn't have us doing a job for them."

Fullerton shook his head. "You are over thinking this. Then just say they're comping you a room, if anyone asks but I doubt they will, Lily. Don't over think."

He almost sounded like Devlin Pierce slighting her for always preparing for the worst case scenario but despite all her planning and organizing for all those other times, this really was the worst case scenario. She feared for her life and for Abby's and Jeremy's. Don't over think.

Don't be scared. Act naturally. She wasn't that great of an actress. Perhaps she could pull it off after all those years of practice with the brides and especially their mothers. Heck, she'd fooled Gretchen the coordinator!

She smiled finally. "Thanks so much. We really needed this delivery. Good night." She was almost pushing him out the door. Abby was already in the backroom pretending to process an empty box of newspapers.

As a band of misfits, they closed up the shop, locking the door and setting the security code. That seemed futile now but Lily did it anyway. Everything needed to appear normal. Normal for whom?

The three moved together down the sidewalk to the cars, almost like the scene from Mary Tyler Moore's old television show when their news team had one massive group hug moving as one across the newsroom. She noticed Jeremy still carrying the pizza and the Hello Kitty sleeping bag. The backpack was now carried by Abby.

Unfortunately, she decided right there and then they were doomed. Surely the Cartel couldn't think this was normal? She shrugged her shoulders as she opened her own car door. On the other hand if they had surveilled Jeremy for about ten minutes they would've realized the threat level from him was less than zero. He was sweet but the elevator didn't go up all the way to the penthouse on that boy. He was perfect for Abby.

As she drove to the hotel she passed the street where she used to turn to go to school. So many years had passed that most of those memories had faded into a murky mess but she still had the scars. There had been some laughs and happy times but she still had the pieces of inferiority haunting her. She wasn't good enough; pretty enough; rich enough. She passed the park where they all used to walk and feed the ducks. Looking in her rear view mirror she saw Jeremy's car right behind her and there was just the glimpse of the top of the Federal Express truck.

Pulling into the hotel's drive, Lily's car door was opened by one of the valets. She handed her keys over and received the ticket. She only had her purse and work bag from the back seat as she waited at the front door for Abby and Jeremy. Thank God he had left the sleeping bag in the car but he was still carrying the pizza box, backpack and a paisley carry-on bag that was obviously Abby's. At least she hoped it was.

The two were holding hands as Lily strode up confidently to the front desk. She could pretend she was confident and maybe it would lower her fear level.

"Hi, we are checking in. Lily Schmidt. I believe we have a suite reserved."

Usually, she was so busy bringing wedding party bouquets into this hotel that she never really noticed the beauty of the chandeliers or the ornate serving tray to the side of the front desk that held water with slices of lemon. She hadn't decorated here since the hotel had hired their own florist, but many of her brides had suites the day of the wedding and she'd bring their bouquets to them. The lobby was lavish, green plants and flowers providing a light but fresh fragrance. On a warm day of stress it soothed. She needed a long bubble bath tonight.

The gentleman checking them in clicked away on the computer. "Yes, we have you." He looked up and smiled. Waving his hand he added, "Peter, will you escort Ms. Schmidt and her party to the Rockhill Suite? Do you have any bags for the night?"

"We're fine, thank you." What must he, she looked at his name tag, what must George think of Jeremy's pizza box? He'd probably seen worse or funnier but the three of them had to look a little strange. They all had sneakers and jeans on. Abby and Jeremy were wearing tees and she was in a black button down top with short sleeves. They were dressed more for a grunge concert than the Intercontinental.

Peter directed them down the hallway.

"I'll be at your service tonight. You'll be on the concierge level and concierge guests only are allowed on that floor. Your keycards just slide in here to go to your floor," he said as they entered the elevator. He was very conversational explaining what floors the gym and pool were on and when food and drinks were available.

"We have hot appetizers, salads, desserts and drinks for guests until eleven tonight if you're hungry."

He looked at Jeremy's pizza box. "There's also a full kitchen in your suite if you need coffee or a microwave."

Lily examined him carefully. His hair was short, no stubble on his face. She watched his hand as he slipped the card into the slot. His hands were soft, a few calluses at the top of his index finger, his trigger finger? Was he the agent Fullerton had mentioned? If he was he wasn't playing his hand; his role was well scripted. So someone else was acting?

The ride ended and they followed him down the left hallway. It was like slow motion as Peter slid his key card into the slot and opened the french doors of the suite. He handed the card to her and then handed one to Jeremy and Abby. She was the only one who said thank you as her two companions' mouths gaped open in shock.

As they entered, they saw the Country Club Plaza in front of them in all its majesty. They were above most of the clay-colored tiled roofs and even some of the newer office buildings. The Plaza area citizens and home owners were trying to retain the ambience of the district, holding off those albatrosses to the edges of the area. Why would they want to block such beauty of this Spanish jewel of the plains? The sun in the west was brightening the painted colors molded into the buildings, the blues bluer, the greens greener, the reds so royal. She'd never really looked at the buildings this way or had the time to examine their beauty. She lived in this city but didn't really *live*. Lily just flitted from location to location, to bride and church and venue packing up, dropping off and going from day to day. She was just surviving. Funny, that's what she was doing tonight too.

Jeremy and Abby continued to do their best imitation of frozen mummies as Lily dug into her purse for a tip for Peter. He didn't take it, instead moving his hand to wave her off. He began to move down the corridor for the tour.

"Let me show you a couple features of the television…"

Before he could finish the sentence, Jeremy was following behind like a pet puppy. She flopped down on one of the huge sofas. She could just sleep here until morning. She heard crying and looked up to see Abby's face.

"Honey, what is wrong?"

"I'm so sorry this is happening to you. It's not fair."

Lily stretched her hand out to present the room. "This isn't fair? I think this is pretty darn awesome. I've never stayed in a suite like this. You should go investigate with Jeremy."

She sat down next to Lily and grabbed her hand. "He's an idiot you know, but he's my idiot."

Lily laughed out loud. She didn't know whether she should agree with the assessment or just let it go. Let it go. Not the time, Lily.

"He cares about you, Abby. I can tell."

Abby nodded. "I know but I'm not sure I want to spend the rest of my life with him."

"Have you two talked about that?" Lily could only imagine what their children would be like and who would be taking care of whom.

"Well, no but I just don't want to be alone…you know." Abby clutched her hand up to her mouth. "I didn't mean, you, but, oh crap."

Lily knew what she meant but it wasn't as if she hadn't thought the same thing on many occasions.

"It's fine, Abby. I know what you mean. You never know but if you think that someone better might come along in the future then maybe Jeremy isn't the best person. You'll know, at least that's what everyone told me. Actually no, not everyone, just my mom." Lily went silent for a second.

"She always said someone would come along and I would always tell her no, I was going to be alone all my life. No one would ever love me. Well, my family loves me, my nieces love me, my nephews and that's going to have to be enough."

"Is it enough?"

"Sometimes, Abby. Sometimes it isn't. I've decided to not over think things right now."

The two smiled at the advice, looking out the large windows of the suite at the sight below them.

"Pretty, huh?" Lily's stomach growled. "I wonder what they have to eat down the hall."

"I was wondering what they had to drink," Abby admitted. "I really need a drink, the alcoholic kind."

Peter was just finishing his tour with Jeremy. "Peter, where's the food?" Lily asked.

"Allow me to take you down there. I thought I heard we have a pasta dish, chicken and beef with vegetables. The appetizers tonight are turkey meatballs in a cream sauce, crab rangoon and I'm not sure about the rest. As I said before there's usually salads and desserts. No need to go anywhere." If he was an agent, he sure knew his cover.

"Lead on." There was never any over thinking when it came to food. Thank the heavens Jeremy was not bringing his pizza box with him.

1. Stop going to sleep watching old mystery shows
2. Take time to enjoy the little things...take a walk on the Plaza, maybe stop and sit outside to watch people walking by
3. Try to get to church a little more during the week...God knew she needed the help
4. Come out of this alive
5. Do the wedding for Saturday
6. Take a chance on something, anything
7. Stop being afraid

Chapter Twenty-Two

Lily stopped at seven on her list. Angela Lansbury was on the television in front of her and Abby was asleep beside her. She barely heard some game on in the other room. Assuming Jeremy hadn't fallen asleep surrounded by his sleeping bag, seemingly his Linus security blanket, he was probably watching the West Coast games now. She strained to hear if he was watching football or baseball playoff games. He may have even snuck out and grabbed some more appetizers from the concierge lounge.

She was surprised that Abby was by her side. She'd explained that this was a real thrill for him and she wouldn't get any sleep if she stayed with him. Lily figured she wouldn't be able to sleep with his games on but she didn't want to think of the two nitwits doing anything else together involving legs wrapped around legs, with her just across the living room. Lily had a light buzz from the bottle of wine they had brought back to the suite. She'd taken a full glass to sip while she had her bubble bath. She'd soaked until her fingers were pink prunes. She'd thought a lot and then she had let everything vanish from her mind for a few minutes.

Lily slipped from the bed and padded across the room to the door of their suite. She felt good in the hotel's fluffy robe. It reminded her of the one her mom used to wear. It was blue but this one was white; hers was chenille and this one a soft velour; hers from Sears and this one designed by Calvin Klein. But when she was sick in the middle of the night and that robe's arms gently enveloped her, she felt better even if she was throwing up all the contents of her stomach.

When they packed that robe away after her death, her fragrance was still lingering. Too bad she hadn't lingered.

She barely opened the door and Peter popped up from his chair across from their door. "Can I help you with anything, Ms. Schmidt?"

"Well, one thing. Have you heard from Agent Pierce?"

His eyes were like steel now and not at all hotel worker worthy. "Ms. Schmidt, there's nothing I can say."

"Well at least you didn't lie to me and say you didn't know who I was talking about. Thanks for that. Goodnight."

As she closed the door she mouthed "gotcha" and she thought she heard a cuss word from the young agent.

She padded across to see the Plaza in the middle of the night. She knew she wasn't the only one up right now but she felt like this view was for her alone. A street cleaner was going by on the street below her. Two waiters were walking across the bridge. She could see their white shirts glowing under the street lights and the occasional red embers from their cigarettes. The bars had closed. At the bus stop was an older African American woman still dressed in her hotel uniform. She was pulling herself up onto the bus. Lord, she looked tired. Bless her. Day in and day out people were cleaning after others, bringing them drinks, fluffing their pillows, making them happy, giving them what they ordered. She was one of those people but tonight she reflected on more than just this view.

She needed and now desperately wanted to make some

changes and if that meant less money, well she couldn't lower her income too much or another fear would raise its little head. Something had to give. And she needed to let go, a little at first and maybe more when she became comfortable with that uncertainty.

Uncertainty…what had Dev said to Abby today? The little minx had never shared their conversation with her. As she went back into the bedroom, she got into bed next to Abby and looked down at her angelic face. She'd interrogate her in the morning.

The sun had been up an hour by the time Agent Devlin Pierce met up with a former buddy from Special Forces. Dev sat patiently outside a Cuban cafe near downtown Miami in Little Cuba. On the table in front of him was the strongest espresso he could find. It had been a long night. He could feel his contact coming up behind before he sat down across from him.

"How long you been here?"

Dev folded his newspaper and placed it on the bistro table.

"Long enough to begin my second cup of espresso. How are you Carlos and what do you have for me?"

One of the ladies from the shop brought out another cup and asked in Spanish if the friend would like espresso. He smiled and in her language ordered a couple of their pasteles. Carlos waited until she had poured and left the area.

"I'm doing the best I can and you aren't going to like the answer I have for you." Dev closed his eyes. All these months and he still was getting nowhere.

"Shoot. I'm ready."

"They are insisting the drugs are still there. Two packages containing one to two kilos each, pure, have vanished. I know they have some people there looking for them and they still think your girl has them. They are mad and embarrassed that all of this happened. They'll do anything to get them back to prove a point."

Dev cussed out loud. The woman was back again with two turnover looking pastries, smiled and left.

"But she doesn't have them. Carlos, have you told them?"

"Over and over, Dev. If I go much further I'm going to blow my own cover. This mistake has cost them and they know you all are after them. The guy at the airport, well he's probably in the Everglades inside a gator by now. They are putting pressure on their contacts in Kansas City. They've shut down that route from South America. Customs is changing procedures."

"I know," Dev admitted reluctantly. His old Army buddy had really placed his life and cover on the line for him. "I have a good idea on who their contacts are and by the grace of God they haven't moved violently on my friend. But things are getting tight. If the Cartel is putting pressure on them, they are sooner, not later, going to put pressure on my girl. Someone is going to get hurt and then they'll never get their drugs. They need to understand that."

Carlos shook his head. "She means something to you?"

Dev paused. "Yes. I am supposed to be protecting her."

"No, you're supposed to be solving this case."

Carlos took a drink as he searched his friend's face.

Dev was concerned about this girl. The furrowed brows, the tight jaw and the way his friend popped his watchband were all tell-tale signs that Dev cared and was scared. He'd seen him this way when they tried to rescue that orphanage outside Kandahar. They'd only been in country six weeks in Afghanistan when they found that building, the Taliban setting up guns right outside the perimeter of their playground.

Across the back of the structure, IED's were strategically placed to eliminate an exit. Dev and Major Plant developed the mission and Carlos had watched them plot every detail. Dev had tightened that jaw, furrowed those brows and popped that watchband for a full hour until just before dawn when they went in.

Carlos could still remember the screams, the children scattering into their cohorts' arms as Dev and he took out those guns and the nasty men guarding them. They'd only lost one child who had opened the back door. They hadn't planned on that. First they saw the swinging door, they heard the crack and saw the pink mist, a true sign of the vaporization of a child that was there one second and with Allah the next. No one could plan on everything but Captain Devlin Pierce sure thought he could, thought he should. The man didn't talk to anyone for a day. It was like John the Baptist in the desert, in prayer and anguish of the uncontrollable.

"We have her in protective custody right now but they'll be releasing her and two others some time today. She has a business and she's going to have to do that work no matter what. They won't be able to stop her."

"Then find the drugs. Shut down these contacts and be done with it."

Dev shook his head. "I don't want to lose anyone. I've got a plane to catch."

Carlos closed his eyes and saw nothing but Kandahar and pink mist. Dev was going to the rescue again and this time he didn't have a plan to plot.

Lily woke to voices in the other room. She had no idea what time it was but the sun was up and shining in her eyes through the hotel's curtain sheers.

"But Babe, I thought you'd come into the room last night."

"I had to stay with Lily."

"Why? She's just fine."

"No, I promised I'd take care of her until her," Abby searched for the words, "until her boyfriend gets back into town. I promised him."

"You gonna ever tell me what's going on with all this? I mean, did you really get a free night from the hotel?"

Lily was entertained by Jeremy's naivety. Bless his little heart.

"Yes, yes we did, Jeremy. Now why don't you go check out the food and see what there is for breakfast."

The door opened and shut and Abby came in to see her sitting up in bed.

Lily's arms were crossed in front of her chest. "So, Dev made you promise to take care of me? What else did you two talk about yesterday?"

Abby's sheepish demeanor answered Lily's questions.

There would be no need for an interrogation. She would give up all information willingly.

"He was worried about you. He wanted to make sure you were taken care of and wondered if you were about to lose it. I told him no and he told me I needed to take care of you until he gets here. I think he's out of town."

Lily felt like he cared but maybe this really was how he treated everyone he protected.

Hopefully he never held hands with some biker dude under his protection!

Lily got out of bed and walked over to hug Abby. "You are a great person. I'm fine and you don't need to take care of me. I'm good. I'm going to try out that rain shower just for fun and then I'm going to join Jeremy for breakfast. You know he will still be eating the free food!"

Abby laughed. "You know it. I'll use his bathroom. I'm starving. This mission impossible stuff really makes you hungry. Do you think Dev has ever hung from an airplane like Tom Cruise in the last movie?"

And her little nitwit was back.

Thirty minutes later, Lily and Abby found Jeremy at a table near the window, still eating.

"Told you," Abby said as she greeted him with a peck on the cheek.

"These are the best little sausages." He pulled one from his plate and showed them like it was a shiny toy to present to mommy.

They finished breakfast and were enjoying another cup of coffee when Agent Fullerton entered the room. He waved to them, got his own cup of coffee and joined them.

"How are we doing this morning?" Lily really liked him. The times he'd come in for flowers for his wife had proved a highlight of her day. He was originally from Michigan but had met his wife at Stanford. He'd played football there but he'd also gained his law degree. When the FBI opportunity had come around they'd already had a son and daughter. Their young family picked up everything for his career. He insisted they were still a tight family. He was such a nice man, a nice man with a gun holstered to his left side under his jacket.

"Wonderful. Thanks so much for the free night at the hotel. It was great but I really do need to get back to work," Lily answered, emphatically insisting on the ruse for Jeremy's sake.

"Yes, I bet you do." He eyed Jeremy who was now eating a sticky bun. "You all going home first?"

"That would be nice," Lily answered. "Then Abby and I need to go back to the shop. I can't disappoint my bride."

"Of course not, Ms. Schmidt. That's perfect. Your homes and then the shop. Sir, where will you be going on this beautiful day?"

He looked in Jeremy's direction and it took a gentle nudge from Abby before he stopped paying attention to the bun, wiped icing off his cheek and answered, "Oh, I'm pooped. I'm sleeping all day."

Lily shook her head. Suddenly he reminded her of Wilbur, the pig in "Charlotte's Web". Lay around, eat, sleep, lay around some more, eat, sleep.

Tom Fullerton turned his head to the side, smiling at Lily.

"Well, so happy you enjoyed your stay. We will be seeing you soon, I hope."

Agent Fullerton got up from the table.

"Thanks, man. It was great." Jeremy waved as the man walked away. "He seemed like a cool dude."

Lily and Abby grabbed their heads at the same time in complete wonderment how the boy had survived this long in the world.

Chapter Twenty-Three

1. Check in with the bride one more time.
2. Check on the timing with the venue...ceremony and reception there.
3. Do preliminary work Thursday.
4. Finish wedding on Friday.
5. Early day...tell Abby eight on Saturday morning.

Everything was going according to plan, at least to Lily's plan. Abby and she stepped back as they surveyed their work at the venue. At the front of the room where the bride and groom would say their vows a trellis stood with flowing ivory tulle and nosegays of flowers placed here and there. The color palette was clean with only whites, creams and greens, and yes there were hydrangeas. Down the aisle they had placed cylinders with floating candles, white petals strewn on each side and white hydrangeas arrangements in glass vases that would be set by the coordinator later on the guest tables.

They'd already given the bouquets to the bride's young coordinator. She was a new up-and-comer who had grown up in Kansas City and already knew just about everyone in the wedding business. Her family had run a restaurant and shop for years in the city. Abby and Lily had already decided they liked her. She was one of them, more worried about the bride and her day than how they looked or how popular they would become from the publicity of the wedding.

"So, have you heard from Dev?" Abby finally had the guts to ask her boss what she'd been wanting to ask her for two days.

"No," Lily answered softly as she packed up their boxes. "I have seen police. Oh and I'm sure we're being watched by the FBI too. There was that one girl on the sidewalk yesterday…"

"Oh, yah, the one with the ponytail? She looked very military."

Lily laughed. She wasn't sure Abby would know military from circus clown. But she'd suspected the same thing. The girl did look military and she'd hovered in the area for over four hours. No one does that no matter how pretty of a fall day it was.

Abby's phone rang. Lily knew it was Jeremy as she saw her assistant move away from her and begin to talk in soft tones. All the boxes were stacked together to take back to the shop. They'd had a long day but the look had been worth all the work. She took the occasional photo for the web page. Lily looked out the windows that overlooked the Plaza. The sun was beginning to set on a very long day, on the end of a very long week.

Her phone rang in her hand. It was an unknown caller.

"Hello."

"Lily, are you hanging in there?"

It was Dev. Finally. Where had he been? Why hadn't he been with her? "Yes, but it has been a long week. Where are you?"

"I've been working on the case but I know everyone has been watching over you." She made the noise that her mother always did when she was exasperated with her.

"Well, yes, they have been doing that. They aren't very subtle either. Even Abby spotted a couple of them."

Dev laughed lightly. "They were meant for show. The ones who are actually protecting you, you won't see them."

She gulped. Really? There were more of them? What had she gotten herself into? How big was this case of his?

"When will I see you?" Her voice had been soft, almost little girl like.

"Soon. You two almost done for the day?"

"Yes, we're heading out as soon as Abby gets off the phone. She's talking to Jeremy."

"How is the little idiot?"

She laughed. "Well, he's grown to full out nitwit now but he's her nitwit so he's fine. He is a good guy. He's accomplished so much with just half of a brain, imagine what he'll do when they insert the other half."

He laughed out loud over the phone. "Now, that's my Lily."

Silence came between them very quickly. It spoke volumes for him. Lily really did mean something to him, what, he wasn't actually sure yet. For her the silence was their old comfortable friend coming between them once more. Who would be the first to end it?

"I'll let you get on with your work. Hang in there. It really is almost over."

She didn't even get to say goodbye before the line went dead. If it really was almost over, then they were too…their friendship, their relationship. It really was almost over.

Lily brushed away a few tears from her eyes and placed her phone in her bag. Abby was walking toward her.

"Jeremy is going to pick me up here and we're going back to my place. Will that work for you?"

Lily looked up quickly with a pretend smile on her face.

"Of course. You do that. It's been a week and you two deserve some alone time, well with your detail outside." She looked out the windows once more and it was pitch black. "I absolutely hate daylight savings time. It's a beautifully colored sunset and then black. It's bad enough that we lose an hour in the spring but in the fall I want to go to bed so early since it's so dark. Hate it."

"Boss?" Abby was searching her face for some kind of an answer when Jeremy came walking into the room. She was really worried about Lily, deep down nauseous in your stomach worried.

"Thought I'd help you out with the stuff."

Abby ran to Jeremy. "You are so sweet, honeybun."

Lily shook her head. Honeybun? She did not want to know how or why Abby came up with that term of affection. But it was sweet of him. Besides, it was nice to have his extra set of hands.

As they loaded the van, Lily saw a patrol car pull up behind them.

"Ms. Schmidt, I'm following you back to your shop. Agent Fullerton gave me the order."

Jeremy hadn't heard. He was too busy loading the last of the leftover flowers into the right side of the van.

"Thank you. Leaving in a second."

Abby gave her a quick hug and kiss and grabbed Jeremy. As they walked to the car she heard the little nitwit ask Abby if the cop was hassling her boss. Lily just shook her head. He was absolutely clueless.

Lily's entourage of one followed her closely back to the shop and parked in the farthest part of the back parking lot, near the alley. She decided she wouldn't unload all the boxes in the dark but she did want to get the leftover flowers into the cooler. Besides, her car was parked near the alley too. She unloaded her bag and the one bucket of flowers. The police officer was watching as she unlocked the door and came into the back of the shop. The cooler's light was bright enough for her to walk across the room without any problem. With the flowers delivered, she locked the back door and began to walk through the front of the shop.

"Lily, don't come any farther." She gasped out loud as she heard Big John's voice coming from the middle of the room. "Please don't. You know I don't want to hurt you."

She was concrete again. She wasn't even near her desk, nor any implement for protection. "You weren't supposed to be here."

She dropped her bag on the floor and kicked it under her desk. She had to do something; had to say something.

"John, why are you involved in this?" Her voice was barely a whisper. She couldn't find the volume switch.

"Little girl, I'm so sorry. I can't tell you any of this. I just need those drugs. Where are they? Just give them to me and we can be done with all of this." His words were more pleas than commands or threats. She could physically hear the anguish in his voice.

"John, I know people, we can get this solved. We can fix it."

She could see the outline of his shaking head. "Nothing can be fixed. Now, where are those drugs?"

"I don't know," she cried out. "I have no idea."

He was rubbing his face in confusion. "I have to have them, Lily."

As a car drove by the flash of the headlights illuminated John's figure, a gun pointed toward her in his right hand.

"John, I can't give you something I don't have."

He shook the gun. "You don't understand what they're going to do to you, to me, to my family…give me the drugs."

She screamed out his name in hopes the officer in the parking lot would hear. John ran toward her and held his hand over her mouth, turning her in his arms.

"Lily, just stop. I'm not going to hurt you, but these people, we just can't mess with them any longer."

There was another flash of light and that's when she realized it was raining. She heard thunder and saw the lightening. The officer wouldn't hear her. She was on her own. All she could think about was the fall schedule. Who would do the weddings? Oh for heaven's sake, Lily Schmidt, stop thinking about the weddings.

"I'm going to release my hand. Don't shout again and don't try to fight me. You know I'll win and if I have to hurt you, well, I don't want to, please, please."

She nodded and he released his hand plus the hold he had on her. They stood only inches apart, looking at each other, searching each other's face for compassion. She saw a frightened man betraying his friend. What did he see? Did he see a scared little girl? Is that how he always pictured her? She'd thought the term of endearment was one of sincere friendship but looking back had he seen someone he could overtake and utilize, betray?

"John," Lily began, "I don't know why you're involved or why we're all in danger, including your family. I'm sure you have your reasons but honestly, I have no drugs."

"They were in that box months ago. You have them."

She shook her head. "No, I don't. If you're talking about those packets and those ice blocks…they're gone. Someone took them."

"Don't take me for a fool, Lily. I've searched this shop so many times."

"Yes and you got those ice blocks," she screamed. Fear was being overrun by anger. "You got the damn ice blocks."

John was confused. "But the drugs weren't in there, Lily. We stole the packets off the flowers and then the ice blocks out of your freezer, but the drugs weren't there." His voice was rising. "Did Abby or that boyfriend of her's take them? Do they know where they are?"

"No, there's no way they did that before you got to them."

"What about your boyfriend? I haven't seen him around. Do you trust him?"

She nodded. "Yes, John with my life. He's a government agent." It was time for the truth.

He shook his head and held the gun down to his side. "I knew he was ex-military. So he was on the lookout for the drugs?"

She nodded again.

"Well, he was a really good actor or he's someone who really cares about you."

Lily felt the tears trickle down her cheeks. She could see the tears in John's eyes with the flash of the lights.

John stopped talking. Both of them could hear the rain on the roof. It was coming down so hard that the cars driving by were blurred images from her window.

Lily leaned against the file cabinet. Her knees were weak. Where was the police officer?

Didn't he find it unusual that she hadn't made it out to her car yet? Oh no, she was Jessica and the officer was Sheriff Amos! The man was probably out there eating a sandwich. Sandwich!

"John," she said softly, "you didn't take the ham sandwich."

"What?"

"You didn't take the ham sandwich." She needed time and she needed her friend to be her friend again.

He smiled. "Right, the sandwich. Sorry about that."

"We found a hard boiled egg later too. It had rolled." Lily was trying anything to calm him down. She could see his eyes softening. No longer did he look like a trapped animal.

John looked at her in the darkness and saw his friend, his very scared friend.

"Lily," he stopped as he saw a figure go by the window. "Lily, grab your bag and go out the back door. You go run to that police car and don't you come out no matter what you hear. Now, go."

His tone frightened her more than any gun. What was he doing? He was releasing her for what reason? She pulled the bag out and slid past him in the darkness. He caught her in his arms and pulled her in for a quick hug.

"I love you, little girl. You have been such a good friend. You take care and let that agent take care of you when he can."

She pulled away, stood on tip-toes to place a kiss on his cheek then ran to the back door and out the back alley.

She was pulling on the handle of the police car's door when she heard the gun fire. Even through the lightening, thunder and rain she could hear the sound. Her friend was in danger. But she had to get in the car. She opened the door. The car was empty.

Chapter Twenty-Four

The rain was pelting the FBI cap he was wearing, the drops dripping onto his cell phone as he texted with Tom Fullerton. Tom would be there in a matter of minutes but he'd already missed the prime suspect. Fullerton had been in Lawrence, Kansas helping his daughter move to her new apartment off campus. Now he was racing across I-70 to get to the boulevard. The case was finally coming to a close.

Dev was speaking to one of the city police officers on-site when he first caught a glimpse of her. She was sitting on the concrete outside her shop, her bag in one hand and a soggy tissue in the other. Her wet hair was so curly he barely recognized her but he knew it was her when his heart had sunk down into his stomach. The officer was explaining how it all went down but he hadn't heard much after "Ms. Schmidt was held hostage for awhile and found the body".

He looked beyond her to see the two news stations' vans and several camera lights wrapped in plastic. He'd been there for almost ten minutes and she still hadn't looked up. Her gaze was on a piece of concrete in front of her, stained with the blood of her former friend. Dev continued to listen to the officer when Tom finally ran up to him.

"What the hell?" he said as he saw Lily on the sidewalk.

"She was here, cop followed her back to the shop. John

was already inside, at least that's what they are telling me. I haven't talked to her yet."

Tom placed his arm around his friend's back. "You need to. And what about the cop? Where is he?"

"Well," Dev began,"the real cop is dead down the street behind the bar and grill. The cop that was following Lily back to the shop is also dead over there." He pointed to the coroner's team blocking off the site.

"Holy..." Tom's voice trailed off. "You need to go to her. I'll take over from here on and we can get her in for a formal tomorrow. But you need to be with her tonight."

Dev completely agreed with his friend. He needed to be with her. He'd probably be cussed at and called every name in the book. She'd be angry. He hadn't been there for her. She'd think that the case, the mission, was more important than her safety. She needed to know he was already thinking the same thing.

He walked slowly over to her, standing directly above her form.

"Lily."

Slowly her face tilted up and saw him. He couldn't tell the tears from the precipitation but her face was completely wet, small crystals of rain falling from one large ringlet on her forehead. He saw her hands shaking and the death grip she had on her bag. Dev crouched down in from of her.

"Lily, I'm here. Let's get you home."

She penetrated his very being with her dead stare. Her eyes held no expression, red from crying. She was tired, finished. It was finally over but he saw no relief or release in her face.

"Where have you been?" The singular question hit his core. He saw the pink mist once more of a lost cause, another who had been hurt because of him and his decisions.

"Let's get you home." Dev reached for her hands to pull her up but she shook her head, screaming out a loud "no".

He grabbed her bag away from her and set it up against the shop's window ledge. He removed his borrowed FBI jacket and slid it across her shoulders. In one move he grasped both shoulders and pulled her up. She landed against him, her head burrowing into his chest. He could hear her sobs; he felt the balled up clenched fist hitting him lightly.

"You didn't protect me. You said you would, but you didn't. Dev, he was my friend."

He held her closer. Tom looked up from the group he was in to see the comforting scene.

He smiled. It was way past time to see those two like that.

He patted her wet head and enveloped her tighter in his arms.

"I'm here now, Lily. Come on, let's get you home. Are your car keys in the bag?"

He thought he heard a "yes" but it was going to be a lost cause trying to find them. He searched around with his hand at the bottom of the bag. She grabbed it out of his hands and pulled out a small purse. She placed the keys in his hand. Lily clutched the bag up against her as she started walking slowly in front of him.

"Tom, I'm leaving my car here. Do you think someone

could drop it by Lily's house?" he asked as he handed his own car keys to his friend as he passed him.

"Sure thing, Dev. Is she...does she need help?" Tom's voice trailed off in the rain. Both men were watching her as she continued to walk by herself out to the parking lot.

Dev shrugged and took out after her. He opened the passenger side and she silently got in. She placed her seatbelt around her but once again she held the bag up for security. He saw a wet, limp file folder sticking out. It was probably next week's orders for her to go over once she got home. He'd make sure she wouldn't do that.

Dev drove through the rain, the wipers on high speed. Occasionally, he'd look over at her stoically sitting there, looking straight ahead into the darkness. She hadn't said one word since they'd left the scene. Her head was bent down as though she was concentrating on her bag and her hands studying each and every seam, inspecting thread she couldn't possibly see in the dark. Yep, she was in shock, numb. Thankfully they didn't have far to go in this rain. He pulled into the driveway and ran across to open her door. She hadn't even realized they were home.

Dev took her right hand and pulled her from the car. She just looked at him with glassy eyes as he locked the car and pulled her again, this time into the house. He'd put the car in the garage later.

He found the correct house key on the second try and opened the door. Automatically, he had unbuttoned the safety on his holster, just in case. It was dark in the house. Apparently she hadn't reset the timer for fall. He sat her in the closest living room chair and then one by one, turned on lights and checked every room. It was clear and she was safe. Lily had been hit hard tonight, he knew that even if he didn't know all the details yet. She'd been a target, she'd seen a shoot out, watched a man die and saw her own friend shot in front of her as he was apparently protecting her. But Dev knew that glassy-eyed look, it was the look of betrayal. Her friend had betrayed their friendship. He knew she'd probably question every relationship she had before the sun came up…and he knew he'd be at the top of the list.

Quietly, he knelt in front of her. He threw off his cap toward the front door as water dripped off his hair.

"Lily, let's get you out of these wet clothes." He slipped his jacket off her shoulders and threw it in the direction of the hat. She was just as soaked as he was. He shook her hands free of the bag and left it on the floor.

She finally looked at him. Her eyes were at the same level as his, red and swollen with every inch of her face covered in tear stains.

"He did protect me, Dev. He did. You didn't but he did."

He sighed. He knew it. He was at the top of the list and the sun was still hours before its rising.

"I know Lily. I know. We need to get you out of these clothes. You have plenty of time to be mad at me."

She stood suddenly and walked toward her bedroom.

"Oh, I'm not mad at you. I expect disappointment. You know it always happens. I'm on my own and have been for a long time. Don't you worry about me."

Dev slid his hand through his wet hair. What the hell was that? He sat back on his heels.

He knew she was in shock but where was this coming from?

She shut the door soundly, leaving him to sit in a puddle developing on the living room rug. A few minutes later she came out in Elmo slippers and a brightly colored chenille robe. Her hair still hung damp around her face but she was now dry. Lily carried a pile of material in her hands.

"Here, you need to get dry too." She handed him black Army sweats, top and bottoms.

What was she doing with Army sweats that might fit him? Was it a past boyfriend she'd never talked about? He knew she hadn't been married before and that minister she used to date surely hadn't been in the military. Then he remembered her brother had recently retired from the Army. Maybe she got them from him.

"Do I want to know where you got these?" he asked, offering a smile to see if it would be returned. Even though he knew the answer maybe he could lighten the mood.

The smile was not returned. "A relative. These are too big for me so I'm thinking they'll work for you and we can throw your clothes in the dryer. Don't expect anything else, Agent Pierce."

He shook his head. Redemption would not be swift but anger would certainly be lingering.

He dried off in the bathroom, changed into the sweats and checked in with Tom to see how John was doing. He had survived the ride to the hospital and had been taken into emergency surgery. They would know by morning if he would survive. Apparently it had been some shoot out on the boulevard. John had been shot multiple times but the presumed hired killer had just one shot in him, straight through the forehead. He was dead before he hit the ground.

He smelled some aroma filtering under the door. Was she cooking in the middle of the night?

Slowly, he peeked out but didn't see her in the kitchen. He heard the television. The floor creaked under his steps as he entered the living room. She was sitting cross legged on the sofa, a huge bowl of popcorn in her open lap. He saw Angela Lansbury on the screen. She was watching "Murder, She Wrote". There were two open beers on the coffee table.

She looked up as he came around to sit next to her. "Is this mine?" He pointed at the open beer.

"If you want it, if not it will be my second. Currently it is unprotected."

Dev winced. Lily turned back to her show. Dev took two long drinks. All these months had come down to a very long week and an equally dramatic, tragic night in the rain.

He watched her through a side glance. She picked each kernel out individually to eat, one after the other, taking the occasional break to drink her beer. The sofa was too short for his legs. Slowly he propped one leg and foot on the coffee table and then the other. His left knee was hurting again. When it rained, it hurt. It was an old injury long since forgotten except when he was in pain. She glanced over at him but didn't make a comment.

"Sorry about putting my feet up on the furniture. Hope you'll forgive me."

She eyed him. Then she examined his feet. "When did you break that toe?" She pointed to his left foot.

"Years ago."

The silence was absolutely uncomfortable.

“So, I just knew you would be watching Jessica Fletcher. How did I know? Because I’m smart? No. Because I’m a trained investigator? No. Because that’s what you do.”

Lily glared at him. His eyes were twinkling. How dare he!

“Don’t mess with Jessica. She may be a busybody but she’s my busybody. Dr. Hazlett is in danger in this one.”

She handed him the bowl, offering it to him. He grabbed a handful. “Heaven forbid. Will he live or die?”

“Don’t be silly. Jess will save the day.”

Dev felt everything she said right now was pointed directly at his supposed incompetency. He would explain everything to her but not tonight. Any explanation he gave would fall on deaf ears.

“Why did you get hooked on this show?”

“My mom and I used to watch it. She loved Angela Lansbury. She was on Broadway in “Mame” and she was in that Disney flick “Bedknobs and Broomsticks” and I just grew to love her.”

“Well, I didn’t know those two pieces of trivia but do you know she played a saloon girl in some western I watched once?”

She stopped munching. “Which one?”

He had felt pride in himself briefly and now it had disintegrated. “Don’t remember.”

“You don’t know the name of the western?"

"*The Harvey Girls,* I think.” The commercial was over and Jess was saving the day.

What was she, a walking Angela Lansbury encyclopedia? She reached for her beer again and he saw her hand shaking. She kept watching straight ahead but he saw little breaks in the granite that was Lily Schmidt. What was she thinking?

Lily placed the beer back on the table. "Mom and I watched the show when she was dying."

He studied her face. He found he liked doing that for some reason. She was mesmerizing in her own way, handling what had happened tonight like a seasoned soldier...a soldier who would fall apart any second. Somehow, Lily or John had hit the panic button on the side of her desk during the chaos. The first agents on the scene explained her calmness as she held John's hand. She had been doing all she could for him until the paramedics arrived. Lily had backed away then and calmly sat down by her shop's door. The agents and then the police had asked a few questions but saw her cold stares and had heard the dead, non-expressive tone of her voice. She was in shock.

One small tear was trailing its way down the side of her left cheek.

"When I was home briefly, now and then, mom and I would watch "Law and Order".

She brushed aside the tear. "Good show."

"Yes, she always thought that since I was in the Army I should know legal stuff so she'd ask all these questions. I never knew the answers until I went to law school."

He could tell she was surprised. "But you're not a lawyer. Why not?"

Dev took a drink of his almost empty beer. "Not sure really. Maybe not enough action. My dad was a little disappointed that I didn't go into practice."

"What did your mom think?"

"My mom was dead by then."

She patted his arm. "I'm so sorry. Did you watch the show when she was sick too?"

"I wasn't there when she died. I was deployed." His voice was flat, devoid of emotion. Years of anger had placed emotion in a small box never to be opened when it came to his mother's death.

Lily smiled slightly. He'd finally shared his secret. Devlin Pierce was finally becoming a human being.

"I couldn't come home. They wouldn't let me so I missed her funeral."

"Who the heck is *they*? How can people have so much control over us? I hate that."

She was screaming. He really wasn't sure what to do at this point. They'd shared their losses and shared the human experience of loss but she wasn't talking about her mother or his. She was angry over what had gone down tonight.

"What can I do for you, Lily? Do you want another beer and maybe another so you can sleep? Do you want to talk all night? Do you want me to leave you alone?" He was grasping at anything to engage her.

She shoved his shoulder. "Where were you? If you had been there John wouldn't have done what he did. If you'd been there you would have protected him and me and that man wouldn't have shot him, killed him."

Her cries were painful and in a matter of seconds her face was wet once more, no rain added.

She shoved him again and again. “You all used me, didn’t you? Just like before…” Her voice trailed off as he grabbed her hand gently and held it in his.

“John isn’t dead. He’s in surgery. It is bad but he has a chance. I knew he wouldn’t hurt you or let you get hurt. John’s a good man but he got wrapped up in a bad situation before we could do anything for him. Lily, I am sorry.”

She looked at his hand hiding her’s. She looked up into his face, searching for something but she just didn’t know what. She needed help but she didn’t know or understand what kind. She needed something, someone. She could call her family but how could she explain this summer and tonight? She felt very empty and alone. Lily could feel the warmth of Dev’s hand. No longer did his touch raise the temperature of her skin. It was a feeling of understanding. But she didn’t want to let him off the hook.

“Dev, will I ever get that memory of tonight out of my mind?” She was hoping he’d say yes.

“It will go away and then it will come back. I’m not going to lie to you.”

She laughed out loud. Now he was the one in shock. “Finally, you’re not going to lie to me. You pick now to do it?”

Dev smiled uncomfortably. He stroked her hand. It was time to break down his own wall at least for tonight.

“Come here. Sometimes this helps.” He placed his arm around her and pulled her near.

Her head landed on his chest, one of her hands laying up against him.

"You know we can stay up and go to church in just a few hours." He murmured into her hair.

Another Jessica Fletcher mystery was beginning. "What is this, a marathon?"

She hadn't answered. Her breathing became even and deep. Dev looked down to see her eyes shut. He turned the volume down on the channel selector and moved one of the sofa pillows to his left behind his head.

Sometime in the middle of the night she'd left his side and thrown a blanket over him. Lily added a proper pillow to the sofa. He woke with the small movement, looked at her with piercing eyes and then moved the pillow and his head down on the sofa. He was asleep as his head hit the pillow.

Lily crossed her arms in front of her as she watched him breathing. She really didn't know what to think about Agent Devlin Pierce. After all this time it was like they started over on square one every time they were together. After last night she knew that was no way to have a relationship, no matter what variety it was.

As she slipped under the covers of her own bed, she wondered about Big John. Her dear friend was in bad shape, worse shape when all this was over. His poor wife, daughter and granddaughter…what would they do when they found out? Lily reached for the light but she pulled back her hand. She needed the light right now. She didn't want to think about darkness and she definitely didn't want to live in it.

The sun was streaming through her window when she opened her eyes. She could smell coffee. She could hear Dev in the kitchen.

Lily dressed into jeans and a shirt and tried to calm down her curly hair. She met him in the kitchen. He was dressed in now dry clothes from last night. He stood there by the counter drinking his coffee.

"Good morning. You slept in for you. It's after eight." He smiled as she looked at the clock. He was analyzing again. Understandably, she'd be in shock for days, weeks but he hoped she could at least function a little.

She smiled and reached for the already poured cup of coffee. He handed it to her and their hands touched. She looked at his chest and arms, the ones that had held her and served as her comforting pillow.

"I love your Elmo mug," he kidded.

"It goes with the slippers. One of my nieces thought it was very important for me to have Elmo in my life." Her voice was softer than usual, probably from the screaming and the crying. Oh my Lord, she had screamed at him. What must he think of her?

"Better than Grover, never really liked him. We need food and I've check your refrigerator. You have nothing. So where should we go?"

She took a sip of coffee. "I can't go."

"Why not? Didn't I just hear your stomach growl?"

He had. She was embarrassed by that, looking down at the floor.

"We always had this rule if you didn't go to church, you couldn't do anything entertaining like going to a movie or going out to eat, well usually you were sick but I wouldn't feel right."

"Catholic guilt, huh? Well we can solve that." In one swift movement he grabbed her keys from the counter, placed both coffee cups on the counter, grabbed her hand and rushed her out of the house. He locked the house and turned to see his car sitting on the street.

"Then, damn it, we're going to church. We can catch the nine o'clock at your church and if we don't pass out from hunger in the middle of Mass we'll go to that little restaurant right down the street. Just pray we have that priest who does the short homily."

She almost felt like a kidnap victim, pushed into the passenger seat of his car and rolling away from her home… to church.

Thankfully, the service was short and they were almost done with breakfast when Dev received a text from Tom. John had survived surgery and had told one of the doctors that he needed to talk to him.

"Important?" Lily asked as she watched him place his phone upside down on the table.

"Yes. I've got to go into work." His words were measured and flat. He sounded like he was going in to fix computers instead of talking to the main suspect in a drug trafficking case.

She nodded. She understood from the words he didn't speak. Maybe John was awake? Maybe John died? She couldn't tell by reading Dev's face. Could anyone read him? She wondered if his family and friends could…maybe his girlfriend? Did he have a girlfriend? She'd never wanted to ask him just in case the answer would be yes.

"Just drop me at home."

"I will but you will have a detail on the house, just like before."

She smiled slightly. "Using me as bait, again?"

His eyes looked straight through her. "No and I don't want to hear that again." They walked out in silence and most of the way home before she broke it.

"Thanks for staying last night. I needed that, the company." She couldn't admit she needed him, not anymore.

"I know." He let the answer fall into the silent car.

When they reached the house, the detail was across the street and Abby was sitting on the doorstep waving as they pulled up.

Lily was out of the car before Dev could reach her side, running for Abby, the two falling into each other's arms.

Abby waved at him as he got back into the car to pull away. As he was leaving he heard Abby say something about a bottle of vodka…

Chapter Twenty-Five

Dev, Tom Fullerton and another FBI agent, Larry Linwood, passed by the hospital floor's waiting area.

Tom pointed toward the long couch where a young woman sat on one end holding a sleeping child on her lap. On the other end sat an older woman, her eyes shut as she sat in the quiet room. Their familial looks were unmistakeable, the younger woman having the same nose and hairline of the older.

It was John's wife, daughter and granddaughter. Dev suddenly felt sick to his stomach. As much as he was angry that Lily had been in danger last night and had been a target through this miserable mistaken tragedy, there was always that other side of the story, the pages that were never printed. There's no way John's wife could've imagined she'd be sitting on that hospital couch on a Sunday afternoon. Dev knew she wasn't well. This would surely push her farther over the edge. That little girl should be playing with her grandpa at some park on a fall day like today or shopping for school supplies with her grandmother. She should be laughing, not sleeping in a hospital waiting room.

Did John's wife know everything that had happened last night and everything that had been happening in the last few months? Or did she just think her husband was doing his job and coming to a security call on his boulevard? She may even have rebuked him for going out on such a night;

it was past his usual hours.

The young woman Dev assumed was John's daughter looked up to see the three men. Tom was checking in at the nurse's desk, brandishing his badge. Dev saw her scared face as she caught his eyes. In war he was used to seeing fear and defiance but her face cut him to his core. Her hopelessness blended with guilty grief. Her actions had created this miserable day, last night and the last few months enveloping her father in actions he would never had done except for her. He sacrificed everything for her…his name, his career, his friendship with Lily and possibly his life. What must that feel like to be a father and to hold that baby in your arms for the first time and then years later go against the very law you upheld for years to protect that baby?

Lord, what a mess. Dev wanted to go over and say something, anything, but it wasn't possible. He followed Tom down the hall with the other agent.

A policeman posted outside the hospital room was talking to an older gentleman dressed in a suit and tie. Tom walked slightly faster as he neared him.

"Charlie, you are a sight for sore eyes. Been a long time." He warmly greeted the man with a heartfelt handshake and partial hug. "Let me introduce you to Agent Linwood, he'll be taking the statement and this is a buddy of mine, Devlin Pierce, with the Justice Department. He's the lead in this DEA investigation. Gentleman, this is Charles Hudson, retired prosecutor and I bet John's attorney."

"You bet right. Good to meet you both." He turned to Dev. "Agent Pierce, John has had nothing but good to say about you in this whole big mess." The attorney extended his hand to him. "He's still in pain but he wanted to get this over and then I'll go to work for him. He's also entrusted me with some timelines and contacts I think you all will be interested in so I hope that can work in his favor."

Dev and Tom exchanged questioning looks. John apparently had been documenting everything? Always a cop.

The attorney shook his head. "I've known that good man since he was on the police force and we worked on some abuse cases together. This is hard for me but I'm doing it for him. Did you all speak to his daughter?"

"No, not yet," Dev responded. "I'd rather bring her into Tom's office maybe tomorrow but let her be for now."

"But," Tom interrupted, "she's not to leave town, Charlie. She's lucky she's not in jail, for now. And we will be expecting a lot from her."

Dev was mildly surprised at the ominous comment. The girl was as much a victim as Lily. She'd made some bad choices but apparently she'd been clean and had been pulled back into a life she had put behind her.

They all entered the room to see John, the man whom Lily had called big, now fragile, attached to an IV and handcuffed to a bed. He looked over to see them enter, smiling slightly at Dev.

"Ah, Lily's boyfriend."

The attorney looked sideways at him, Tom smiled and the other agent began setting up his equipment.

Tom murmured to his old friend, "long story".

"Actually, John, I'm…"

John stopped him with his free hand. "A good man."

Dev took a step back as Tom explained with the attorney's additional comments, how they were going to proceed. He was also encouraging John to assist Agent Pierce in his DEA investigation as much as he could. John was facing federal charges and any help would make it better on him when the time came for sentencing. The timeline and contact lists would even help his daughter's case.

As John's statement was recorded, Dev listened intently. Compassion was needed. This was a good man in an awful no-win situation. He continued to describe the tearful call from his daughter, the threats from her former dealer, the searches he had done at Lily's. He was a friend of Lily's and she wouldn't think anything of him checking on the shop. Even when Lily's code no longer worked, he contacted the security company and a friend there told him the new system and how to re-program and re-set once he entered and exited. He had goofed on one occasion.

Tom and Dev looked at each other. Lily would be getting a new service to keep her and her shop safe if Dev had anything to say about it. Tom would be visiting the company the next day to emphasize the term SECURITY and to possibly bring charges against John's "friend".

John had decided to leave the freezer in disarray so Lily wouldn't know what was missing and to try to pin it on some break-ins that were occurring in the area. Some of his police comrades had shared specifics of the thefts over lunch one day.

"I took the freezer bags, the ones I thought were the heroin. I took them home, defrosted, cut them open and all that was in there was the chemical gel that freezes. But I left them at the drop spot at the shopping mall down the way. I have the address and the spot in my notes. A Cartel contact picked them up. I had to go in one more time. Last night, well, I never wanted Lily to know."

"We had a camera set up when we changed the security system, John. Your friend didn't know that," Dev interjected. "We didn't tell Lily we suspected you, but she knew. You said something at lunch that tipped her off. You read a note on her desk. No one would've seen that but whoever was in the shop in the middle of the night. It was a plant for Mrs. Notte, remember?"

John wiped his forehead with his free hand to remove the forming beads of sweat.

"Oh Lord. You have to believe I would never let them hurt her. She's my little girl too." He looked point blank at Dev. A small tear appeared and rolled down his cheek. "She must hate me."

Dev couldn't answer. Vulnerable was not a good look for Lily Schmidt but she'd been more than that last night. She'd been lost, betrayed, alone. He couldn't and didn't want to remember what she looked like when he'd grabbed her into his arms. Yes, she had been in shock but she was not weak. She wasn't one of those women who was a clinging vine shouting "help me, help me you big strong man". She laid up against his chest but she never sunk in for him to be the only one who could get her out of a jam. He hoped she'd understand when she knew the entire story. His new friend had a heart bigger than her brain sometimes.

"So, they flew my daughter and granddaughter up here. I figured they wanted to make sure we were all together when they took us out but they told her she had to bring those packages back to Miami. I never told my wife anything but she knows something is up. My daughter and I have had too many whispered conversations and too many daddy phone calls this summer. We didn't know someone else was on that plane, someone following my child the entire time and last night, well, when I tried one more time…" John took a deep breath. "It's fuzzy with the storm but when I saw that figure I knew what he was there for…he was going to kill me first and Lily was just in the way again. Then they'd go after my family. Months ago I was suspicious when a couple of men slammed my wife up against a canned goods aisle at the supermarket. She injured her hip again. Then we found out about her cancer returning. I just wanted to keep everyone safe."

He shut his eyes and his breathing became labored. "I tried to protect Lily. I made her stay behind the desk and I met him at the door. That's when it all went wrong. I don't remember much past that but I got him. Didn't I?"

Dev reached for his hand through the bed railing and the hand cuff. "Yes you did and you protected Lily."

"It's going to be your job now," John murmured as the machine alarms went off. "But there's somebody else out there, boyfriend. You gotta get him, you gotta…"

"We need someone in here," Dev said into the speaker beside the bed. "His blood pressure is plummeting. We need someone stat."

The FBI agents pulled their chairs back against the wall to allow the staff a quick entry. "Hang in there, John." Dev continued to hold his hand.

"You're a good man. She needs you but don't you hurt my girl. Please try not to hurt my other girls too, please, promise me."

Dev tried to shrink as small as he could as two nurses and a doctor checked monitors, listened to his heart and injected drugs. He just kept holding Big John's weakened and imprisoned hand.

"I promise, John. I'll do everything I can. You have my word."

"You Army?"

"Yes, sir."

"Knew it. I believe you. Bless you." Dev could barely hear his words as he faded into unconsciousness.

The monitors were beeping with warning bells and blips. Finally, the doctor pushed Dev aside and began a cardiac treatment. Dev faded back into the corner of the room. Fullerton and the other agent removed themselves but the attorney stayed near the doorway. He was watching the frantic resuscitation of his old friend and compatriot in crime fighting from so many years ago.

Dev's thoughts were of those three females in the waiting room. Without thinking he dashed out of the room as the staff was preparing to move the bed at high speed. He assumed they were taking John back to surgery.

"Mrs. Temple," he yelled as he ran down the hall. "You need to come with me now. Mrs. Temple!"

She was on the edge of the waiting area when he slid in front of her. He grabbed her hand and hauled her behind him. She was able to meet her husband's bed in the hallway before the other elevator.

Dev stood back, leaning against the wall, sliding down until he was crouched on the floor with his head in his hands. How could any of them ever heal? If John died or if he lived there would be an inconsolable world of hurt that would soon be their reality. He felt a hand on his shoulder and knew it was Tom.

"That was a nice thing to do."

He didn't dare look up. He saw his own tears falling onto the floor.

"She needed to say goodbye. The love of her life may die and everyone needs to get a chance to say goodbye."

Inside his head he kept saying that word over and over again. *Goodbye, goodbye, goodbye…Mom.*

Later, Dev texted Lily and told her he would see her tomorrow. They needed her statement.

He made her look out her window to report that the police detail was indeed there.

"Yes. Took her a sandwich and soda. Thinking of asking her in for dinner. Making roast," she texted back.

She sounded natural, not in shock at all. She was being Lily…now she was going to entertain the policewoman. She took in people into her world like others took in puppies and kittens. From Abby to Jeremy, Mrs. Notte, John, Neal, him, all those brides and moms and their relationships with her were the proof.

"Take care of yourself. Get sleep. See you tomorrow," he texted back. It was the last text he would send. Eventually, Tom and the other agent went on their way but he stayed. He'd gone down to the food court in the hospital and bought sandwiches, coffees, waters and couple of milks and returned to the waiting area. Slowly he approached the three females. The young woman was checking her phone, John's wife had her hands folded in quiet prayer and the little girl was at the low table playing a video game.

"Mrs. Temple, I thought you all might like something to eat." He laid the assortment on the table.

"That was very kind of you, Mister?"

The little girl was all smiles as she noticed the Happy Meal right in front of her. "Dev. I know your husband. I'm friends with Lily, the florist."

"Oh, yes, you're her boyfriend. How wonderful. You shouldn't have done this for us but I certainly appreciate it."

The little girl patted her on the leg. "Gram, can I? The fries are warm."

"Yes, baby," Mrs. Temple said as she smoothed the hair on top of her head. "Alise," she said as she motioned to the other woman, "this nice man is dating Miss Lily, remember her?"

"Yes, Momma."

Dev could tell she was hesitant, afraid. She knew who and what he was and he certainly wasn't a nice man, nor was he dating Lily in her eyes.

"Thank you for the food, sir." She answered as he had expected but grabbed a sandwich anyway. They must have been starving. He was too but the coffee would do him for now.

"Have you heard anything about your husband?" He finally asked a question after they had eaten.

"He's still in surgery again. That's all we know. Thank you so much for coming and getting me."

He took a sip of coffee and didn't respond. In a war zone sometimes human kindness could get you killed but the only thing that would happen to him here was a crack in his armor. He would still be alive at the end of the day, but his heart would be a little more worn around the edges.

He couldn't help himself as he watched their interaction. Watching and analyzing had always been his forte even as a child. His mother was always scolding him for his absent-mindedness in church and other serious occasions, but actually he was studying. He was figuring out if that woman really loved her husband, or if that girl had been at a party the night before or if the priest was not feeling well. That behavior had become second nature for him and he utilized that skill in war and now in this job.

Alise was nervous, her hands shaking a little. She wasn't on drugs from what he could tell besides there was no way she could've sat there all day without a hit of some kind if she was. She was guilty. There might not be any crime to hang on her but her father's mortality was in the balance and hung on her, at least that's what she was probably thinking. And her mother knew absolutely nothing. She probably wondered if her mother would still speak to her, want her when she discovered what had been going on. And Alise was worried about her own child and what all this would do to her, what sins as a mother she would have to pay for?

He saw Mrs. Temple rise quickly from the couch, turning to see her join a doctor. The man immediately grabbed her by the shoulders. Dev raced to the duo in time to catch her in his arms.

He heard the scream from the couch and the little girl asking what was wrong. He moved Mrs. Temple to the couch and could see a nurse running toward the scene. The mother's screams of pain were primal, guttural, the hurt felt by all of them around her. Alise moved to comfort her mother. The nurse checked her vitals and patted her hand. This woman was dealing with cancer and now the death of her husband, and soon, so much more. Her vitals would eventually stabilize; her life would never be the same.

Painfully, he saw the little girl, another of John's little girls, crawling away from the scene backwards until she could go no further and hit the wall. Dev walked away and joined her on the floor, his long legs sticking out across the floor.

"How are you?"

She didn't answer. She was still holding onto the toy that had come with her meal, clenching it like it was her last tie to this earth. If she let go she would sail into nothingness.

"It will be fine. Right now your grandmother and your mom are having a hard time."

"My Grandpa J is gone, isn't he?"

He gulped. What the hell had he gotten himself into now? His first thought was to lie. No, he learned one thing from Ms. Schmidt…lying didn't work with those you loved. It definitely wouldn't work with a beautiful, innocent little girl.

"Yes. He was hurting and now he isn't."

"God has him?" She looked right up into his eyes. Lord, save him. Only truth could be answered.

"Yes, God has him. You know your grandpa was a special man and he loved you very much."

"I love him too." Her gaze went to the small toy in

her hand and so did Dev's. They stared in silence. As her mother and grandmother calmed down, drank some water and asked questions of the very patient doctor who was still there, Dev heard the occasional words…a bleeder, loss of too much blood, his heart…and John was gone. He also heard FBI mentioned a couple of times and autopsy. Lord help them all now as reality ventured into the cloud of sorrow.

Alise finally turned toward her daughter and faintly smiled. Her eyes softened and she mouthed "thank you" to Dev. He nodded, reached for the small video game and handed it to his sidekick.

"Show me that game you were playing, please?"

"Sure. You just don't want me to worry about all the grown up stuff, right?"

"That's exactly right. But I want to see that game too." She smiled at him and began to show him the frog, the castles and the lily pads. Lily. He needed to talk to her before any news stations reported the death and he needed to do it in person, no text would work.

He had followed Mrs. Temple and the girls home and ordered a police detail on them just until they could make sure everything wrapped up…the Cartel, the drugs and the contact in the city.

The little girl, Angelica, had wanted to hug him before he drove away. She'd tugged on his pants leg until he noticed.

"Yes, Miss?"

"You need to come down to my size." Her mother stood right next to her, nodding in his direction.

"She probably has something to tell you."

"Oh," he said as he knelt down on the pavement in front of his pint-size new friend. "What is it, Angelica?"

She hugged him around the neck. "I know you are a policeman just like Grandpa J. You are very brave just like him. Bye." She kissed him quickly on the cheek and then ran into the house. He continued to kneel, his left hand touching his face where she had left her mark.

"When will things happen to me?"

He stood up slowly as he thought about that question.

"Well, we have a few loose ends, some statements and we will figure this all out, together," he answered seriously as he looked into her eyes. "Right now we have some drugs to find, still. We have someone to arrest in town, and we have to deal with the men in Miami and South America."

She looked down to the sidewalk. "I meant with me… do I go to jail now?"

"No, you go inside and you stay with your family. They need you," he answered as she raised her head in surprise. "But you know you don't leave town. That car over there will be watching over you all until we can wrap this up. We will be in contact. Get some rest, try to write down anything and everything you can offer in a statement, I mean names, dates, times, money, drugs, anything."

"Thanks." Alise began to walk up the path to the front door.

"Oh and," he yelled, "don't let that little girl down ever again."

It was almost eight in the evening when he knocked on

Lily's front door, leaning up against the frame. He'd already checked in with her detail and informed her of the news. Apparently the policewoman's father had worked with John. It would be sad news all around the city.

Lily opened the door attired in her usual Sunday night relaxation wardrobe of shirt, sweats and sneakers. She looked him up and down, noticing the suit, the loose tie and the open collar. He looked tired, actually worn out and very worried. She had no idea what she looked like. Her day had been a Sunday but it wasn't feeling like a normal day. She'd cleaned the house, every so often, stopping to grab her head and to scream out loud in anguish. One time her detail had knocked on the door furiously yelling if she was in danger. Her heart hurt. Her friend, her friend....

"Hi." He had no more emotion left in his body or his voice. He felt like he was returning Michael's body back to his parents again. He actually was not thinking about anything past this moment, or these next few hours ahead with her. Hopefully she would allow him to comfort her, as best as he could. Hopefully, she could try to work through the shock she was feeling and he could help her, if she let him. If she let him.

"You look like a man who needs a drink." She motioned for him to come in.

He immediately took off his jacket, throwing it on the back of a chair as he came into the living room. Next he jerked his tie off and unbuttoned two buttons on his shirt. Her focus zeroed onto the gun holstered on the side of his body. He noticed she was watching some British show on PBS. Thankfully, it wasn't the news.

She watched him carefully. She knew that if he stroked

his fingers through his hair that he was nervous, upset. As he sat down on the sofa he played out his tell.

"I'd love a beer but water is fine too."

She rushed into the kitchen. What now? What on earth now? She knew it was more about John but she knew in her heart she didn't want to hear anymore. She'd heard enough to last her years and seen enough to never be able to remove the visions from her memory.

"Beer I can do. I have the one you like."

He didn't answer. She flipped the cap and hurried into the living room handing it over to him.

Surprisingly, he scooted over on the sofa and patted the cushion next to him.

"I need to talk to you. I know last night was hard on you. No one should have to go through that but now…"

She balled her hands together. She was suddenly so very cold, just like last night.

"It's John."

Dev nodded at her pronouncement. His eyes weren't twinkling. The beautiful shining green color was dull and murky. He'd had a long day but she saw something more than just red tired eyes. She saw a vacancy and she understood immediately that her world was once more minus a human being.

"Oh God. He's really gone." She couldn't control the river of tears falling no more than she could quiet the sobs as he laid the beer down quickly and gathered her into his arms. They both fell back against the back of the sofa, repeating last night's behavior. She wasn't just his mission or the focus of a case. He wasn't sure what she was except he needed to hold her right now and be there for her. He'd promised.

"I'm so sorry, Lily." He repeated it over and over until her sobs quieted. She never looked up at him as he comforted and rubbed her back, still holding her securely in his arms.

How long had it been since he'd held someone like this, with no expectation of heading off to a bedroom? This was too intimate in so many ways. He found he couldn't help himself around her. He *had* to do this, to be with her this way and to help her in any way he could.

The PBS show was over; his shirt was wet from her tears before she jerked up suddenly. "What happened? I mean I know what happened but you were going to talk to him, he had something to say to you, right? And now he's dead." Her voice was hard and accusatory.

Maybe it was just his imagination? Maybe the shock was rearing its ugly head?

"We did talk. You know he was protecting you and his family." Dev tried to read her expression but he received a blank stare. Apparently she had cried herself out.

"He, well, there was a bleeder. They took him in for a second surgery. Eventually his heart gave out."

She shook her head back and forth. "No, no. So that's it? It's all over, isn't it? But what about his wife, his daughter, oh my God, his little Angelica?"

Dev didn't answer. Nothing was really over, especially not for John's family. There were times like these when your fight or flee feeling took over your body. He wanted to flee; she wanted to fight.

“The whole thing is over now.” She had commanded and so it needed to be.

“No.” The simpler the better in answering would be his only defense and it wasn’t a very good one.

“No?” Lily stood up and looked down on him. “I saw a man killed last night and I saw my very dear friend shot. I heard shot after shot…do you know what that’s like?”

Finally, he looked up directly into her eyes. He was serious, deadly serious. Of course he knew what that was like. Seemingly, darkness always made it worse. The black hole of night could be illuminated with night vision for that one shot aimed perfectly into a man to do the most damage. He knew what it was like and he hated it. He hated that she had to see and be part of it. He hated that he lived with those memories every day, some for seconds, others for minutes and those occasional weekends when those thoughts moved in and stayed way beyond their welcome.

“I’m not going to answer that question. We have people who can help you work through this.”

“You have people,” Lily laughed. “Well isn’t that nice. What more has to be done? How much more do you need from me…you want some blood? John already gave it.”

She held out her arm, showing her veins to him. “What more, Agent Devlin Pierce?”

He placed his beer down and stood up moving past her toward his jacket and tie. “We need to find the Cartel’s drugs.”

“Well I don’t have them, Agent Pierce.”

“And the Cartel doesn’t have them either, Ms. Schmidt.

So where are they?"

Her face hardened even more, if that was possible. "You think I have them? Are you accusing me now?"

He picked up his things and headed to the door. "I think I better go."

"I think we can agree on that. You never answered me. Are you accusing me?" He stopped and turned to face her as he moved to leave.

"No, don't be ridiculous. But we will need you to come into the shop tomorrow and maybe we can all figure out what the hell happened to them. You'll need to make a statement too at some point. I'll talk to Tom and our DC office about when and where that will happen. But the drugs need to be found."

He was on the sidewalk when she yelled. "Do I need to bring an attorney?"

He kept walking to his car. "Bring whoever the hell you want. It's Monday. The shop is closed so you'll be available. I'll text you with the time." His response sounded like an order, a direct one.

He stared at her standing in the doorway as he started the car and backed out into the street.

He'd probably only see her one more time, tomorrow. That was a good thing. All of this, she had gotten under his skin. This uncomfortableness was overwhelming. Again, vulnerability was never a good look.

Then he saw her fall to the floor, crumpling like a paper doll. He pulled back into the driveway and ran toward her as she came up to her knees. He'd waved off the patrol cop.

He pulled her up to him and held her there.

"I'm so sorry, Dev. I don't know how to get through this. I'm so sorry I said those things."

He held her head to his chest. "Me too. It's been a long day. We will get this all sorted out. Let's get you back inside."

He walked her toward the sofa and brought her a glass of water. She was wiping away more tears.

"All I'm doing is crying and screaming. I feel useless and I feel like I did something wrong, but I didn't did I?" She looked up to him for answers.

"You have done nothing wrong. None of this has been your fault. You're going to have to talk to somebody or this will eat you up alive, trust me. I know." And he did know. Even at that you'd talk, learn skills to adapt your behaviors for what you were feeling, that feeling of helplessness and blame was never gone. It became part of you. It would remind you in the simplest of times that you were fallible, that your choices created your life and sometimes others' decisions molded you into a different person, whether you liked it or not.

"We both need to get some sleep after last night and then all this," he continued. "Do you want me to stay tonight?"

She laughed, wiping her nose on her sleeve. "My detail is going to get suspicious if you keep sending them home at night, don't you think? Let them do their job and you get some rest."

Dev wondered if she even knew what she was implying. Part of him, the tired part, wanted to just stay the night, to hold her when the memories flooded her thoughts, soothe her fears and to just be a friend. That's what they were, friends.

The other part of him, what he considered the real Devlin Pierce, made sure her door was locked behind him, said goodnight and left her side to spend a fit-filled, sleepless six hours in a hotel bed.

Chapter Twenty-Six

1. Meet at shop no later than two today
2. Check schedule for the week
3. Need Abby as much as I can in shop
4. Get through the week???

After last night's encounter with Devlin Pierce, Lily Schmidt was not feeling particularly proud of herself, nor did she know what she was feeling. In fact, she was numb. She'd been a crazy woman, first crying in his arms and then going straight over the line into anger at him. It hadn't been his fault that a horrible mistake created another horrible mistake which created chaos in her life and the ultimate loss of her friend. It was the Cartel's fault; they'd goofed. Some little guy at the airport had missed a box, a very valuable box. It had been shipped to her. They had some of their drugs but some were missing and she needed to try her very best to help find them. But she didn't have them.

And in the midst of the shock, confusion and grief had she actually almost asked him to sleep with her? It wasn't as if she hadn't thought about it, well, she wasn't going to ask him but she thought…what had she thought? He wasn't interested in her that way but there were times when the lines blurred. She knew she wasn't imagining it. Or was she? Was she so desperate for love and attention that she made so much out of so little? She was a victim, a suspect. She was a woman just trying to survive at this point with emotions all over the board. She needed to prepare for this meeting but she had no idea how to do it. It wasn't like the SAT's when you could study for days and months for entrance into a college. Besides, she was pretty sure she had no idea what the answer was.

Lily knew she had to give a formal statement but that probably needed to be done downtown somewhere. She'd told any agent and police officer Saturday night who would listen to her, all that had transpired before her eyes. Actually, she hadn't seen anything while she was barricaded behind her desk, but the aftermath was still very clear in her memory. The sounds of the yelling and gunfire collected in her brain creating a scrapbook of muddled, terror-filled thoughts. Her imagination threw all caution to the wind. As she walked down to the shop from the parking lot, her imagination took a backseat to reality…John's blood had left a discoloration of the sidewalk.

That night he'd seen the figure in front of the glass window. He'd pushed her down under the desk and thrown the chair in front of her.

"You don't move, little girl. Don't you dare come out until your boyfriend comes and gets you."

She saw him hit the alarm button at the side of the desk and as soon as he walked away, she hit it again. The last time she saw his face was a final look and a contrived smile before he moved toward the front of the shop. She'd heard yelling and then pop, pop, pop, a pause and then pop, pop.

She was praying over and over. Maybe she heard more shots but she couldn't really remember because of the storm. She heard the sirens and then saw the lights of the patrol cars reflected on her back wall. Slowly pushing the chair away, Lily crawled out.

The first sight was of John's body laying between the door and the sidewalk. The glass door was almost closed except for his two legs wedging it open. She stayed on her hands and knees as she saw two agents with guns drawn, opening the door farther. The police were close behind.

Their flashlights illuminated her face and blinded her momentarily until they came to her side.

The next few minutes were a blur as they raised her up and sat her down on the chair. Their voices sounded like the Charlie Brown cartoon characters on the old television specials. There was a buzzing in her ears and she couldn't focus. She kept telling them what had happened… John had saved her life. They didn't need to know anything else.

When she saw John try to raise his head, she moved to his side, holding his hand at first, then placing pressure on his wound.

"You're going to be fine," she had lied. It seemed like hours before paramedics pushed her to the side and began working on John. He had slowly raised his right hand to wave at her as they took him away.

She told everyone who would listen that John had saved her life. Lily remembered his kind face, his soothing voice telling her she was going to be fine. She really doubted that. She continued her story when she noticed that no one was working on the other body in the street. Finally, someone covered it with a sheet. She watched them move in slow motion and barely noticed the stretcher to the left of her.

Lily slowly slid down the wall of the building and sat down on the sidewalk, her knees up and pulled into her body. Her head laid on top of them. A female agent had come over and wiped off her bloody hands. Finally, finally Dev had come.

Lily blinked a couple of times. She was fixated by the spot on the sidewalk. A life came down to a spot, an abnormal shading of an irregular form in the concrete. She'd once heard you weren't really dead and forgotten until no one said your name ever again. John, John, John… she'd repeat every time she walked through her shop's door now. Being at the shop would never be the same again; coming to work every day through that door would never be normal again.

She had to wake up out of this dream. Lily took a deep breath in and then looked around the boulevard. Everything was still there and life was going on. But there were two dark sedans parked illegally on the street in front of the shop. Lily looked in through her "autumn leaves" themed front window to see agents inside her domain. Taking a deep breath, she entered and fixed her gaze on Dev but Agent Fullerton came up to her first.

"Lily, we really appreciate you coming in today. We know you've been through a lot for several months and we can't do our job without your cooperation, so we thank you so much." He pulled her own chair out for her and sat across from her, at her consultation table. She laid her once soggy folder, bag and purse on her table. Dev joined them to stand in front of her.

Tom Fullerton motioned for her to sit across from him. The other men in the room seemed to be going over every inch of her shop and she knew what they were looking for…what they were *still* looking for.

Nervously, she fingered her keys still in her hand. “I really like what you guys did with my place,” she joked as she nervously looked around. The shop was a wreck with broken items on shelves, papers in disarray and open cooler doors with wilting flowers. She looked up to Dev and stared into his eyes. He looked tired and finished, finished as when you are done talking to someone and you just want to say goodbye.

Fullerton smiled and opened a notebook in front of her.

“Lily, here’s some of our facts.” He began to list dates, times, places, speculations. She was sick to her stomach. She was angry when she remembered they’d been watching her inside her own shop the entire time of this mess. She’d never thought of the cameras after Agent Pierce had installed them. But she had either forgotten or never been told about some of the microphones. They could hear them the entire time! She was angrier, if that was possible, when she realized they’d known about John for a very long time. Apparently, there was also another one or two accomplices. Oh my God. She wanted to knock the smugness off Agent Pierce’s face. It was smugness she was seeing, wasn’t it? Maybe she should have brought her attorney.

Wait a minute. She continued to listen to Tom Fullerton. He was doing what she did almost on a daily basis…making a list, going down that list, accomplishing jobs, and getting the work done. She breathed in and out slowly, listening more intently, not looking at Agent Pierce.

“Which leads us back to…where are those kilos of heroin? They aren’t at the wholesaler and from the notes

John gave us they were in the box that was shipped to you with the dead hydrangeas, with the packets of preservatives which were drugs too. Where did those freezer bags or blocks as you call them, go?"

Wait, John had given them notes? Her temporary confusion would have to be answered later. She must've looked like a deer in the headlights of an eighteen wheeler. This was going to hurt.

"I don't know. I just don't know."

"Did your assistant handle them? Did she do anything with them?"

"Abby didn't do anything with them," Lily yelled out. They weren't going to hang this on Abby. "I just don't know. We probably put them in the freezer and used them."

Fullerton shook his head. "Then they should have been collected in the first burglary."

"Oh, yah, the ham sandwich escapade." She drummed her fingers on the table to distract herself, buying some time to have her memory check in with some miraculous piece of information.

"This is getting us nowhere," Tom lamented as he looked up at Dev. "Until we find those kilos…"

He let that threat hang on the air. It was no skin off his nose, only her's, literally perhaps. Would the Cartel send a second wave? She wasn't quite sure how the South American group took care of florists but she saw in the rain Saturday night what they did to others who crossed their paths. She didn't even have a gun for protection.

Dev came closer, blocking Fullerton from her view. He

crouched down in front of her. "Lily, use that remarkable memory of yours and tell me where those two blocks are."

Dev grasped her hands in his, their eyes locked in concentration. This would've been romantic if not for the importance of the situation and a half dozen other agents in the room.

"Think back to that delivery. You left the packets on the dead hydrangeas. There were two ice blocks in the box, right?"

She nodded slowly, her eyes shifting to the left trying to see that day again. The ice blocks were in good shape and…

"I put them in the freezer."

Dev's head fell down in exasperation. "But they weren't there when John stole from the freezer. Could you have thrown them out? Did you use them for a delivery?"

"I used them that weekend. I had the boxes at home in the garage…" She looked at him in panic, removing her hands from his.

"Oh my God," she gasped as she threw her own hands up to her mouth. "They weren't in the freezer that night… they were in my garage and I brought them back to the shop after the break-in."

Dev knew she remembered. He just hoped they could retrieve them. He didn't know how much more of this interrogation of sorts he could handle. He'd rather interrogate the Taliban than Lily. If she prayed out loud one more time he might send her to her maker!

"Lily? Where are they?"

Her face had turned white and she began to cry. "We used

them that weekend on a wedding. It was hot, remember?"

She was looking at Dev as though he was the key to this whole cockeyed caper. All the agents seemed to nod in unison. They were getting somewhere now but the electricity in the room proved to be somewhere in between slow excitement and having your teeth pulled.

Dev was trying to understand her thought process. "It was hot. You used them on a wedding. Which wedding?"

"That wedding!" she yelled. "Oh no. I bet they were in the bottom of those boxes!"

"Lily, I'm tired of this," he said impatiently. Enough already. He head a team of agents surrounding him who wanted the information now. It was time, way past time to end this case.

"Which wedding? I need name and location. Now."

The last word was said as though he was commanding, demanding something from his troops. He was impatient and she knew that she needed to get it out. She looked around the room and saw the myriad of faces, men breathing as one and waiting for her to spill the information. She would be ruined. Absolutely, this was the end of her career. Pack the shop up, sell everything, put the house up for sale and just hope her sister would understand when she ended up on her doorstep in Fredericksburg.

"The wedding was the one in the country club area… with Gretchen. I left the empty boxes with her."

Dev understood completely.

"I'll take Lily and Fullerton with me. I want two of you to follow but hold back when we get there. Lily and I'll go to the door. No need to make a big deal out of this."

He pulled her up to stand in front of him and grabbed her purse. "You did great, Lily, now let's get this over with."

He was softer now, he was Dev now, not Agent Pierce.

"But what if they've thrown them away?"

He was already pulling her along behind him and out the door to one of the cars.

"If they have, then they have and we can announce to the press that some of the Cartel's shipment was permanently lost. We can announce the death of a hit man, a burglary, the end of this case and just say that some of the Cartel's shipment was destroyed or lie and say we found them. That should end it. If we put the story out all over, they'll look like fools and back away."

She heard him. She was putting together all the puzzle pieces. Months ago, they could've lied and said they had found the drugs. Months ago, they could've ended it and maybe John would still be alive. They had purposefully set out to find some Cartel connection here in the city and they had used her to do it. She had been bait from the very beginning.

It sounded like cut and run for the DEA and the FBI but she would be left behind to lose her business, her life, what little she had. Would it be over for her? Easy for him to say but so much harder for her to exist with all that publicity…the wrong kind of publicity. Of course, she'd be out of danger. Wouldn't she? Did the Cartel watch the news and read the newspaper? And John was still dead.

Once inside the car, Dev drove and conversed with Agent Fullerton. She sat in the backseat watching the houses go by. These were some of her favorite neighborhoods. She'd miss them. These were the streets that she drove on Christmas night when she was all alone. Possibly she would be considered a voyeur but she so enjoyed the open curtains framing tableaus of families seated around festive dining tables and Christmas trees serving as decorations for the end of another memorable holiday. She'd drive around street after street until she hit the parkway and ended up at the Plaza, the mother of all lighting spectacles. Surprisingly, it was never busy on Christmas night. You could drive freely, watching the diners scurrying to their evening reservations.

And why was it that the lights looked so much brighter on Christmas night? Was it some sort of magic deposited as a gift from Kris Kringle to Kansas City? It was magic but now this was reality.

It didn't take long to arrive at the long familiar driveway where just a few months ago such happiness had lived. Dev parked and opened the door for her. She noticed Fullerton followed closely behind. She glanced back to see the other two agents parked on the street in front.

"Now, I'll introduce myself and Tom and of course they'll know you, then we'll…"

"No," Lily interrupted. "No, I'm going to talk to them. You two stay right here."

She was back in control. If they were going to take away her Christmas, her life, her work and her reputation then she would finish it her way.

"You used me as bait. You have been telling me what to do and now it's time for me to do what I need to do. It's my business after all that is at stake. Me, not you. You go back to DC, you go back to your office," she said pointing at the two men, "but I'm here. Me. These are my clients, my friends."

She emphasized every single syllable, every word and looked directly into Devlin Pierce's eyes. Enough. They had been greedy government agents; now the mission would be on her terms.

Fullerton and Dev stepped back as she went up to the door. The two men looked at each other, understanding she had a lot on the line, and she had taken even more over the last few months.

Dev had already realized she wasn't any ordinary human being but now she was really proving her worth.

Gratefully, her former bride's mother opened the door and immediately smiled as she saw Lily. She hugged her and looked past to see the two dark suited gentlemen accompanying her former wedding florist.

"Irene, we need to talk about the wedding flowers we had for your daughter's wedding. These gentlemen here," Lily motioned to them, "are from the FBI and the DEA. We need to know what you did with the boxes after I left that day. May we come in and talk?"

Shocked was not the accurate word for Irene's demeanor but she motioned them in. Once they were all seated Lily explained the entire situation, how she had used ice blocks to keep the flowers cool during transport and had left the boxes in the garage for Gretchen, along with the now infamous blocks.

"Did you throw them all out or did someone use them after Gretchen? You would have seen them. They look like the ones you use in your cooler for picnics, camping." Lily thinly smiled at Dev. He smiled back knowingly. There was no way that Irene, nor any of her family had ever used a cooler, especially not for camping. On second thought she might have forced her husband to "Shakespeare in the Park" and had the maid or the cook pack them something in a cooler.

"I know exactly what happened to those boxes," she proudly announced. "This will solve everything."

Three faces smiled back at her.

"Gretchen said she could use them for an event she was doing the next week. I believe she took all the boxes and if those blocks were in there then Gretchen has them. There, so that's where they went. Wonderful, isn't it?"

Three faces frowned, and of the three, two were showing great discomfort. "Gretchen took them?" Lily had to be sure she had heard that correctly. "Gretchen?"

"Yes, Lily."

The silence was sickening. It really was all over now. Lily could start shredding the business cards as soon as she returned to the store. She had that bride last year who sold real estate and thought her house was cute. She needed to find her number tonight. Updating the resume would be second on her list. She began to make lists in her head again. Dev's voice interrupted the fourth item.

"Thanks so much. We will be in touch if we need anything else. You've been so helpful." Agent Fullerton was handing her his card and thanking her for her assistance.

Dev almost pushed her out of the house and into the car. Fullerton was on his cell phone calling the other sedan's occupants.

"Lily, check your phone for Gretchen's contact info and call her, please." He was all business. She acted before she could react.

Gretchen was answering within a minute.

"Yes, Lily, what do you need?"

"Tell her we are coming to her right now, dropping in," Dev prompted.

She knew what to do. "Gretchen, where are you right now? Oh, your apartment across from the Intercontinental? I need to see you right now. It's about a really big client and I need your help desperately, immediately. I just don't know if I'll be able to handle it and I know you'll steer me in the right direction. Number 829. Great, I'll be there in just a few minutes." Lily thought she was going to vomit but needed to add one more piece of bait. "I'm leaving the client off the parkway so about ten minutes? Great, thanks so much, you are such a love."

She hung up with a bad taste in her mouth, not just the little lies but the taste of subservience run amuck. Looking up to the front seat, Dev was watching her in the rear view mirror. They were stopped at a traffic light. She couldn't place a word of description on what she was seeing from him. There was a softness, perhaps pride in her and in what she had just accomplished? Maybe it was just pity for some little shop girl who got herself in a big mess. A lot of people enjoyed a good train wreck.

He was driving down the parkway and turning the corner into the Plaza area. Only a few more blocks and they'd be at Gretchen's. Great, just great, Lily kept repeating in her mind. Number four on her list was to begin packing and maybe sell all the china. Number five, explain to Abby that they were going to have to close after the news stations got wind of all this. By the time she had reached number fifteen, perhaps her longest list to date in her head, they were in front of the high rise apartment and Dev was opening the door once again.

"I'm not telling you anything on this one." He patted her on the back. "You've got this."

"You know what's going to be the absolute worst part of this?" She paused as she took a deep breath. "She's going to know we were never dating and that it was all a ruse. I hate that."

She was looking down at the pavement as the three of them walked into the lobby. Fullerton showed his badge to the doorman who punched the button for them and opened the secure doors.

Silence was the norm one more time between the three of them until Dev whispered down in her ear.

"I'm saying this only once, Lily. I hate that it was a ruse too."

She still didn't raise her head. She wiped her left eye and patted her cheek dry. He seemed to know she needed that right there and then. It was kind of him. She appreciated the pitying. Even though they weren't alone it seemed as though Fullerton didn't hear what had been meant for only her ears.

Lily had collected herself by the time they reached Gretchen's door. Apparently the door man had alerted her and there she was with the door open, striking a pose like an old Hollywood siren.

Gretchen looked every bit the star, tons of makeup and

an ensemble of a leopard tunic over tight leather leggings. For heaven's sake it wasn't that cool outside to be dressed for "The Graduate" seduction scene.

"Darling, oh and you've brought guests, your boyfriend and I don't seem to know this other young man."

Lily rolled her eyes and Agent Fullerton was looking around to see if someone had followed them up.

"Hello, Gretchen, may we come in?" Lily asked but just kept walking with the two agents in line behind her. Gretchen's smile vanished as they all stood in her elaborately decorated living room. This wasn't a social call.

"What is this about Lily? I don't understand."

"Well, you will," Lily motioned to Fullerton. "This is Agent Fullerton of the FBI." He quickly showed her his badge.

"And this is not really my boyfriend. This is Agent Pierce from the DEA. We need to discuss the wedding we had at the Hayden house earlier this season."

Gretchen wasn't a very good actress but her nonchalant face reminded Lily of Nora Desmond, bored with life and quite possibly in need of a colonoscopy.

"Everyone, sit, please. Agents, may I get you something?" She was acting the perfect hostess and Lily just knew she was already plotting revenge.

"No, we're good," Fullerton answered. "We need to know what you did with the boxes from the wedding. Mrs. Hayden said you took them with you to use the next week for some function you were working on. Actually, we need to know where the ice blocks went that were in those boxes."

"Well, I don't know. That was months ago." Lily shook her head. The woman was rude to everyone even federal agents.

Dev sat forward on the sofa. "Gretchen, if you can, could you possibly try to remember? It would be so important to me, to us, if you could tell us where those items are or what you did with them?" Lily was suddenly nauseous again as Dev held eye contact with the coordinator and had that little slip of a smile. His eyes were actually twinkling; he was flirting with her. Lily looked out the window. She knew he was just getting his information but jealousy was rearing its ugly head for no reason at all. Besides, she was still mad at him. Had the words in the elevator been an act like this? Or had they been a whispered wish to fall on her heart?

"Well, honey, let me think," Gretchen sat forward too, her leather-clad legs now touching Dev's. "I had that event at the Nelson." She pulled her phone out to check her calendar.

Lily watched her contort her face as though she was in actually pain from the stress on her little brain. She probably was. Thinking took a lot of effort for someone like Gretchen. And why couldn't she just say the event was at the art gallery, or on a Wednesday? Why say the "Nelson" dramatically as though it was some English nobleman's castle?

"It was for the Junior League."

Dev nodded and Lily continued to be sick to her stomach. She looked over at Tom Fullerton and grimaced. His face showed nothing, absolutely nothing until Lily sighed with disgust. A thin smile formed on his lips and he winked at her. Lily's patience had never been her strongest attribute. Right now she just wanted to grab Gretchen's phone and shove it up…

"Oh yes, that wedding off the parkway. I had you leave the boxes in the garage. It was so hot and I needed them to transport the bouquets. I saw those blocks in there. I threw the boxes away."

Dev's head dropped first, followed by Lily's and Tom's. They were sunk. "But I kept the blocks. Is that important?"

Now they were all drawn in attention at the woman.

Dev casually responded. "Well, it could be. Where are they now or do you even still have something as simple as those things?"

Really, really, Dev, Lily wanted to scream. All of this anguish and he was treating her like a queen? An idiot queen at best, but still after the interrogation she had been through and the trials of this entire situation, Lily was losing her patience.

"Gretchen, do you have those two damn ice blocks or not? If you do, where are they?" Lily yelled out loud. She thought she heard Dev and Tom both cuss.

Gretchen viewed her with contempt. She stood up from the sofa and promptly left the room. Dev glanced at Lily but saw Tom Fullerton holding his head in his hands.

"What did you think you were doing?" His eyes were no longer twinkling. He definitely wasn't her boyfriend now.

"I was getting us some information. As long as you were taking, I thought maybe you all were going to go out to dinner and dancing. I'm so done." Lily's announcement had Fullerton laughing out loud and Dev glaring.

"Way to go, Lily. I should never have involved you in any of this."

"Well, I never wanted to be involved but you all decided to catch more Cartel bad guys so we are even, Agent Pierce."

Dev didn't respond. Now he was looking at the view over her head. He figured she knew they had been using her all along. It was for the mission.

"Enough you two," Fullerton whispered. "I'm beginning to think you two need to go to dinner and get a room."

Silence. Unpleasant, uncomfortable silence coupled with a lack of air filled the room. They didn't look at each other and there was nothing more to be said. Gretchen entered the room and solved everything. In each hand was a white package of mush.

"Are these what you boys are looking for?"

Nora Desmond had produced the scene stealing moment of the play!

"I'm pretty sure these are the ones. I was keeping them for when I went down to the lake. I use them in the cooler when I catch fish."

Lord, Lily thought. Gretchen fished? Actually she could see the barracuda doing that, gutting her fish, enjoying it, thinking about whose career she would gut next?

Fullerton took over as the real professional in the room, producing evidence bags from somewhere in his suit and thanking her so much for her help in "a very important investigation".

"Will this be on the news?" Gretchen really did love publicity, good or bad. "I can't believe I've solved your very important case."

Lily was muttering in her head as Gretchen coyly gave the bags over to Fullerton. "I thought they were blocks," Dev whispered.

"Blocks, bags all the same difference when they're frozen. They keep the flowers cool in shipment and when we're transporting. You can use them over and over again." Lily refused to look at him, to see into those eyes that were obviously studying her every move since she disappointed him.

Gretchen was signing something Fullerton had produced and smiling sweetly once more.

She glanced over to the other two on the sofa.

"So, you two were never dating? Lily, I never knew you were such the little actress. You're always such the nice professional. Bravo, dear, bravo."

And then Gretchen applauded in approval. She winked at Dev.

Lily stood up, followed by Dev. "Thanks, Gretchen, I'll just add that to my new resume." Gretchen laughed and then eyed Dev up and down in her own Gretchen manner. "Well, honey, the way you two acted I didn't know anything was up. You just looked like you were a couple. If he's single, Lily you should grab him. I know I would. I mean those shoulders, those eyes…"

Lily just kept walking to the door. Time to flee. "Yah, yah, yah, ruggedly good looking, yada, yada, yada."

"We'll be in touch, ma'am," Fullerton said as he finished his paperwork. "Here's my card.We'll be contacting you to come downtown for a statement at your convenience but we certainly thank you for your time and assistance."

"You married, Agent Fullerton?"

Tom couldn't get to the door fast enough. "Yes, ma'am for years now. Pleasure to meet you. Thanks again."

Once they were all sequestered in the elevator, laughter broke out.

"Tom, I think you could have yourself a girlfriend," Dev announced.

"Only because you were taken, boyo!"

The laughter ceased.

Chapter Twenty-Seven

Dev's list wasn't very lengthy. It just included one item…to finish this case. John's funeral would be tomorrow, the end of a very long week. Once the drugs had been confirmed, Lily and Gretchen's statements had been taken in Tom's office and all the assorted paperwork was completed, the press was informed locally and nationwide. Dev's contacts with the Cartel confirmed to him that any hit was off on Lily and all could continue as normal, whatever that was now. The good guys had won; the bad guys had lost. The bad guys would continue to be bad and the good guys would try to stop them. That simple…right!

But there was just one more thing. He drove up the long driveway and parked a little past the front door. Dev was followed by two more vehicles. They stayed in place as he got out of the car and proceeded to ring the door bell. He didn't look like an agent right now. He looked like him on a weekend in jeans, sneakers and a pullover sweater. Fall was really settling in on Kansas City and a cool breeze blew colored leaves around his feet.

"Yes, sir?" A man, apparently a butler, stood in the open doorway.

"I need to see Garrett Notte, please."

"May I tell Master Notte who wishes to see him?"

Dev cleared his throat. "Lily's boyfriend, from the flower shop his grandmother goes to." He needed to perform the act of a lifetime.

"Oh, well if it's about the occasional items that Mrs. Notte picks up sometimes and forgets to pay for, you need to contact her son. I can give you his card. He'll be more than happy to pay for her forgetfulness."

"No, it's not about that, please get him." Interesting? Lily hadn't told him about Mrs. Notte's shoplifting. That sweet old lady had a few secrets after all. Didn't everyone?

The butler left and a few seconds passed before Garrett Notte stood before him. The young man eyed him suspiciously and then smiled.

"Oh yes, I've seen you in the shop. I've been meaning to see how Lily and Abby are doing after all that mess this past weekend."

Mess? That's what murder was to him? He calmed himself down…you are Lily's concerned boyfriend.

"Mr. Notte, Garrett, I needed to talk to you about something."

The young man shifted from one foot to the other. "If you're here to talk about Abby and me…"

"There is no Abby and you," Dev said sternly.

"I understand that now. I misread some cues from Abby. You know she and I are from such different circles but I thought we could have some fun."

Dev was suddenly nauseous from the pompous behavior of the country club cadet wanna be.

"You'd be lucky to have Abby, buddy. So, you won't bother her anymore." It was a command, one given with authority and no ambiguity.

"Of course," Garrett answered quickly.

"Now, I really came to tell you one thing," he paused to tap down his anger. "You will never go around that shop or talk to Abby or ever bother Lily again. Somehow I know, you little jerk, that you're involved in all that went down this weekend. I don't know how but you are. You *will* leave my girlfriend alone."

Dev stopped to let the words sink into the young man's brain of mush. He thought he could faintly smell marijuana on his clothes. He gently grabbed his shirt for affect and definitely smelled the remnants of weed.

"You leave them alone and you'll never have to see me again, but if I have to come back, you won't be left standing. Do you understand, Garrett?" Dev was just a couple of inches from his face.

Garrett, in shock, just nodded quickly and stepped back as Dev released him. He was still standing in the foyer with the open door when Dev left the house and marched down the steps.

He stopped at the base and nodded at the DEA agents

waiting, along with Tom Fullerton.

"Did that feel good?"

"It would've felt better if I'd hit him, but for now, I'm good." Dev smiled as he watched the federal agents roll into the house. Garrett was presented with a search warrant in one hand and silver cuffs in front of his face.

Dev got into his car and drove away. There'd always been a dark hooded figure, another contact in the city. John's notes at his attorney's office had given them so much more detail and all the puzzle pieces had fallen into one complete picture. He saw Garrett escorted out to the waiting car from his rearview mirror as he drove down the drive. Every puzzle piece had been linked and this last one, the hooded figure, was now sliding into the back of a federal sedan to be processed.

The case, this case in Kansas City was now closed. The mission had been completed.

Chapter Twenty-Eight

1. Only one wedding...Abby will finish up Friday and be in early Saturday morning
2. Agent Fullerton and Dev will pick me up at eight in the morning
3. Formal funeral, take lots of tissues
4. Wear waterproof makeup

After the church service, the cars formed a three-block line as they snaked their way to the cemetery with a full police escort. The church had been filled that Friday morning to give respect to a man many people knew as friend, as the gentle giant of the boulevard.

Big John was gone but not forgotten to so many and he had been exposed…as a hero. The news reports mentioned his heroic acts of protection, including a shoot out with a known hit man. There was no mention of drug activity but coincidentally the DEA was running a mission to shut down Cartel contacts in Kansas City at virtually the same time. Imagine that.

Lily didn't add much to the quiet conversations in the car. Agent Fullerton drove and occasionally Dev would look back at her from his place in the passenger seat. Usually he asked if she was fine or if she needed water. He'd already given her two bottles for the backseat. She watched the scenery go by and the occasional motorcycle officer who was directing the line.

She'd never been to a police funeral and she still wasn't sure she wanted to be there. The church service had been quite enough, complete with bag pipes blaring "Amazing Grace". She'd look to Dev now and then but his face gave nothing away. He had on his "hardened soldier" face.

Once the cars were parked at the cemetery, Dev helped her out of the car, offering a hand of assistance. It was going to be a long walk to the gravesite. She was cursing silently her choice in footwear, heeled tall boots. But he never let go of her hand as they walked across the grass and through the dry leaves of fall, holding hands like a real couple.

It wasn't until they stood across from the family on the other side of the casket that he released her hand to stand at attention. She realized this was the first time Dev had seen her dressed up with heels, makeup and a professional outfit of a pencil skirt, button down shirt and wrap sweater. He and Tom Fullerton were in their classic Secret Service dark suits, every wrinkle gone, every pleat pressed. She stood in between them. No longer was she a victim or someone to be protected. They were equals; they were friends.

While prayers were being said at the grave she noticed the similar military stances of both men, feet about a foot apart, hands clenched in front of them, sunglasses on the eyes to shield their views. She felt very safe. Of course all the police surrounding them didn't hurt either.

Oh no. There were officers lining up on the ridge for a gun salute and another with a trumpet. She couldn't stand the playing of "Taps". Its hollow, long notes meant death for her not goodnight. She wondered how many times the men standing on either side of her had heard that trumpet tribute.

John's wife and daughter sat on either side of his granddaughter. Her feet dangled in the air as she scooted forward on her chair. Usually her gaze was toward the casket and the hole in the ground but one time Lily saw her smile and wave. Dev broke attention and waved back.

Lily looked up at him but he didn't flinch. Why was John's granddaughter waving at him?

The clergyman was finished with his part of the service, now the police took over. Dev flinched at the first couple of shots. She watched from the corner of her eye. She could see every muscle tighten. His arms were now at his side. Lightly she touched the top of his hand and he reached around to hold her's in his. He never looked down at her but he needed that touch. "Taps" was played and his hold tightened. During the flag removal and folding, his right hand reached up in the sharpest salute she had ever seen. Tom Fullerton did the same, but she was mesmerized by Dev's actions. The flag was presented to John's wife and a few words ended the service.

Soon mourners were walking away and saying their final goodbyes to John. Others hugged his family. It remained quiet as the large crowd dispersed with hushed murmurs and stifled crying.

Tom moved away to speak to a high ranking police officer. Dev continued to hold her hand, finally asking if she was still fine. He removed his sunglasses with his other hand and placed them in his pocket.

Lily nodded. "I need to say something to her." She looked in the direction of John's wife.

"We'll go together."

They waited away from the gravesite until John's family was walking toward the funeral sedan. The littlest member came running to Dev, jumping up into his arms until her face was even with his.

"I knew it was you." She touched his face with both little hands as if she was making sure with her own physical examination.

"Well, hello, you," he smiled at her, shifting her weight for a better hold. John's wife smiled at Lily as she reached for her with both hands.

"Oh, honey, how are you?"

How could she ask how I was when she had lost her husband, Lily wondered. The two women hugged for several seconds. She introduced Lily to her daughter and explained the florist's relationship with her father.

All three women watched Angelica and her animated facial antics. She and her new-found friend were making popping noises with the sides of their cheeks. Dev stopped when he noticed their stares.

"You look nice today," Angelica told him.

Dev smiled. "You do too, sweetie. Pretty dress."

"Grandpa J likes this one." Her smile faded as she played with the crisp knot on his tie. "You sure he's with God, Dev?"

Now his smile vanished. "Yes, I know he is, angel. I do and he's going to watch over you." She gave him a soft kiss on his cheek.

"You mean when you're not around?"

He whispered in her ear. "Count on it."

The ladies waited patiently but it was time to go. Angelica squirmed a bit and Dev lightly placed her on the ground. She immediately bounded into her mother's arms.

Alise passed in front of him toward the car. "Thank you for all you did for us."

Dev nodded but said nothing. Lily suspected he couldn't. She saw him gulp a couple of times. He popped his watchband.

John's wife patted her arm. "It may take me a while but I'm going to visit your shop, Lily. We will stay in touch."

"Yes, we will." Lily gave her one more hug before releasing her. As she walked past Dev, she mouthed "thank you" to him and went on her way. The two of them were left looking at each other.

"Your case is closed now."

He shifted his weight back and forth. "Yes."

"So, now what?"

"More paperwork for me, a few more interviews for you, maybe a court case…" Dev was uncomfortable as the recipient of questions that needed answers. She was working her way up to a very large question, one that he couldn't answer. Thankfully, Tom joined them and it was time to go. It was time to drive away, take Lily back to her shop so she could go to work and way past time for him to go back to Washington DC. It was time to go home. The day had really come…the case was indeed over.

Chapter Twenty-Nine

1. Pack
2. Finish emails back to DC
3. Make sure Tom has everything he needs from me
4. Have receipts in order to turn in
5. Meet Aunt Pat for dinner

"Well, you're a thousand miles away already, Dev." His aunt eyed him suspiciously as he slid a drink coaster back and forth on the table. He hadn't looked up when the waiter brought their waters and menus.

"Did you say something?"

"Dev, what are you thinking about? Something about work?"

He picked up the menu and scanned the items. He knew when he walked into the grill he was going to have a steak tonight. He wasn't going to leave a city known for its meat before he had one.

"No, the case is over. Good guys won again." He stopped. Not all the good guys won.

Surprises didn't usually happen to him but Big John's duplicity had proved the exemption to the rule but he'd had his solid reasons. Winning gave way to disappointment in humankind. Again. John's betrayal of Lily's friendship infuriated him more than he could convey to her. When John placed her in danger, even to protect his family, it was inexcusable. Dev would never forget her voice on the phone the day she had made the discovery that they knew for weeks. She had sounded like a wounded animal, pitiful and fearful of what was to come. But when she figured out that she'd been the only one not aware of all the facts, she'd become an enemy with rightful grounds for her anger. Tom and he had weighed that so many times of what she would think when she finally found out, but they needed Lily to be Lily which meant she knew nothing of all the chess pieces moving on the board. The game had to be played to catch rooks, maybe even a king or queen.

The waiter returned to take their orders. Once that was completed, Dev returned focus on his water glass rather than his dinner guest.

"Devlin Pierce, what is going on? Don't tell me nothing."

His head shot up to look at her as though he was a five-year-old boy caught at the table passing food to the dog. For a brief second he had heard his mother's voice unwavering in a reprimand. Aunt Pat had her sister's tone when she was demanding attention. She had his now totally.

"I'm going to miss this city. It's hard to go back to DC when you've been somewhere, well normal."

She eyed him.

"Devlin Anthony Pierce, it is not the city. It's her isn't it?"

"I haven't thought about it that way."

Sometimes her nephew could be a complete idiot. She

knew he was intelligent or he would never have graduated from West Point and law school with honors. She knew he was a tough guy, managing to come home safe and fairly sound from deployment after deployment. But he could be denser than a concrete wall.

"Stop being so analytical and aloof. You know sometimes people do get together through their work environment. Your job is just a little more unusual than some with certainly different situations. It's so much easier to meet over the coffee pot, the copier or at the microwave. It's not like she's a murderer for heaven's sake."

He shook his head and shifted uncomfortably in his chair. He felt as though he would soon be interrogated. He'd leave before she grabbed a pitcher to waterboard him.

"It isn't that easy. She was a witness, a suspect, well not for long, a victim and it was my job to protect her. We used her and before she figured that out we had become friends."

"Hah," she laughed out loud as she crossed her arms over her chest. "Friends, is that what they're calling it now? You have some feelings for this girl, woman…how old is she? You're not robbing the cradle are you?"

He shook his head at the assumption. "I don't like your insinuation. She's over thirty and her birthday is December twelfth."

"So she knows who she is by now."

He rubbed his chin and leaned on the table with both elbows.

"You make it sound so simple. I'm not sure she does know who she is. She's a real enigma. She's confident in her work and unsure in her private life. She's smart but she makes these lists to remind herself of this or that and leaves post-it notes all over just in case she forgets or loses her list. She's so neurotic about those lists she's rubbed off on me and now I'm doing lists in my head." Dev sighed and continued.

"She's funny as hell and I haven't laughed so much in so long. And she gives as good as she gets. She knows something about everything; loves politics, music, theatre and sports. She even know's sports. It's a man's dream."

He stopped short of saying anything more after that admission. He could tell his aunt was seeing right through all of his smoke and mirrors rhetoric, of course she was his mother's sister. Damn genetics.

Aunt Pat came closer across the table and took both of his hands in hers. The intimacy made him nervous. He wouldn't be able to lie to her now. "Devlin, is she your dream? For so long you've been doing everything for your family, your friends, your country. Maybe it's time for you to do something for you."

He removed himself from the closeness to toy with his water glass. "I don't know. Really. She is a surprise and nothing I was looking for and someone very unexpected. I mean, she's not even my type."

"What a snob you are, boy! My gosh, do you think I was ever looking for an early balding pudgy insurance salesman? No, I wanted Ed John, an all-American basketball player so I could wear heels and still have him loom over me. But I fell in love with a man who was three inches shorter than me and had a BMI that was over the limits for his age from the time he was twenty-one. You know what I did? I threw away all my heels. He always said the more he loved me, the more insurance he sold so it was a win, win."

She looked away, fighting back the tears and pushing them aside with her hand. "I bought a pair of heels last month, finally, but I had to return them because I couldn't walk in them. I miss that man every single second, minute, hour, day and more at night than you could possibly imagine. I slept next to him all those years and sometimes in the middle of the night I wake up, still hearing him snoring. I'd give anything to hear that sound again, to be woke up in the middle of the night so I could throw a pillow at him."

Aunt Pat turned to look him straight in the eyes. "Devlin Pierce, when you find love you don't see the facade, you see the heart and the soul. This woman has gotten to you."

"But she's not my type."

"Why not?" This truly was a full investigation by Aunt INC.

"Well, she's short and barely comes to my shoulders and then there's her hair. It's short and curly and I love a woman with long hair. I never know if her eyes are green or brown, mostly because her lashes are so thick I can't see them. She has a nice nose, lips, short neck and she's not athletic at all."

Aunt Pat was completely disgusted. Her sister would've kicked him in the shins by now. "So, the kids will have you for all that hiking and running stuff."

He laughed nervously. What was the woman thinking? "I think you're getting way ahead of yourself."

What had he become that he couldn't see what was obviously right in front of him?

"And I think you're a coward. I never thought I'd see the

day when a highly decorated former special forces soldier would shy away from someone who might have the ability to offer him a life he always wanted. It sounds like you two are compatible from what you've told me before. Is she too much over the top, a talker, a whiner?"

"No, don't be silly. She has complained some through this ordeal but she's had the right. She was angry when we used her trusting nature. When we were together we could be silent. It used to be uncomfortable but now the silence is a soothing feeling. It feels natural."

Their steaks came. If meat could be beautiful then they would have won the pageant.

Briefly, he was allowed to dig in, swallowing only food, not his pride.

"I know you've lost your mom and some of your friends. You don't talk about your time in the Army and you certainly haven't shared your feelings about your mom. So, I just want you to consider one thing."

He kept eating but he was listening. Her tone was softer, not judgmental at his obvious discrimination based on the looks of someone.

"If you heard tonight she had been hurt, or worse killed, would your life be changed in any way? That's it. I want to enjoy the rest of the night with you, maybe let's go to a movie. But just think about it."

Dev placed his knife and fork on the plate and took a swallow of water.

"A movie sounds good. I appreciate your concern," he paused setting his glass down, "and I've wondered that same thing almost since the moment I met her. I'm not sure I could go on knowing she wasn't here in Kansas City in that little flower shop making those brides happy every weekend. Happy?" He'd had those feelings the night he saw her in the rain, sitting on a sidewalk, her world turned upside down.

Aunt Pat smiled. "Delighted. I would love some non-athletic, plain looking great nieces and nephews. They'll remind me of my husband."

A couple of customers stared at him as his laughter filled the restaurant. He looked out the window to see Lily's car rounding the corner but she wasn't looking into the building. She had flowers in the back and this time really was on a delivery. She'd passed him by and didn't know it. He didn't like how that felt at all.

Chapter Thirty

1. Find special ribbon for Jordan wedding
2. Have Abby work a few extra hours Friday
3. Do buckets and prep work
4. Change window decor... Thanksgiving will be here!
5. Set up appointment to look at drip on back faucet
6. Make sure I get some sleep

Lily pushed the buttons on the security pad automatically. She was a robot this Monday.

She looked wistfully down the sidewalk, half expecting John to saunter down, greeting her with a much needed caramel macchiato. She wiped back a tear as she looked down and saw the discolored concrete. How long would that be there?

Lights and computer were turned on and she listened to the phone messages while she put her lunch in the fridge. There were a couple of calls to return but it would soon be her down time. It was cool every morning now and she couldn't wait to wear sweaters and leggings daily.

She went to the front of the store to check on the door when she saw Devlin Pierce walking up the sidewalk from the parking lot. He looked like a federal agent today with those blasted sunglasses, polished shoes and a sedate blue tie. He stood out like a shining light wearing the brightest white fitted shirt. He looked like he belonged in some romance novel, the soldier who returns from serving his country to the states where he serves his country. He meets woman after woman until he meets “that one” and she means everything to him. They would live happily every after until the terrorists tracked him down, kidnapped his love and wrecked havoc on their perfect world.

Really, Lily, she asked herself. The reality was that she hadn’t seem him since the funeral. She could still remember the final news account…

"The FBI, in coordination with the DEA, have ended a sting operation to stop a cartel shipment of drugs from reaching the open market in the Kansas City area. Several area businesses were integral in assisting the federal agencies.” She could still see Gretchen holding those two bags like she was the new model in a hand lotion commercial.

She opened the door. “Hello stranger.”

He was close enough she could smell his light cologne. Removing his sunglasses, he looked into her eyes. “I’m sorry. I’ve been busy wrapping this all up and making a few changes. May I come in?”

Lily waved him in. “I don’t suppose you brought me coffee?”

“I thought about it.” His words lingered on the air and they both knew that the other was thinking about that discolored sidewalk out front.

He sat down in one of the consultation chairs. “I wanted to say goodbye and thank you again. We really couldn’t have done it without you. Seriously. You were our rock star.”

She sat down, actually, fell like a brick. It was over. Her

daydreams and thoughts could now be put away like an overly used book with its pages weathered and torn.

Dev saw something in her face. Perhaps it was fear, disappointment or simmering anger? He needed a translator to understand Lily. Like with any foreign language, there were times of understanding but then someone would speak too quickly and lose you in mid-sentence. He was lost in this silence.

"Lily, I'll stay in touch. You may see Tom now and then and frankly, he loves stopping in to see you and Abby. His wife loves the flowers." He was using the word love too many times.

She stared at him blankly. What did she want or need to say to him? That she cared for him? That she loved him? Her last relationship had been such a disaster. Dev was just doing his job all along. Put this case in the file cabinet and move on.

"Lily, say something, please," he finally pleaded. He couldn't take the silence, the hurt he was now seeing clearly.

"Goodbye."

Dev sucked in air at that one word. He stood up to leave. Robot woman stood as well, walking past him to reach for the door to show him out.

"Agent Pierce, I won't say it was a pleasure but it was very nice meeting you, and to know you. Thank you for all you did for me. Tell Agent Fullerton that his wife will love my leftovers... they have no calories."

He saw professional Lily, the one who could be crying and screaming on the inside but telling the bride exactly what she wanted to hear on the outside. She had hated lying but he had taught her the skill of artful omission and she had become an exceptional student. She was punishing him and rightly so. She was moving on and so was he. It would be easier this way. For both of them. But was this really want he wanted?

"I'll tell him. Take care. I've got to catch a plane back today so I better get going." He extended his hand to shake hers. Awkwardly, she moved one hand from the door and the other to his, lightly touching his hand. She felt that warmth again.

"Bye now." She was pushing him out the door like an appointment that had lasted too long.

He looked back once, shaking his head, slowly making his way to his car.

No more twinkling eyes, no more sudden heatwave whenever he touched her for any odd reason. You have a busy week making everybody else happy.

"I want to be happy," she yelled out loud. She refused to cry. She needed to go to work.

She began on the emails. Mrs. Carson wanted to make her corsage into a wrist. The wedding for the first part of December was wondering if the church would be decorated for Christmas.

There was a text on her phone…from Dev.

"Lily, I will miss you and I want to stay in touch. You weren't just a damsel in distress."

Her hands began to shake. She didn't know if she could just be friends with this man, if that's what he wanted. She wasn't sure what she wanted right now.

"Lord, what should I do?" She looked up in prayer and ignored the text.

Sitting in his car with the engine running, Devlin Pierce was completely dumbfounded. He had been summarily dismissed as if it were his final day at a very bad job. Basically, the boss had told him to get out, nice knowing you, we're done now, scoot. But he didn't want to be gone.

On the way over to Lily's he had made a list in his head. Saying goodbye had not been on it.

Instead, Lily had built a wall hiding what she really wanted. He couldn't climb it, at least not today. He pulled the car out of the lot and began driving to the airport. As he drove through the Country Club Plaza, he sighed. He really was going to miss walking those streets, the food and the people. He was headed back to traffic, politics and everyone knotted into never-ending circles. By the time he turned in his rental and shuttled to KCI, he'd almost stopped making lists in his mind. But he couldn't shake number one on the list. He'd meant to kiss her goodbye.

He hadn't been her knight in shining armor, nor had she been the damsel in distress.

Dev took the Metro from Reagan to the Alexandria, Virginia station, walking the three blocks to his townhouse. He turned the key and opened the door to another planet. There was a stack of sorted mail on the coffee table. His Dad had taken care of all that and considering the clean smell in the home, his maid service had made sure everything else was in order.

Everything was in just the right space, clean and orderly. It was an analogy of his life prior to this investigation, until Lily. She'd made a mess of everything. She'd come into his life like a tornado throwing everything he knew before her around in circles. But more than that, she'd attacked his heart and made him feel.

He looked around. It was a beautiful thing to have order, no stacks of unread magazines or Elmo slippers residing near the door. There were no post-it notes. He peered over to the kitchen with its bare countertops. His wood floors were shiny, his sink glistened.

It was time for him to embrace the obvious. He missed her. He missed her humor, conversation, her endless post-it notes and lists and he missed those eyes.

Lily's eyes held her world in them. They had been convincing today, leading him to believe she'd always be there on the boulevard in her little shop, arranging flowers and fulfilling dreams come true.

Funny, he'd never heard any of her plans for a day of her own, almost as though she weren't worthy of a "day of her life".

He took a sip of red wine and licked it from his lips. The television was on and he faced it but he wasn't watching. Still thinking of Lily, he took a larger drink.

What would she look like as a bride? What would her gown look like? He'd only seen her in a dress a couple of times. She was very professional at the funeral.

But what would she do with that hair? She'd have to get married in the winter to have any chance of keeping it in place. The veil would cover it. Undoubtedly she wouldn't be wearing heels.

There was a photo in the shop that proved she'd had a life with heels, makeup and longer hair. Lily stood in the middle of several friends, drinks in hands, wearing a black turtleneck, fitted jeans and hair that swept away from her face hitting at her shoulders. She was thinner, wearing black boots with heels. Her smile as wide as her face had drawn his attention to the wall where the photo hung by her desk. Her face shined.

Now she was basic Lily. Had she put that other girl in a box and shoved her into storage forever? Would he have liked that girl as much as he liked this one?

He downed the remaining wine and stood up. It was time to go to bed. He needed to be into work early in the morning. As he began the steps to his bedroom he was thinking about her again. He was seeing those lips.

He cussed out loud. He hadn't even kissed her.

Over a week later, Dev had started his run as the sun was coming up. Even though it was a Saturday morning, he couldn't sleep in, frankly he hadn't slept. Last night he'd spent a quiet, restless evening reading the newest spy novel until he decided around midnight to turn off the lights. He laid there listening to the wind blow through one of the few trees on his block. Around three he walked downstairs to get a drink of water and to look outside. He grabbed the book and went back to bed, this time the reading finally putting him to sleep. He'd forgotten to shut off his alarm and woke at five. He gave up in his attempt at slumber a half hour later.

Usually, Alexandria would be waking up but this was the weekend. You saw mostly runners, a few walkers and bikers and those neighbors standing like the walking dead as their dog sniffed around for just the right place to relieve itself. The coffee shop was open. He stopped, grabbed a newspaper and a coffee. By the time he left, the world was coming alive and he felt like a run down the parkway.

Serious runners and those just looking good used the parkway that wound near the Potomac River and finally dumped into the Memorial Bridge area. When Dev had briefly served at the Pentagon he'd become used to the breathtaking scenery of the Jefferson, Lincoln and Washington Memorials not to mention the Kennedy Center and Georgetown all along the path.

As he came back through the older area of Alexandria he saw an area florist loading the van for the day. The huge sprays were all white with greenery, roses and those ever-popular hydrangeas. At least now he knew what they were. Dev looked at his watch. Lily was probably loading her own van right now.

He thought about her quite a bit when it was quiet. He laughed out loud every time he clicked on the television and found Jessica Fletcher solving another murder mystery. What a nosy writer! That woman had the gall to insert herself into cases over and over. She always figured it out. She was always impeccably dressed and not one hair was ever mussed.

He missed seeing Lily's hair curl up as the humidity rose. He missed their conversations, the laughter, her questions and uncertainty…he missed her. His aunt called him a coward and maybe he was. He definitely was running away from something.

He pulled up less than half of a block away from his home. His father's car was parked outside. He bent over placing his hands on his legs. His breath was visible on the air and it seemed to be turning colder. Thanksgiving was next week.

"Damn." His father was here to have the mandatory turkey family day talk or as he preferred to call it talking turkey, his father's own interpretation of a holiday inquisition. You going to be in town this year? Do you think you can make it this time? We missed you last year and the year before, so are you coming this time?

Dev raised up sighing. So many holidays had passed. He wasn't sure he knew how to sit around a table and share a meal, enjoying the company of genetic relatives. He'd sat at other tables over the years in Iraq and Afghanistan, at his turkey, steak and lobster, visiting briefly with his brothers in arms and even a president once. He was finishing his pumpkin pie when George W. Bush entered the hall for a surprise visit. Dev was picking up his plate when the President came next to him, bringing his own tray.

"If you can, sit back down." Dev made time.

Family was different for some reason. Oh, he knew the reason. Death had taken the heart of their family. He put on a smile and entered his own house with caution.

"Hey Dad," he yelled as he came through the front door. He could hear him in the kitchen making coffee.

"In here." Dev was already standing at the edge of the kitchen. "Boy, you look tired."

Dev came beside him to wait for the warm liquid. "Long run this morning. You need milk?"

"No, I'm good. I brought something unhealthy." He opened the white box next to him to offer doughnuts.

Dev brought out a couple of plates and loaded three onto his before offering the plate to his father. "This will do me."

"Well, you did run. I can't do that anymore at my age."

Dev shrugged. "Oh believe me, I can't either. Age is catching up with me."

They sat down in the living room, his father across from him in the leather chair. The doughnut eating offered silence but he could feel his father watching him. The questioning was about to commence but the doughnuts were too good to escape.

His father eyed him closely as Dev took a drink of coffee. He might as well get it started so it could end.

"What?"

"You didn't get back with that socialite, did you?"

Dev hadn't expected that beginning volley. "What? No, not her." His dad saw something.

"Not her? Hmmm, someone else?"

Silence was the better part of valor besides, what was there to say? He enjoyed working on weddings? That he'd found his creative side?

"I don't know." He really didn't, did he?

"Where'd you meet her?"

Dev relaxed a little. His father never seemed this interested in his personal life so he'd play along for a bit. He smiled. "On an investigation out of town."

"She's not in jail, is she?"

Dev laughed out loud. "No, Dad."

"Oh thank God." His voice expressed relief. "When do we all meet her?" Dev took a final drink, placing his cup on the coffee table.

"I don't know. I'm not sure what I want to do about her."

"What does she want to do?"

Dev was stymied. There was so much between them—mileage, professions, silence and unrequited feelings.

"Dad, I, she, we," he was stammering. "I have no idea. We haven't talked about being a couple. We have a good time but we're friends."

His father shook his head. Here was his highly accomplished son who didn't have a clue about life and living stammering like a fearful child.

"Dev, sometimes I think that by the time you figure out what you want it might be too late. For someone who goes full tilt into danger, killing all those dragons around the world, you sure don't take any chances with your heart. Don't end up alone, please."

The last word hurt Dev. His father was alone now but at least he'd had a family and a life with a wonderful woman.

"Is there something wrong with the woman? Is she a little off or of a different culture? Do you hate her values? What?"

"No, nothing like that, Dad, she's just not the type of woman, well Aunt Pat said I was being a snob."

Jack Pierce laughed out loud.

"She's probably right but I'd say you're a jackass. Not your type? I just knew I was going to marry Cheryl Ladd or Lynda Carter. One was blonde, the other a brunette and neither knew I was alive. I ended up with your mother and her curly light red hair that made her look like little orphan Annie when she was caught out in the rain. Remember how frizzy her hair got in the humidity?"

"Yes." Dev was thinking of someone else's hair and becoming very uncomfortable in the process.

"And your mother was so short. I was always getting stuff for her out of the high cabinets. She was so slim and then she had you kids and she never was again. Remember, I was going to live with Charlie's Angel or Wonder Woman but I ended up with your mom. I never regretted that my plan was changed by her plan." He could see his son was thinking, hopefully listening.

"I'm sure your aunt was better suited to give you advice but maybe you need to give yourself a break, maybe let this woman show you who she is and who you two could be together."

His father stared into his coffee cup. "You know I haven't told anyone this but there's times in the house that I hear her in the morning, making breakfast and humming that song…"I Could Of Danced All Night". There's nothing more disappointing than walking into an empty kitchen. I miss her every day, Dev."

They both shared a moment of silence.

"Dev, can you two sit in a room in complete silence knowing each other is there with no need to talk?"

Dev nodded affirmatively. "Can you laugh together?" He nodded again.

"It's easy to walk away when you don't care but it's so hard when you do. I see you feel for her, but you're not shallow, son, you just might be in love."

His dad stood up, grabbed both of their cups and took

them to the kitchen, returning with his jacket in his hand.

"I've said more today than I have in years so I'm shutting up now, except are you coming for Thanksgiving?"

Dev looked up. The question had finally been asked. "If I'm in town." His dad patted him on the back on his way out. "Good enough."

Dev sat silently in his car. He was continuing to stare at the front door of his parents' home. But it wasn't his parents' home any longer. It was his Dad's house. It was the place where he had lived as a kid. With Mom not there it just wasn't the same structure, nor was their family but Dad was trying. He was trying too. This would be his first Thanksgiving at home in years. After Mom died the family time diminished significantly for all of them, not just in his absence but maybe that had something to do with it.

He sighed out loud. He wasn't beyond saying that he helped to separate a very close family.

He was sure that they worried about him constantly, even now. His Dad would remark "you know you can get hurt even in the Reserves and with the DEA" and he would admit to him there was always that possibility. Heck, he'd almost crashed three times on I-95 just this morning.

Driving was dangerous, flying was dangerous, walking and running on the street was dangerous and Dev knew that you didn't have to be a soldier to have something happen to you one day, to never return home that afternoon from work.

He looked down at his phone and opened the contact list. He hit Lily's name and stopped before the call went through. He texted instead. He didn't want to interrupt her holiday, one of the very few she actually celebrated with a day off. If she had a wedding tomorrow she'd probably start working sometime tonight.

"Lily, just thinking about you and hoping you're taking some time off today. Enjoy. Happy Thanksgiving."

Short, direct, meaningless but that's not what he was feeling. He'd been lying to himself for a couple of months now and his Dad's words the other day brought the truth to the surface. He was frightened of Lily Schmidt and how she could single-handedly dissect his heart, insert feelings, close it up and send him on his way to recuperate alone. His fear broadened when he thought about a life with her; the fear grew when he thought of a life without her.

Maybe she didn't care about him? He'd pushed her away so many times along the way claiming his job was in the way. Finally, she shut the door on him. Obviously he'd given her mixed signals, heck he didn't know what he was doing. She had too. He saw the looks she gave him, could feel the heat when they touched.

She was nothing he wanted but she was all he wanted.

"Crap," he said loudly. He grabbed the bread from the passenger seat and finally got out of his car. It was the easiest contribution he could make to the dinner.

He walked slowly up the sidewalk and stood at the front door. His hand was on the doorknob when his phone buzzed. His Dad opened the door at the same time and stared at him blankly.

"I'll take the bread, you answer the phone."

"Damn." He looked up at his father and held out the phone as though it was the object of his very own destruction.

"Dad, the text, I'm so sorry. I've got to go. I've just been called in." His father's eyelids shut as if he were in prayer. He nodded. "Devlin, come in and say hello."

"Dad, I've got thirty minutes to get there."

"I understand. Stop debating, come in, wave and leave. I'll explain to everyone. Please."

And that's exactly what he did. He was running back down the sidewalk to his car in less than five minutes.

Chapter Thirty-One

1. Check with Abby and Jeremy about Saturday's deliveries
2. Make sure Neal has red roses
3. Spend time in a nice warm bubble bath and have a glass of wine
4. Try not to dwell on another birthday
5. Try not to think about HIM

Lily was processing the red roses that had just arrived when Abby entered for the day. "Hey boss, what needs to go?"

Lily pointed to the four arrangements on the back counter. "Here's the order sheet and make sure the cards are attached. You can deliver now."

"Didn't we do the daughter's wedding last year?" Abby studied the name on one of the cards.

Lily nodded. "Yes. Remember, her dad had a heart attack two days before the wedding and was in the hospital the day of? That was so sad. He was looking forward to his only daughter's wedding day. Well, he lasted another year."

"Oh and by the way, Jeremy and I can take those deliveries Saturday, no problem."

"Oh good. I can have a weekend with my sister then." Lily's sister usually didn't come into town by herself but she was participating as godmother for one of her best friend's children. "Beth and I are going to celebrate my birthday with a spa session on Saturday. She has the baptism on Sunday and has to be at the airport by three. We'll have just enough time to enjoy without getting sick of each other."

"And then she's back to Virginia? Near some agent?" Abby giggled. When she saw Lily's glare she didn't continue. You did not poke the boss. Besides, she knew Lily was struggling with the few emails and texts from him now and then and the occasional voice messages on the shop's phone. He always hoped she was doing well.

About the time Abby began to pick up the first arrangement for delivery, the shop's door opened.

"Hi there." It was a delivery man from Prescott's Bouquets carrying an enormous bouquet of white hydrangeas. "Do you all believe this is a flower delivery for a florist?"

"Who's it for?" Abby went to the front to grab the flowers. What was Jeremy, her perfect little idiot thinking, sending her flowers?

"The card says Lily Schmidt. You all have a nice day." He handed the full bouquet over into Abby's hands.

"Oh boss, you have a gift for your birthday."

Lily finished her work with the bucket of water and the roses and wiped her hand on a towel. What had her sister done? She looked into the shop and saw the large arrangement. Really, Elizabeth? Flowers?

"There's a card."

"Fine. I'm coming." If Beth wasted money on these she would wonder where her head was these days and that wouldn't predict an enjoyable weekend as planned.

"December birthdays are junk," Lily admitted as she grabbed the flowers. They were exquisite and they must have cost a fortune from Prescott's. That shop always did the high priced charity events and most of the Kansas City society functions.

She placed them on the counter and read the card. "Lily Schmidt, Happy Birthday."

"So? Did Elizabeth send them?" Abby couldn't stand the anticipation as she watched Lily pull the insert card out. Lily said nothing, just staring at the card for a few minutes.

"Beth didn't send them. Agent Pierce did."

"Shut the door!" Abby clapped in delight. "He remembered your birthday and that you've never received flowers on your birthday. Of course, he could've just pulled a file and found your day." That statement prompted another glare. "What did he write on the card? Come on, you have to share."

Lily smiled at her assistant. "Yes, I suppose I do just to keep you quiet. I mean, these are beautiful. He wrote…you deserve the best so I'm sending you my mother's favorite flowers. Happy birthday. I miss you more than you know. Dev…"

"He misses you, and remember when he lied about his mom's favorite flowers when he didn't have a clue what a hydrangea was? What a crack up. And this is the first time you're getting flowers, and from him?"

Lily nodded. She'd never told anyone that except him. He'd remembered her secret. When she'd told him the information had just slipped carelessly in conversation but he had made it important, and now he had solved the injustice.

"It's a good birthday this year. I'm good." Lily decided if she kept reciting those positive statements they might become her reality.

Chapter Thirty-Two

1. Begin New Year...eat healthy, exercise, start compiling tax info
2. Inventory all vases
3. Email Abby schedule
4. Two consultations Tuesday and Wednesday
5. Stop by store...need milk

During the winter, Abby only worked a few hours here and there leaving Lily fairly on her own. They had a wedding in a couple of weeks but for now she was alone in the store. Income was always tight during the winter and this year was proving to not be the exception. She usually did a few deliveries here and there, Valentine's Day arrangements and the occasional funeral work but her bread and butter weddings really didn't begin again until after Easter. It was a vicious cycle one that made her happy for the time off and neurotic because of the time off.

Her lists were fairly short in January, most of the time jotted on post-it notes stuck to the calendar. As she sat at her computer her mind wandered more than worked. She was thinking about him.

Dev had called her Christmas Eve on her cell phone to wish her a Merry Christmas. He sounded tired. He said he'd been out of the country and hoped she'd received her birthday flowers. She thanked him for the thoughtful gift and the joke hydrangeas but he did admit they really were his mom's favorites, he just hadn't known what they looked like.

They talked for almost thirty minutes, like a comfortable couple who knew each other very well. Abby was thrilled he had asked about her and Jeremy and was actually happy to hear they were still together. He wondered if Fullerton had kept in touch and she was happy to report he was a weekly customer. The FBI agent had even brought a large tin of popcorn in for the holidays on a day when Abby and she really needed it. She told him how pretty the city was right now and he admitted he wanted to see the Plaza at Christmas sometime. He'd even said maybe next year.

"So you are fine now?"

"I am. I had a good end of year and now it's pretty slow. That's usual."

"No, not talking about work, Lily."

She'd pushed back a few tears when he had asked her that with such concern. She cleared her throat before answering.

"Yes. I'm glad that this year is almost over. Hopefully this new one will be better."

"When are you visiting your sister up here?"

"Not sure yet."

"Well, I want to see you when you do. I could even pick you up from the airport if I'm in town."

She really wanted to see him. She wasn't sure when the anger over the secrets, lies and being used left her. Her head understood why he did what he did but it had been harder for her heart to catch up. Apparently, it was doing just that.

"You know, Dev, I'd really like that."

"Well, we'll do it then. But I have some trips coming up so don't plan anything until May." She couldn't do May, nor anytime after that until the end of the year.

"I'll email you when I'm thinking about it and you can tell me if you'll be around." They really were just talking as friends. Her heart hurt but her head was content if that was the only relationship they were to have. What an idiot she had been that last time she'd seen him. She could've at least hugged him, kissed him on the cheek for all he had done for her. She would miss him in her life even if that relationship would only be friendship.

"That's all we can do, keep trying. Better let you go. Mass tonight, right?"

"Yes, Christmas Eve. I'll sleep in tomorrow and drop in at Patsy and John's around one in the afternoon. They're having Italian and have invited me."

"You know so many people. Remind me again who they are."

"Patsy, the cake lady and her husband John, the one with the horses. You talked to him about engineering when we were decorating the cake at the Hilton."

"Nice couple. He knew his stuff. He should be retired now. Tell them hello. Is the weather good enough for you to drive all the way out there?"

His amazing memory was one thing she didn't know if she would ever get used to. John had just retired a few weeks ago and their house and stables were a good hour drive south of Kansas City.

"No snow or ice here in fact it looks like tomorrow will be in the fifties. Little chilly today but I can wear a new sweater and that makes me happy."

"Good. You're prettiest when you're happy. Merry Christmas, Lily. I'll talk to you soon."

"Sure." He had said she was pretty and better when she was happy. Had she been happy with him?

"You have a good Christmas too and be careful," Lily muttered. Her voice was catching. "Thank you so much for calling. You made my Christmas." Lord, she sounded like she was talking to a client.

"One of the best things that has happened to me, Lily, in the last few years was that drug case in Kansas City. I want you to know that meeting you was something I hadn't expected. You know, we both plan things, sometimes we over plan. You were such a surprise. You mean a lot to me and I hope this year we can really stay in touch."

Lily could tell he was carefully parsing each word. He was attempting to tell some sort of truth but it was muddled by some uncertainty.

She had to relieve his pain. "I value our friendship too." "I'll talk to you soon."

This was painful. "Bye, Dev." And he was gone.

Lily focused on the computer. It was now a new year and he was still gone.

Chapter Thirty-Three

1. Get a coffee and just breathe
2. Lunch with Abby
3. Close the shop for the rest of the week
4. Church tonight...go early to get a seat

It was a beautiful Holy Thursday complete with a Cinderella blue dress colored sky with fluffy white marshmallow clouds and a warm sun that announced that spring was in full swing. Winter had been winter. As that season left, the bridal season would begin right after Easter and she wouldn't have time to breath like she did today. After finishing lunch with Abby and completing a few tasks she needed to get done, Lily closed the shop's door and put on the security code. As her finger planted on the key pad she shook off the memory of her friend dying in the street on that rainy night.

Multiple snows and de-ice treatments had turned the concrete where John had laid back to its normal color. Normal? It would never be truly normal again. She looked down the sidewalk and saw the open table at the coffee shop. John wouldn't be waiting. She still missed his common sense approach to life and that huge smile that made her feel so secure, until that night. She knew there was so much more to the story of his involvement but she had never pushed with nosy questions. Part of her really didn't want to know. Some day maybe, but not today.

With Lent almost over it was time to treat herself to a caffeinated beverage (she would never give up caffeine for forty days again) and to sit outside enjoying the almost perfect day. Was there ever a perfect day and would there ever be one again?

Actually life was fairly quiet. The wedding season would bring a storm of clients and dilemmas but she could weather just about any storm after last year's problems. Almost a year of uncertainty, danger and the multitude of questions that had come with every day had been too much in her little organized life. She used to be so sure of herself. She always acted that way in front of the rest of the world. That night at the hotel she had realized that deep inside where no one could see she was a ball of unintended nerves and unbalanced decisions. Had she kept any of those resolutions she'd made? She had wanted so much more for her life.

She sipped her coffee, breathed in deeply and saluted John heaven-bound with her cup. As she watched people drive by, she could hear the conversation at the other table. The lovely blonde was complaining that her professor just didn't understand her spirit…really? Was there ever a professor who understood your spirit? Maybe in Berkeley but not in Missouri. Gosh, college was a long time ago. She wasn't even in the career she had planned all those years ago.

Most days she didn't think about the "what ifs" like the path not taken or the man not married. She had thought she would be an editor for a large newspaper or maybe teach history to eager high schoolers. Maybe she had chosen wisely. As far as the man not married, looking back on her past serious relationship, she'd known from the beginning it wasn't going to work. Put another star in her decision making skills column.

She owned her own business. She was successful in Kansas City, a small ever-growing pond with lots of big fish who kept trying to devour the smaller fish who just kept swimming in the crashing waves. She was living comfortably despite income being tight now and then.

Personally, she was alone, not lonely but there were those nights when she thought of him, of Dev. She was better with Agent Devlin Pierce, even Abby had mentioned it at lunch.

Something was missing without him and those twinkling eyes. Even danger was better with Dev.

She'd received a message from him the other day when she had been out of the shop making deliveries. He had just left a short "hello, just checking on you" message that sounded more like a mandatory phone call than a chance to talk to her. He should've called the cell but he didn't. It was a call made out of duty, his responsibility to check in on her. He was duty-bound.

That awful responsibility gene! She also had it oozing in her DNA. She was tired of how it programmed her life. This wasn't the life she was meant to have but now there was no getting out of it, really. She had clients, she had bills, she had stuff! She couldn't just pack up, leave and head out on some nomadic route.

"Breathe," she muttered out loud as she looked up to the sky. But everyone else had left. Her mother and father had passed away, her brother had moved first and then her sister. She still had aunts and cousins here but that was it. Maybe she saw them once a year and talked to a couple every other week. Her friends had all begun families and had no time for the only single woman in the group. "Drop by when you can," they'd say but they didn't tell you what time or day of the week. She understood what it meant… move on, we're too busy with our lives to be part of yours.

She had resolved to change and some days she did like today. She refused to allow her life to be all about work from now on. The break today was just a small step in a new path. It was almost four in the afternoon by the time Lily left the outside table and headed home for a little dinner. The light on her landline was blinking. She hit the button expecting to hear the dulcet tone of the robot caller…do you have unexpected bills and need assistance from the federal government…instead it was Dev.

"Hi Lily. I've been away working. I'll try to catch you this weekend. Take care." Ah, it was the duty bound check-in call.

"Take care? That's it?" Lily yelled at the machine. "Say something else, Agent Pierce!"

But there was nothing else. She listened to the message one more time and then hit erase. Why didn't he just call her cell? She knew why…she would answer that! She wasn't going to waste any more time over this man. She was in her thirties. She didn't have the luxury of fawning over some man until he decided she was the one. They had something. She thought it was love. Her breathing always stopped when she heard his voice but maybe it was desperation for a kind of future she wasn't meant to have.

She was alone, on her own. She just needed to get used to

that and stop wasting tears and thoughts on a life that was never going to happen. She would end up a fifty-something wedding florist making other women's dreams come true, never even revisiting her own again. She was done wasting time. Yet, she'd had such resolve and hope just a few hours earlier.

God and she were going to have a little talk tonight.

Lily arrived at church early. You didn't just show up right before Holy Thursday services and expect to sit down. There would be a throng of people, usually the same familiar parishioners who attended the very solemn celebration of the first last supper. She enjoyed the quiet, the reverence of the atmosphere. Eventually the organ music began softly. She closed her eyes and continued to pray.

Holy Week had always been special for her since childhood. She'd told Dev how her mom and she spent hours in church that one week of the liturgical year. Her mother had preferred Good Friday and its solemn hours of prayer but Lily's favorite was tonight. Yes, it was the same every year, with the same readings and almost always the same music, but it was always a new beginning. It was the ebb and flow of the Christian tidal wave; the history of the Church in all its magnificence. There was peace in knowing that the tragedy of the crucifixion brought the mystery of the resurrection. Winter brought spring, sin brought forgiveness and maybe, just maybe this year God would bring her an answer to her depressing questions. Maybe she would have that new beginning.

The lights were dimmed a bit as the singers took their positions. It was time to begin. It was time for the self-reflection to stop and the focus on the Lord to begin. Self pity wasn't an option when you were looking up at a cross, at a man who died for your sins. Lily felt like a piece of garbage when she thought about it that way. Catholic guilt was indeed a powerful energy.

As the priest began the service, the congregation rose in unison. The church was packed but people were still trying to move into the full pews. Lily was still trying to talk to God about her dilemma when she felt someone move into the pew next to her. As she moved her bag off the cushion and placed it under the pew, she never missed a note of singing. There was one more hymnal in front of her and she just picked it up and handed it to the individual next to her. His hand touched hers as she finally looked over to see a familiar military college ring.

"I knew you'd be here," Dev whispered.

Lily stopped singing. She turned fully to peer into those green twinkling eyes and couldn't speak, physically couldn't utter a word. She thought she heard a voice from heaven. "You're welcome, Lily. Now stop whining."

"Close your mouth, Ms. Schmidt unless you're going to sing."

Instantly she turned back to her hymnal and tried to find her place. She discovered she couldn't sing either. Lord, was this a dream? She glanced to the left again. He was still standing next to her. He had his "agent" looking suit on but no tie. He wasn't singing either. He glanced toward her and smiled.

He just smiled. He was tan. Where had he been? Why was he here now? This was the nicest surprise since her sister had tied balloons on her sports car one birthday morning. Was this an answer to all her questions or was it just the beginning of more questions? Really, she didn't care. She just cared that he was next to her at this very moment. Stop planning, Lily, just live.

Apparently it was time to sit down. This fog of a dream allowed peeks of movement around her but physically she could feel the reality of his shoulder up against her own.

"What are you doing here?" she whispered.

"Going to church with you."

She couldn't take her eyes off of him. Lily had never been this distracted in church. He seemed different but maybe it was because she wasn't a crime victim anymore. Why would he be here? Had something happened and they were back to square one with their case?

Dumbfounded was a meek representation of what she was feeling.

"Not work. I'm off for a few days," he finally answered as he looked directly into her eyes. He reached over and took her hand in his. "I had a change of plans and I made a new list. At the top of that list was you. I came back for you."

Lily was transfixed at their interlocking hands. He was smiling warmly at her and at her only.

He raised their hands up and softly kissed hers before laying it back down. "Did you hear me?"

She nodded. "You made a list. That's beautiful."

He had to stifle his laughter but he watched as a tear trailed down her cheek. Lily didn't know why or how this was happening but she wasn't dreaming. There were hundreds of people around with their presence telling her this was indeed real. It was becoming the most real night of her life.

The services continued but he never let go of her hand. The contact that used to be an intense fire was now a warmth transforming her doubts.

At times they had to release their hands but then his hand slid to her back. It made her feel like they were really together. Lily took a breath and released it slowly. Finally, she wasn't alone. He was there for her. He came back for her. There was not one "to do" racing through her thoughts. There was only peace, finally.

At the end of the service, the officiant explained that everyone should leave in silence.

Usually that wouldn't be a problem for rule-following Lily Schmidt but she wanted so badly to pepper Dev Pierce with so many question. She didn't know what to begin with and now she couldn't at all. Even out in the darkened parking lot parishioners were speaking in hushed whispers or maintaining complete silence.

Lily was holding her car key in her right hand as they walked together in the darkness. She always felt safe with him not just because of what he did but because of who he was. As she walked, she continued to stare at him in disbelief. She had asked for direction and an answer, and in walked Devlin Pierce. Was she to really take this as a sign from God?

Finally, she was standing next to her car and Dev stood in front of her. "So here we are."

"Yes."

Dev moved in closer to her as cars pulled out of the parking lot. One came dangerously close to them.

"Damn, do they always have to drive like that here?"

Lily laughed out loud. "You know they do and is that any way to talk on Holy Thursday? You just got out of church, Dev."

He moved his weight from left to right foot almost uncomfortably. Why was this so difficult? "I know this may not be the right time, I mean Holy Thursday, Good Friday, Easter…I know how important your faith is to you. It makes you, you. This is definitely not the right place."

"Dev, what are you trying to say? Is there something wrong? If there is, it doesn't matter what time or place."

He smiled. "You know, you're right. It doesn't matter does it? It might as well be here in front of God and everyone else."

She looked around the emptying parking lot. "Well, there's not so many left now."

He slipped his left arm behind her back and pulled her close to him with his right. She was looking up into those eyes, his chin close to her forehead.

"I've been waiting a long time to do this and I'm sorry it took me so long to see what was right in front of me."

Before she could say anything, he dropped his lips to hers in one long kiss making up for all those times he'd thought of kissing her. She smelled like flowers. Of course she did. When he finally pulled away, her arms were around his waist and her eyelids remained shut.

"I'm sorry it took you so long too," she muttered breathlessly as she opened her eyes.

He smiled down at her face and saw things so much differently. She had always been right there waiting for him in her own independent way. They were going on an adventure neither one of them had planned, or was she making a list in her head right now? He kissed her once more, deeper, if possible, just in case. He didn't want her thinking about anything but this kiss.

As he brought his head up, he whispered into her ear.

"I'm pretty sure this is a sin."

Lily brought her arms around his neck and pulled him closer for another kiss in front of God and everyone. Now that she had him she wouldn't be letting go anytime soon.

"Not yet, Devlin Pierce, not yet."

The end is just the beginning for Lily and Agent Devlin Pierce. Watch for their next adventure in The Lily List Mystery Series.

C.L. Bauer offers a peek into the flower and wedding world she knows well in her hometown of Kansas City, Missouri.

Visit www.clbauer.com or email clbauerkc@gmail.com.

Welcome to Lily's!

C.L. BAUER

C.L. Bauer grew up and lives in Kansas City, Missouri. Her first novel The Poppy Drop, A Lily List Mystery was well received by the top 100 Books of Independent Publishers when it launched in 2018.

The Lily List Mystery Series features the highly organized, post-it note, and list making florist Lily Schmidt. Readers have enjoyed the adventures of the mystery loving woman and the wedding stories that are highlighted in these novels. Ms. Bauer draws on true events from her family's wedding and event flower business. With over one hundred years of serving families on their special days, Clara's Flowers has received numerous awards in the wedding world, including "best of" and "legacy winner" for service and design.

C.L. Bauer's first love of writing provided an early career in journalism. During high school, she began as a sports reporter, became an editor in college, and continued professionally in every writing medium including advertising and creative direction.

The author enjoys her family, travel, a good book on a rainy day, bulk post-it notes, and meeting her readers. She can always be swayed to feast on Mexican food, watch a hockey game, and drink the occasional fruity libation. If you've read her novels, you already know she loves Kansas City during the holidays.

You can reach C.L. Bauer on all forms of social media including her author pages on Facebook, Instagram, Twitter, Amazon, and Goodreads. Please review this and any of C.L. Bauer's published works. They are widely available for purchase in print and e-book forms. She's available for book club discussions virtually or in-person.

As always, happy reading!

Sign up at www.clbauer.com for this author's newsletter, promotions, pre-order information, free chapters, and upcoming publications. Contact C.L. Bauer directly at clbauerkc@gmail.com.

Coming in 2021...A Lily List Mystery Exclusive! Can't get enough of your favorite characters? The Exclusive novels feature more adventures with Lily's friends. Mysteries, murders, and more romance are coming your way!

Printed in the USA
CPSIA information can be obtained
at www.ICGtesting.com
LVHW020824181023
761088LV00011B/103

9 781736 346006